KATIE GINGER lives in the South East of England, by the sea, and apart from holidays to very hot places where you can sit by a pool and drink cocktails as big your head, she wouldn't really want to be anywhere else.

When she's not writing, Katie spends her time drinking gin, or with her husband, trying to keep alive her two children: Ellie, who believes everything in life should be done as a musical number from a West End show; and Sam, who is basically a monkey with a boy's face. And there's also their adorable King Charles Spaniel, Wotsit (yes, he is named after the crisps!).

For more about Katie you can visit her website: www.keginger.com, find her on Facebook: www.facebook.com/ KatieGAuthor, or follow her on Twitter: @KatieGAuthor

Also by Katie Ginger:

The Little Theatre on the Seafront

Summer Season on the Seafront

KATIE GINGER

ONE PLACE. MANY STORIES

HQ
An imprint of HarperCollins*Publishers* Ltd
1 London Bridge Street
London SE1 9GF

This paperback edition 2019

1
First published in Great Britain by
HQ, an imprint of HarperCollins*Publishers* Ltd 2019

ISBN: 978-0-00-833973-9

MIX
Paper from
responsible sources
FSC® C007454

This book is produced from independently certified FSC™ paper
to ensure responsible forest management.

For more information visit: **www.harpercollins.co.uk/green**

Printed and bound in Great Britain by
CPI Group (UK) Ltd, Melksham, SN12 6TR

To my wonderful mum and dad for their continuous support.

To my brave mother-in-law, Eileen.

And in loving memory of Steve, who I never knew,
but I love all the same.

Chapter 1

Sarah scanned the plethora of Chinese food before her and tentatively picked up her fork to skewer a mini spring roll. When Dean, her date, had suggested he choose the restaurant she'd been excited at the prospect of a fancy meal. His profile on the dating site showed a nice guy with good taste. He liked walking his dog along the beach, old black-and-white movies, and fine dining. She therefore hadn't expected to be sat in the Szechuan Palace All You Can Eat Buffet staring at unappetisingly grey egg fried rice and beef in black bean sauce (well, that was what the label said, but it more closely resembled bits of old innersole in tar).

Like the meal, Dean also wasn't exactly what it said on the tin. The black-and-white, extremely soft-focus photo had been cleverly taken to hide his receding hairline, and by using a headshot he'd kept the rather rotund and protruding beer belly well hidden from prospective mates. This could only have been in the hope that what his profile had called a 'fun' personality would win the day. It wouldn't. At least, not in Sarah's case. According to Dean, a fun personality meant constantly interrupting to talk over her, and making childish, full-on racist jokes about Chinese people, even though he was cheerfully tucking into his second plate of food and wearing bits of it on his shirt, presumably to save for later in case he got hungry on the walk home.

Instead of the traditional Chinese music, the local radio was loudly playing cheesy Nineties' pop. Sarah knocked back the remains of her second glass of cheap house white, grimacing slightly as acid with a hint of vinegar slid down her throat. Britney Spears decried, 'Oops, I did it again' over the noise of the other diners and Sarah watched Dean's second chin wobble as he continued talking about himself, just as he had done all evening. So far, Sarah had heard about his ex-wife (a bit of a heifer since the divorce, apparently) and the latest goings-on in the Arsenal football team (a shambles according to Dean, the expert), and watched a video on Dean's phone that was supposed to be 'bloody hilarious' but was actually just a bloke far too old to be on a skateboard, continually falling off as he tried to ride it down a handrail. When Sarah didn't find it fall-off-your-chair-funny, Dean had helpfully suggested she cheer up.

Thankful that, on seeing her date, she'd had the foresight to order a bottle, Sarah refilled her glass and took another gulp of wine. An image of Finn MacDonald's strawberry blond curls appeared in her mind and Sarah admonished herself for not having left earlier. The trouble was she felt sorry for Dean. Everyone got nervous on first dates, especially if they'd been out of the game for a while. Maybe underneath it all he was a nice guy. When she'd started dating again, she'd felt constantly nervous and said stupid things so, as a generally kind-hearted soul, Sarah had given Dean a second chance. Plus, at that point they'd only been half an hour in and she was starving. But time had passed painfully slowly and the last hour had been verging on water-boarding levels of torture, zapping her appetite. No, there was no denying the date hadn't got any better. However, as Dr MacDonald had so far failed to notice her existence on the reception desk, and the puddings looked quite nice, Sarah decided to make one last valiant effort to find some common ground.

'So, Dean, your profile said you like old black-and-white

movies. What's your favourite? I love—'

'Ah, yeah, bit of a cheeky one that, really. My mate Dave told me to put it in there. Said the girls like that sort of thing. I don't really like that many.' He shoved the final piece of chicken ball into his mouth and licked sweet and sour sauce off his pudgy fingers. Sarah worried she might throw up in her mouth and focused on one of the Chinese lanterns swaying to and fro above her head. 'I only really like one and that's *Raging Bull*.'

'But wasn't that made in the Seventies or something?' she asked, confused.

'Yeah, but it's still black and white, innit?' He gave her a wink, all the while chasing a piece of food that had evidently got caught somewhere in a back molar. Dean pointed to her still virtually full plate. 'You going to finish that?'

Sarah gave a resigned smile and pushed her plate towards him. 'No, you can have it.' That was it. There was only one thing left to do and that was to cut her losses and leave, but first she had to nip to the loo. 'Excuse me, Dean. I won't be a minute.'

'Right you are.' He leaned back and took a large glug of beer.

She didn't really need the loo. What she needed was space to text Lottie, her best friend. They'd only recently become besties, since meeting on the committee of Greenley Theatre. Lottie was the chairman – well, she'd been acting chairman back then, having been asked to take over the position by her nan, Elsie. Now, having made the theatre such a success, she was full chairman. Sarah was secretary on the committee and since she'd joined the local amateur dramatics group, the Greenley Players, they'd got to know each other even more. But it was Lottie's determination, combined with her kind, gentle nature, that had ensured their friendship developed quickly. Sarah had been so lonely till she met Lottie, and the rest of the players.

Once inside the cubicle, Sarah sent Lottie the SOS message. For her and Lottie, SOS meant Sort of Scared. Which she was, on several fronts. Dean's capacity for consuming Chinese food verged on the terrifying, and knowing that if the date continued he may well expect a kiss at some point filled Sarah with the sort of fear she hadn't experienced since watching *Chucky* as a kid. Lottie knew that after receiving the message she had to wait fifteen minutes then text or call pretending Sarah was urgently needed to do something vitally important elsewhere.

After sitting on the toilet seat for as long as possible (any longer and the other diners would start to think she had a dodgy tummy) she headed back to the table. Sarah retook her seat and watched in wonderment as Dean continued to clear the remains of her dinner. 'So,' she said, trying to fill the awkward silence and cover the noise of Dean masticating like a cow. 'What other things do you like, Dean?'

He finished chewing and swallowed, his cheeks pink from the effort. 'Well, I like football and you know ...' He shrugged. 'Blokey things.'

'Do you go for long walks along the beach? You said on your profile you take your dog.' She loved strolling along the beach and wanted to know if and when Dean went so she could avoid him.

'Nah, that was another cheeky fib. I normally take Ted to the dog park near my house. I like being near home in case he gets a bit humpy and I have to bring him back, sharpish. Last week he tried to hump a pug and I can tell you, that pug was not happy about it at all.'

Knowing Ted was a huge Labrador, Sarah was tempted to enquire about the mechanics but thought better of it. Right on cue her phone rang. 'Sorry, Dean. I won't be a minute.' But Dean was scraping his fork across his plate gathering up a stray noodle. 'Hello?'

'Not going very well then?' asked Lottie. Sarah could hear the smile on her face.

'Oh, no,' she replied dramatically, with an exaggerated gasp. 'You're where? The hospital? What's happened?'

4

'Is it the worst date you've ever been on? Even worse than three-teeth Terry?'

'That's terrible.' Sarah glanced up at Dean who was oblivious to her feigned distress and gave her a gummy smile. 'Are you okay?'

Lottie giggled. 'Are you going to pretend that I've broken my leg again?Because seriously, Sarah, people are going to cotton on sooner or later. According to you, I've broken my leg about twenty times this year.'

Sarah felt a slight pang at Lottie's words but only because they were true. She had been on more bad dates than good ones. Why did people have to lie on their profiles? Life would be much easier if they didn't. She let her mouth form a circle of surprise. 'How bad is it?'

'Oh, it's terrible. Terrible! It hurts! I think it might need chopping off! To be fair though, it's a pretty useless leg, what with it breaking all the time, so I probably wouldn't miss it. Perhaps we could turn it into a prop. Does anyone in *The Tempest* get their leg chopped off? Either that or I could bash Sid over the head with it whenever he annoys me.'

Sarah heard a muffled 'Oi!' in the background and had to bite her lip to stop a smile from creeping out. Sid was Lottie's boyfriend. Soulmate, really. And a nice guy. They were the cutest couple ever.

'I'll be there right away,' Sarah said, her voice full of concern. Lottie giggled.

'Okay. Byeeee!'

Sarah placed her mobile in her bag and looked at Dean who couldn't have cared less if she was there or not. He was busy watching another video on his phone, guffawing and snorting with laughter. Sarah couldn't see what it was but found the donkey noises quite disturbing.

'You off then?' he asked, looking up from the screen. She stood up and grabbed her jacket from the back of the chair.

'Dean, I'm so sorry, but my friend's broken her … arm and she needs me to go and get her from the hospital.'

'Christ, that's bad luck. Hey, are you still gonna pay your half before you go?' He picked up his beer but paused, putting it to his lips. 'Hang on a minute. You can't drive, you've had too much to drink.' A flicker of suspicion passed over his eyes and was instantly replaced by a flash of hurt. 'You're not trying to make a run for it, are ya?'He was joking but his tone was uncertain and the way his expression changed made Sarah's heart twinge with guilt. Poor Dean. It wasn't his fault he wasn't her type. Sarah ardently believed there was someone out there for everyone, even first-date disasters like Dean. Someone, somewhere, was waiting for Dean to find them. Someone who hated black-and-white movies, dog walks on the beach, and from the smell of grease hitting her nostrils, nice food. But that person wasn't her.

'Don't worry, I'm going to get a taxi,' she added hastily. 'I just can't leave her there all on her own.' The excuse seemed to work and he smiled.

'Right you are then.'

Dean's balding head glistened in the light and Sarah felt a wave of unutterable sadness. Was this really what her life had come down to? Escaping second-rate dates with men who had no real idea how to treat a woman? With an inward sigh, she laid some cash on the table. Sarah always carried cash for first dates just in case she needed to make a quick getaway. No one wanted to wait around for the waiter to bring a card machine and then faff about. She'd learned those lessons long ago. 'Here you go. I hope you enjoy the rest of your night.'

'I'll probably finish up here and nip along to The Bell for a swift one with the boys.' He rested his hands on top of his belly. 'Are we doing this again, then?'

A drop of Hoi Sin sauce had stained his chin. It was a round, fleshy chin, not like Dr MacDonald's which was smoothly chiselled and sometimes scattered with blond stubble. He was the only thing that made working at the doctor's surgery manageable. Stunned that Dean even thought a second date might be on the cards, Sarah was momentarily unable to speak. Then checking her phone again for dramatic effect, she said, 'I'll call you sometime,' before darting out of the door just as Bewitched were cracking into 'C'est La Vie'. Sarah rounded the corner and hurried on until she was away from the Szechuan Palace and its overpowering aroma of spicy fat.

A cool sea breeze blew on to her face and eased the heat from her cheeks. It was early July but the sun had been shining since the end of May. Temperatures were higher than she'd ever known and even at nine-thirty in the evening it was still warm. The sun set slowly behind the pier painting the sky in streaks of gold, and the few clouds that were dotted about were like patches of purple velvet. The waves lapped gently on the shingle beach and music carried on the air from the pubs that lined the promenade. As the relief subsided, Sarah's heart became heavy. Once again, she'd have to trawl the dating sites and go through all the hassle of arranging another date. The nervous excitement she used to feel at the prospect of a date was now replaced by a bored drudgery. All the magazines said she had to get out there to find the one, but she was quite fed up of it now. And what did you do if the one you thought you were supposed to be with had no idea you existed? Sarah had been single for ages, until Vince, but that hadn't ended well and she was still unable to think about it without a stabbing in her heart. Their relationship had been the best three months of her life, but she'd misjudged the cheating git completely. She'd learned her lesson then that whirlwind romances didn't work out and there was no such thing as love at first sight. To cheer herself up, Sarah concentrated on the thought of taking her make-up off and getting into her pyjamas as soon as she was home.

A beep resonated from her pocket and she read the message from Lottie. 'I've got half a bottle of wine with your name on it and Sid saved you a Cornetto if you want to come round?' A grin lifted the corners of her mouth. She was so lucky to have Lottie, but wished she was as lucky as Lottie and Sid had been in finding each other. They were one of those couples who were just meant to be together. Sarah gave a heavy sigh and pushed her brown hair back. There was something decidedly miserable about being 31 and single in a town like Greenley-On-Sea. As much as she loved her sweet little home town by the sea, she was running out of men to date. It was another reason Dr MacDonald was just so perfect. He wasn't from around here and was clever, funny and a great doctor. Everyone loved him.

Looking down at her phone, Sarah texted back, 'See you in five minutes,' and headed off towards Lottie's house. At least she had rehearsals to look forward to tomorrow – though the Greenley Players' rendition of *The Tempest* wasn't going quite as smoothly as they would have liked. Even with four weeks to pull it together. And who knew, maybe Dr MacDonald would walk into work on Monday morning and suddenly see her for the first time, or bump into her on the street and realise he'd loved her all along. A girl could dream, after all.

Chapter 2

Nate glanced out from centre stage at row upon row of happy, smiling faces and paced about reciting his lines. The floorboard that always creaked underfoot moaned as he circled the stage. He ended up at the same spot he always did, and the spotlight shrunk until only he was lit. An imperceptible change the crowd would barely notice, but it made what he had to say even more impactful. In a second, it would enlarge as the action moved on. Hell, it was hot. The old West End theatres didn't have air conditioning – it was impossible to make any changes to the historic listed buildings – and he was boiling in his costume of heavy denim jeans and a thick shirt. Sweat soaked the back of his neck and ran down between his shoulder blades.

The words came to him as second nature, like breathing. They'd been said so many times every intonation was ingrained on his brain, just as every move was imprinted on his muscle memory. He'd enjoyed playing the part of George Milton in a new adaptation of *Of Mice and Men*, and the critics loved it, but he was secretly glad that the eight-week run was coming to an end as exhaustion was creeping in. The final push to the finish was always hard and it was the exhilaration of performing that carried him, and the rest of the cast, through the last few shows.

Thankfully, there were only a few more days to go. He concentrated on his co-stars as they recited their lines.

Thanks to its reception, offers of work were flooding in and Robin, his agent, was busier than ever sending out audition tapes. His career was on the up and had reached the point where he was automatically asked to take some of the theatre industry's main roles, even some TV ones, but not all of them. Robin assured him that would come soon. It was just a matter of time. At 38 his success had come a little later than he'd have liked, but his star was still rising. As he looked up to see one of the actors slightly raising his eyebrows at him, Nate realised his mind was wandering again. That was happening a lot lately. Since that regrettable night with Hannah Salgado he'd thought more and more about his career and his marriage, and everything he'd risked. Tonight, coming near the end of the run and with a choice of what to do next, he couldn't stop worrying about it all coming out and everything he'd worked so hard for falling apart.

He'd been childish at first, blaming Hannah for their one-night stand two weeks before. Then he'd blamed his best friend Marcus, whose stag do it was, for letting him get so drunk he'd ended up in bed with her. But Nate knew there was no one to blame but himself. He was still a married man. Okay, he and his wife, Emma, were just about to start divorce proceedings but still, the ring remained on his finger and that should've stopped him. He and Emma had been married a long time, and together since university, but slowly she'd fallen out of love with him. Perhaps it had been the pressure of them both being in the industry. Certainly, as his career had grown while hers had stagnated, her jealousy had turned to anger and she'd drifted further and further away from him and into the arms of other men. It had broken his heart. They'd been keeping the marriage together for the sake of their careers, looking for the right time to announce an amicable divorce, and it had been hell.

The lighting subtly changed again to illuminate Nate against the now darkened backdrop, and that was his cue. The performance was reaching its dramatic climax and he focused on the words as he spoke. True emotion came forth, as it always did, until a voice from the depths pierced the silence that fell between him and the audience. A sudden wave of nausea rose inside him and every muscle tensed. He knew that voice.

'Look at you giving it the big star, Nathaniel Hardy. Forgotten to return my calls, have you? Just been too busy? Or am I not good enough for you now?' Nate paused, trying to figure out if he was mistaken. But no, he definitely wasn't. Despite her Spanish surname, the voice that came from the dark was pure Essex. 'What's the matter, Nate? Got nothing to say this time? You thought you could palm me off, didn't you? Thought I'd just disappear like some slutty one-night stand. Well, I won't!'

The audience gasped. Nate swallowed down the bile, hoping he wouldn't be sick. Saliva gathered in his mouth and his head spun. It was like being drunk. What the hell was Hannah doing here? The theatre was silent and the air thick and unmoving, lit by fractured beams of light. He'd thought Robin had dealt with this. Nate had told him and Emma about his indiscretion the very next day after realising what a fool he'd been. When Hannah had un-subtly mentioned the media finding out about what had passed between them, he knew he'd been used. At first Nate had thought they were just two lonely people who wanted a night of comfort. Only afterwards did it become clear she was after a career boost in hitching herself onto him. It had been a major error of judgement and one that he couldn't undo however much he wished it.

Emma couldn't have cared less as long as it didn't get out. She had irons in the fire that something like this could ruin, plus her dad, a big-name producer, would get caught up in it too, He'd do his absolute nut if this came out just now. Robin had advised Hannah to keep quiet for the sake of Nate's and her own reputation. Though Nate's marriage might be over behind closed doors, the world didn't know that, and he couldn't afford for them to find out. If this hit the papers, which it would now, all the offers that had been coming in so fast Robin couldn't keep up, would disappear. He'd no longer be the sweet-hearted, loyal husband he'd always tried to be. The darling of the chat shows and women's mags because he'd been with Emma since university – since before he was famous. He'd be a cheating bastard. They had no idea that things had changed for Emma and he'd slowly been coming to terms with it. They didn't know she'd fallen out of love with him and he simply wasn't what she wanted anymore. They'd planned to split in a month, announcing it through their respective agents before divorcing quietly. The papers would have been sympathetic then and it would have played out nicely with neither blamed, only each admired for their grown-up attitudes. Now a silly drunken one-night stand was going to ruin everything, and it would become a sordid mess.

'Come on, Nate,' Hannah began again. 'You're an actor, you must have something to say. You're not exactly shy and you certainly weren't that night at my flat.' She was standing up, seven rows back. Even the ushers approaching her looked scared, her normally pouty face held in an angry grimace. She'd clearly planned for this moment. An expensive dress poured over her curvy figure, her make-up impeccable despite the heat, and long black hair hung down in curls that, he knew from Emma's pre-awards-show routines, took an expert hand. Why was Hannah doing this?

Muttering crept forwards through the audience like a ripple on water, landing at his feet. Nate knew he should say something, but he had no idea what. His mind was gripped with panic at the consequences of his stupid actions, brought on by too much drink and far too much heartache. He'd loved Emma and admitting their marriage wasn't working anymore had broken his heart. It had been exhausting putting on a brave face for the paparazzi. And then, one night, when he'd finally managed to get away from them, a chance meeting after one too many flaming sambucas had brought Hannah into his life. There she was, this gorgeous model telling him she'd just broken up with her boyfriend. Nate, fuelled by beer and shots, had let the pain and loneliness he'd worked constantly to keep at bay wash over him. The hurt of Emma's rejection had finally become too much and he'd stupidly been swept away by Hannah's flattery, by the little-girl-lost persona, and one thing had led to another.

The guy playing Lennie stepped forwards. 'Excuse me, madam, I think you should leave. You're ruining the performance for everyone else.' Nate stared at him, knowing it should be him saying something. Every moment he kept his mouth closed he looked even more of an idiot. The audience – his audience – were agog.

Hannah folded her arms over her chest in a defiant stance, making sure her enormous boobs rested on top. 'Do you know what this scumbag did?' she asked, gazing around, playing to the crowd. Some people turned away, embarrassed, while others began filming on their phones. God, this would be all over the internet within ten minutes. His career was over. That was it. It was all going to fall into the toilet. The media wouldn't be kind. It would be a highly publicised betrayal of his childhood sweetheart for a fame-grabbing model. They'd never know or understand the reality. He wasn't an arsehole. Just an idiot. Robin would probably drop him. He wasn't big enough news to weather a storm like this. And Emma would hate him even more. Hannah gleefully continued. 'He told me he loved me. He told me he was going to leave his wife and—'

What? No! Jesus Christ on a bike. Had he been so drunk he'd said that? He had no recollection of it, and it didn't sound like him, but the night had passed in a blur. Nate couldn't even remember if the sex had been any good he'd been that drunk. Shit. This was all going wrong. So, so wrong. Why was she here now?

'—and now …' Hannah turned towards him and smiled. 'Now, he's trying to pay me off to save his reputation. Well, his agent is. Nathaniel hasn't come near me since the night we spent together having sex! Lots and lots of sex. Which was crap by the way! But he's too much of a coward to even face me himself, aren't you, Nathaniel Hardy? Have you told your wife about us yet?' Her head stopped wiggling and she glared triumphantly.

No, no, no, no, no, thought Nate. This wasn't right. He knew he shouldn't have done it, still being technically married, and he'd regretted it straight away, but did he really deserve all this? He couldn't – *wouldn't* – have said he loved her. Nate had only ever said that to Emma. And he was sure he wouldn't have promised more than a single night of no-strings sex. She wasn't his type. He'd never before been the sort to just jump into bed with someone. It was always the emotional connection he wanted. The curtain began to close, protecting him from the audience and Hannah.

'Nate,' whispered Lennie now they were shielded. 'What the fuckery is going on? That silly tart's ruining the bloody show.'

'I'm sorry,' he muttered, his brain slow and sluggish. 'I'm so sorry. I didn't know she was here. I thought it was all dealt with. I'm sorry, I'm so sorry …' Nate's legs wobbled beneath him and he collapsed onto one of the hay bales used to set the stage. In the play he was on a farm in California. He'd been there recently. LA, to be exact. For a small film role. He wished he was there now, or anywhere else for that matter. The erratic breathing returned, not helping his light-headedness at all. The lights seemed to be moving and Nate held his head in his hands trying to stop the flashes drifting across his eyes.

One of the female cast members tutted and turned her back on him. She thought he was a cheating bastard. And he was. Technically. But he couldn't break his agreement with Emma and tell the truth of her numerous affairs now.

'Nate,' the theatre manager said calmly, as if this happened

14

every night of the week, 'after we remove her from the audience, are you okay to carry on?'

Was he? He had no idea right now. His world was tumbling down around him. Could he perform after this? He thought of his training, and something inside him clicked. He nodded. 'Yes. Yes, I am.'

Hannah's voice could still be heard in the background as what sounded like three or four different ushers tried to remove her from the stalls. 'Get off me, you fucking idiots. Do you have any idea who I am? Don't push me. You can't do this. Oi!' Her screeching faded and the theatre manager spoke once again to Nate.

'Are you sure?'

Nate looked around at his fellow actors. He couldn't let them down, or the audience who had paid good money to come and see them. The play had been ruined enough for them already because of him, he wouldn't cheat them out of the last twenty minutes. That was his only good bit of luck. They'd been so near the end when she'd started shouting, he didn't have long to get through. The sneaky minx had obviously been waiting for the pivotal moment of the play. Pulling his shoulders back, he said, 'Yes. I'm sure. Just give me a few minutes to get myself together.'

'Okay.' The theatre manager deftly moved the curtain aside and stepped onto the stage. 'Ladies and gentlemen, I'm terribly sorry for the disruption to tonight's performance. We're going to have a fifteen-minute interval and then the play will continue. Thank you all for your patience and your support.'

The quiet mumbles erupted into a loud chatter that filled the room. Nate couldn't help but wonder what they were saying about him. Nothing good, he was sure. Lennie turned to him. 'Are you okay, mate?'

'Not really,' Nate replied, studying his visibly shaking hands. 'Just give me five minutes.'

Nate rushed from the set, through a door at the back and

down the steps to the dressing rooms. Using his hand to steady himself, he sped along the corridor and burst through the door. Collapsing into his chair he let his head drop into his hands. It was stifling in the small, messy dressing room. The London air was dense with heat and there was no breeze to cool him, only the whirring of a small desk fan that did nothing but blow droplets of cold sweat across his forehead. Nate's face was ashen as he stared at his reflection in a mirror brightly lit by the bare bulbs encasing it. He wasn't really seeing himself, just a pale version of the man he'd been when everything was going well. It was like he was looking at someone else now. Nate swigged from the bottle of water beside the abandoned make-up brushes, tossed aside as the thrill of the five-minute call and the eager anticipation of performing filled him. A buzzing from his jacket, hung on the back of the door, told him he had a phone call. Grabbing it, he saw it was Robin. Word was out already.

Repressing the urge to ring back, Nate closed his eyes and recalled the lines he was about to recite, mumbling them to himself. At the start of his career he'd thought the phrase 'The show must go on' was a joke but right now, he really wasn't laughing.

* * *

The applause was subdued during the final bows and once the curtain had finally closed Nate didn't wait around for the rest of the cast as he normally did. Tonight, there would be no congratulations on a job well done. Not for him anyway. Instead, he did his best to get back to his dressing room without speaking to anyone. The cast didn't know what to say to him, which was funny considering they were actors. They simply exchanged awkward glances that they thought he didn't see.

A horrible queasiness rocked his body as he closed the dressing-room door and took his mobile phone from his jacket pocket.

He had several missed calls, text messages and voicemails from Robin. Nate was beginning to feel angry now and wanted to know how everything had gone so horribly wrong. He felt so guilty, but Robin had promised he'd sort it. It took a ridiculous amount of time to find Robin's number because his fingers felt like they were wrapped in cotton wool and wouldn't go where his brain directed them. Several times he scrolled too far one way then the other. His whole body was shaking so much it took every last bit of energy to concentrate on what he was doing.

Robin answered straight away. 'Nate?'

'Robin, what the hell has happened? I thought you'd dealt with it?' Nate began to change out of his costume, undoing the dirty, dusty jeans his character wore, pulling them off and with one hand slipping on his own smarter ones. Where the hell was his top? Robin sighed and Nate could picture him scratching his forehead, like he always did when he was stressed. His thick cheeks would be red, his blood pressure rising. 'Robin, she's here saying—'

'Yeah I know. I've seen but I did handle it, Nate. I told you, it was made clear that she needed to keep that night strictly between you two. No press and no further contact. She was … compensated accordingly and I thought she'd taken it well.'

'Well, she clearly bloody hasn't.' Nate tilted his head and pinned the phone to his shoulder then undid the cuffs of his shirt. Taking the phone again he pulled the top over his head and grabbed his own T-shirt, threading through one arm, then the other. He knew he sounded like a complete dick but controlling the panic was proving difficult. Robin's voice was so loud Nate could hear him even when he moved the phone away to pull the top over his head. Nate sat down and pushed back his dark hair. 'Has anyone told Emma? I can ring her now. I just don't want the first thing she hears about this coming from her agent, or worse, some shitty, insensitive reporter knocking on the door.'

'I've already called her,' Robin replied, calmly. 'I told her I'd deal with it and that everything else remains as you guys agreed. Suffice to say, she went off like a rocket.'

Nate pinched his temples. 'What do I do now, Robin? This is going to be all over the net tonight and then in the papers tomorrow. They're going to think I'm a complete scumbag.' Nate's voice cracked slightly. Emma already did, and he hated himself for still caring so much about a woman who hadn't loved him in years. 'I'm surprised she's not taking the opportunity to put it all on me and get out while she can.'

'Think about it, Nate, if the press go digging about in your private life to find out if you've done this before, what else might they find? Her affairs could be uncovered. She's better off letting this die, but she doesn't want you to come back to the house tonight.'

'What?' It felt like a punch in his ribs.

'She said she doesn't want to see you right now. Not until she's processed what's happening.'

He paced around. 'Processed what's happening? It was a drunken one-night stand after our marriage was over! She had an affair with one of her co-stars for nine months before I even knew we were in danger.'

'Never mind about that now,' Robin replied. 'The paparazzi will already be outside the theatre and you can't go home so I've arranged for you to go somewhere else.' Nate blew out his cheeks. He felt a stinging in his nose and gritted his teeth, refusing to let his emotions get the better of him. 'But listen, I'm sure we can still work this to our advantage.'

'How? How can we possibly do that? I look like some shady love rat. Like Hugh bloody Heffner.' There was no answer for a moment and Nate opened his mouth to speak but then Robin began again.

'I've arranged for you to go somewhere and I've got a car waiting outside. I'll pack you some stuff tomorrow and send it on.'

Nate shook his head. 'I can't just leave the show. There's still three nights left.'

'Your understudy can take over. We'll say you've got pneumonia and you're recovering. You need to distance yourself from this.'

'Pneumonia? But it's July.'

'You can still get pneumonia in July. Stop being difficult.'

Outside his dressing-room door, the theatre came to life again as costumes were collected, props were organised for the next day and people bustled around. 'I'm not being difficult, but no one's going to buy it. And I haven't even got clean pants.'

'What are you, the Queen of bloody Sheba? Just wear the ones you've got on now. Turn them inside out or something, I don't bloody care! And I don't care if they buy it or not. The story will die quicker if they can't twist your words.' Robin sighed heavily. 'We just need you out of the way for a week or two until they find something else to write about, which they undoubtedly will.'

'So what exactly do you want me to do?' Nate pressed the heel of his hand into his forehead.

'Get in the car that's waiting – it's taking you to stay with an old friend of mine in a little seaside town where the press won't bother you.'

Nate moved to the open window and closed it. The stage door was busier than usual, probably stacked full of reporters pushing past the fans who had paid good money to see the show and hoped for a quick photo or autograph with the cast. 'And where's that?' he asked, unconvinced this plan would work.

'Greenley-On-Sea.'

19

Chapter 3

Greenley was always quiet at this time on a Sunday morning. The only people around were fishermen, walking towards the pier ready for the day ahead, their rods and nets slung over one shoulder and a great box of bait carried in the other hand.

Sarah met Lottie outside the theatre, ready to begin the next rehearsal of *The Tempest*. 'Morning,' she said, forcing the words out of her scratchy throat. Stopping beside Lottie, she took a final glance at the still, blue-green sea. At one corner of the beach, a bright ball of white light threatened to blind her where the sun rose at its own leisurely pace into the sky.

'Hey, you,' said Lottie, fiddling about trying to unlock the revolving doors. 'How are you feeling this morning? You were a bit tiddly when you left last night, but then from the sounds of it you had to get a bit drunk to get through your disastrous date.'

'If that's a nice way of saying I was off my face and talking at a million miles an hour, you're right.'

'Umm … yes,' Lottie replied, grinning, her blonde ponytail swishing as she turned her head.

A low groan escaped Sarah's mouth and she rubbed her temples. 'Urgh. I think the nice white wine you bought mixed with the God-awful vinegary stuff I had at the restaurant and caused some sort of chemical reaction. You know, like those volcanoes kids make with vinegar and bicarbonate of soda. My stomach's all weird and bubbly.' Right on cue it gurgled loudly and she repressed a burp. Lottie raised her eyebrows as she dropped the keys back in her pocket.

'Was that you?'

'Sorry.' Sarah placed a hand on her stomach. 'I feel like I've died and been re-animated, or at least my stomach has.'

'Ooh, now there's a thought. Maybe we should do *Frankenstein* one day?' said Lottie, excitedly. 'Mrs Andrews can be the monster.' She giggled to herself then turned to Sarah. 'I don't know why you didn't stay over. I've got two spare rooms and Sid doesn't mind.'

Sarah didn't know why she hadn't taken up Lottie's offer either. She wished she had now. The roundabouts on the taxi ride back to her house had acted like a centrifuge, rattling around the horrible wine and greasy food from the Szechuan Palace with the four Cornettos and two very large glasses of wine she'd consumed at Lottie's. This morning her mouth felt like a small furry creature had setup home, turned it into a bedsit, then died. Even after a breakfast of Alka Seltzer and half a slice of buttered toast she wasn't sure she'd make it through the rehearsal. A gentle summer breeze filled her lungs, making her feel marginally better, but then a sheet of used chip paper drifted up and wrapped itself around her ankle. She bent down, picked it up, then put it in the bin. 'Where is Sid anyway?'

'I left him in bed, snoring his head off.' Lottie's face always changed when she spoke about Sid, as if a light turned on somewhere in her soul and shone out like a beacon of pure joy. Sarah had been truly ecstatic when they'd got together. Although walking in on them full snog backstage after the opening night of last year's Christmas pantomime had been a little embarrassing. 'He said he'd meet us here.'

'Okay.' Sarah looked up at the old building admiring its

Victorian elegance. The long square front of grey stone was mostly fixed up now, though they still needed to change the rotting poster cases. The windows either side of the door gleamed in the sunlight and the domed canopy above the elegant revolving door had just received a fresh coat of blue paint. 'I love this place.'

Lottie pushed one of the large glass panels of the revolving door, and followed its circular motion inside. 'I do too, it's amazing isn't it? But that reminds me, I've got to organise someone to clear the guttering before the summer's out.' Sarah was just about to grab her phone and make a note when Lottie tugged hers from her back pocket and did the same. Their love of organisation was one of the things they'd bonded over. That and both having lost someone close to them. Lottie had lost her beloved nan last year, and Sarah her mother a few years ago. Sarah was happy to speak about her mum, even though it was painful to remember her, but she quickly changed the subject whenever her dad was mentioned. That he was in prison was a fact of which she was deeply ashamed. He'd always been a respected accountant in the town but got greedy when he didn't get as much of a bonus as he wanted. Then her mum had been diagnosed with cancer. Terminal cancer. Meaning he wasn't there at the end. There were other things too, but those she had buried so deep she didn't dare think about them, afraid of the hurt that would erupt. She hadn't even told Lottie, studiously avoiding the subject whenever it came up. 'Come on,' said Lottie, leading the way. 'We need to have a bit of a clean before we start.'

Sarah followed Lottie in and clicked on the light. The revolving doors opened into a small square balcony that had steps on either side leading down to the seats. The ceiling was painted in Greco-Roman murals, some a bit naughty, and each wall had floor-to-ceiling columns evenly spaced along it. Everyone commented on what an unusual set-up it was, but the Greenley Players all agreed it made their theatre extra special. Just like Lottie. Lottie didn't act, admitting herself she was rubbish, but she was great at sourcing costumes, organising props and generally bringing it all together. To think that a year ago, before Lottie got involved, the building was falling apart, there was no amateur dramatics group, and the mayor planned to sell the theatre to plug a hole in the council's budget was astounding, but now, it was a thriving part of their community, loved by everyone. 'I still can't get over how nice it smells when you walk in here,' Sarah said, taking a deep breath. 'It smells like cupcakes.'

'That's because I've got approximately forty-eight plug-in air fresheners on full whack,' said Lottie, making her way down the central aisle to the stage. 'It costs me a bloody fortune.'

Sarah followed Lottie down the aisle in the centre towards the stage, pausing to pick up a small scrap of paper left under one of the seats. 'I've told you, you don't have to pay for things out of your own money. The budgets have been re-done and we've got a special one for maintenance and cleaning that covers things like that. We're doing really well, Lottie, you should make sure you get your money back.' Lottie placed her handbag on one of the chairs and smiled at Sarah.

'Okay, I will. I promise.'

'Things seem to be going well with your plans to turn us into a charity. Even our beloved mayor's on board this time, isn't he? He was verging on positive the other night.' Sarah had been at the meeting and the mayor was their most vocal committee member.

'Oh, you know what he's like. There's a lot of paperwork to do and he much prefers being seen as the mayor, throwing his weight around and looking important, to actually doing mayor things and you know … helping.'

Sarah nodded. She knew only too well. Last year, during their campaign to save the theatre, Mayor Cunningham had been less than supportive. Now Lottie had these amazing plans for it to become a charity which would mean more funding possibilities and he was, as usual, being negative and annoying.

Slipping her handbag from her shoulder, Sarah dropped it onto a chair beside Lottie's. 'I'm actually starting to feel hungry now. I could murder a coffee and cake.'

'Did someone say coffee and cake?' asked Sid, striding in with takeaway cups and a pack of muffins. This was why Sid was a keeper.

'Hello you,' said Lottie, smiling as if she'd never seen him before. 'Dragged yourself out of bed eventually then?'

'Only for you, my darling,' he replied in lofty tones, then handed a cup to Lottie, and one to Sarah. 'I thought you could use this. And one of these.' He brandished the chocolate chip muffins and Sarah nearly ripped his hand off as she grabbed them.

'You're an absolute star, Sid. Thank you.'

He gave his usual lopsided, cheeky grin. 'Well, you were completely trollied last night. I'm surprised you're upright this morning.'

'It is a bit of a challenge,' Sarah replied, breaking a piece off the top of the muffin and placing it in her mouth. The sweet chocolate soothed the ache behind her eyes. Lottie gave Sid a kiss on the cheek before taking a sip of her coffee. As Sarah and Lottie were nibbling their muffins, while Sid took huge gigantic mouthfuls, a few of the newer members of the Greenley Players arrived ready to rehearse their big summer play. There were only two performances, but the Greenley Players all wanted to show they could handle some Shakespeare. Lottie welcomed them just as Mrs Andrews, long time Greenley Player and prima donna, strolled in.

'Good morning, fellow actors.' Mrs Andrews strode down to the front in three-inch beige suede high heels and skintight cream trousers. Her long flowing cardigan billowed out behind her, as did her honey blonde hair. She paused with her back to Sarah. 'Lottie, darling, I really must talk to you about Ariel. I'd like to play the character a little stronger than we first agreed. I just feel there's so much I could be doing. I mean, I really think I should be playing Miranda, but still …' Sarah flashed her eyes mischievously at Lottie. They'd heard this all before. 'I don't want to complain but …'

Sarah wanted to say, 'Yes you do, Mrs Andrews. You've done nothing but complain since we started rehearsals.' But she swallowed it down and shoved some more muffin in her mouth instead. Next time they were going to have to give her a leading role just to stop her moaning. Especially as Sarah had had two. She was playing Miranda now in *The Tempest* and had played Jasmine in *Aladdin*, their Christmas panto. She'd also been the lead in *Much Ado About Nothing*, but that didn't count because it had been such a disaster no one wanted to think about it.

'Well, that's really something you need to discuss with Conner,' said Lottie diplomatically. 'Since he's directing. And with Gregory, as he's playing Prospero.'

Mrs Andrews tossed her hair over her shoulder. 'I just want to get this sorted, Lottie. With the builders still working on the extension and all the stress with that …' She dramatically laid a hand on her forehead. 'I could really do with something going smoothly for a change. My talents are not being utilised at present.'

They'd heard about the ongoing saga of the two-storey extension for the last two weeks not to mention the months of wrangling with the architects, but Sarah had very little sympathy. The enormous addition to Mrs Andrews' six-bedroom townhouse in the posh part of town was so she could have her own spin studio, complete with fancy disco lighting and expensive sound system. She didn't teach spin, she just didn't like working out with all the other riff-raff at the gym. Even though she used the super expensive one in town that was more like a spa.

'I understand,' Lottie replied, her voice neutral. 'Just chat to Gregory when he gets here. Actually, where are Gregory and Cecil? They're normally here by now.'

That was odd. Gregory and Cecil, owners of the town

bookshop, were usually the first to arrive. Pulling her phone from her bag, Sarah checked that Gregory hadn't sent her a message. When she looked up, Mrs Andrews had left Lottie alone, so Sarah shook her head to confirm she hadn't heard anything. The other players were milling about chatting excitedly, and some had made their way onto the stage and were making a circle of chairs ready to read through the play. Rehearsals were at that wonderful stage where everyone was finding out about their characters and reading from the script, so it didn't matter if you couldn't remember all your lines. Sarah's stomach knotted at the prospect of having to learn everything off by heart, she was really struggling with *The Tempest*. Gregory, who had experience of acting on the West End a long time ago, had been helping her, and she found his presence reassuring.

Just as she was about to call them, Gregory and Cecil arrived. They moved down towards the stage huddled close together, doing a weird run, skip, hop kind of thing, like over-excited children. Uncharacteristically, they gave everyone only a brief hello, rather than their usual exuberant welcome complete with air-kisses, before sitting together at the furthest end of the front row. Frowning, Sarah picked up her coffee cup and went over to them. As their whispering quietened, she felt a stab of hurt at their secrecy.

'Hello, Sarah, darling,' said Gregory. He and Cecil stood and kissed her on each cheek before re-taking their seats. 'How are you?'

'Hungover,' she said, taking another bite of muffin. 'But fine.'

'Don't talk with your mouth full, dear,' said Cecil, and she playfully narrowed her eyes at him.

'Another disastrous date was it?' asked Gregory. He was wearing an exquisite linen suit, complete with open-neck shirt.

'No – well, yes. Sort of.'

'You can tell us all about it later,' Gregory said, then gave Cecil a conspiratorial look.

Sarah frowned. Something was lingering in the air around Gregory and Cecil, and the coy smiles tugging at their heavily tanned faces told her they had news of some sort. She hoped they weren't setting her up on a blind date again. Unless it was with Finn. 'What's got you two all excited?' she said. 'I haven't seen you this worked up since we saw Kit Harrington in *Othello* and you were planning on throwing your pants at him.'

Gregory took a deep breath then leaned in and spoke in almost a whisper. 'I've got something to tell you, but you have to keep it top secret.'

'Okay,' Sarah replied, hesitantly.

His eyes scanned around quickly, checking no one was listening.

'The one and only, totally gorgeous, heartbreakingly swoonworthy Nathaniel Hardy is currently asleep in our spare room.' Gregory sat back with a silly grin on his face. Sarah opened her mouth, closed it, then tipped her head. *Nathaniel Hardy, the famous actor?*

'Are you telling me fibs?'

'Scout's honour,' Cecil replied, giving the three-fingered salute, but Sarah didn't believe him for a minute.

'You were never in the Scouts. You told me you refused to join because you didn't believe in camping.'

'Darling, why would you ever go camping when there are luxury spa hotels?'

'Not the point,' Sarah responded huffily. The coffee and muffin hadn't settled in her stomach and she felt a bit sick. 'Why don't you tell me the truth or just say it's private? There's no need to tell lies.'

Gregory leaned further in and took her hand. 'I'm not lying, my darling. This is top secret and you can't tell anyone.'

Sarah's brain refused to compute. It was one of the oddest things Gregory had ever said to her, and that was saying something. She felt a bit like she'd read one of those odd newspaper

27

headlines that pop up every now and again like, 'Alien Crop Circles Found in Chigwell'. You just couldn't believe them because if aliens did come to this planet, the last place they'd want to visit is Chigwell. 'Nathaniel Hardy?' she asked. 'At your house? Right now?'

'Yes. Yes. And yes.' Gregory smiled like he'd just been given Chris Hemsworth naked, for Christmas.

'Why?' was the only thing Sarah could think to say in a vain attempt to understand all this nonsense.

Cecil sighed in exasperation. 'My darling girl, haven't you seen the papers?'

'No, of course I haven't. It's ten-thirty on a Sunday morning and I'm hungover as f—'

'Thank you,' said Gregory, disapprovingly.

'You're lucky I'm here and dressed. I nearly didn't make it at all, or I could have turned up in my jimjams.'

Leaning backwards, Cecil wriggled his phone from the pocket of his trousers and began tapping away.

'What are you doing?' Sarah asked.

Cecil held up a finger, then resumed typing. 'Hush.'

'I just want to know wh—'

'Hush,' he said again, before turning the phone to show her the website for one of the tabloids. A giant headline read, 'Love rat heart-throb ditches loving wife for debauched night with glamour model'.

Sarah's eyes widened and her mouth fell open. 'He did not!' This was incredible. Like most of the women in the UK, Sarah fancied the pants off Nathaniel Hardy, especially since he'd played a suited and booted villainous bodyguard on TV. Those well-fitting suits were mouth-wateringly attractive and he had a strong square jaw. Plus, he was supposed to be a complete darling, loyal to his first love despite starring alongside some of the most glamorous women in the world.

'He did,' said Gregory. 'I got a call at about ten o'clock last night from an old acting chum who's now an agent in London – Mr Hardy's agent as it turns out – and he said one of his clients needed to get out of town for a bit and could we take them in—'

'So we said yes, of course,' cut in Cecil, his cheeks tinged pink with excitement. 'Who's going to say no to something like that? We'd have taken in anyone. And then he said—'

'And then he said it was Nathanial Hardy,' finished Gregory. 'Honestly, I thought I'd died and gone to heaven!' He placed his hand over his heart. 'So then he turns up at about midnight, in a black car with tinted windows. No bags. Nothing.'

Sarah pulled back and scowled. 'Not even spare pants?'

Cecil rolled his eyes. 'Not that we could see, dear, no. No toothbrush either. Luckily, we've always got people staying so we have a supply.'

'Of spare pants?'

'Of toothbrushes. What is it with you and pants?' Sarah gave a cheeky grin while Gregory gave a great yawn. 'I couldn't sleep a wink last night knowing he was in the next room.'

Sarah's eyes flitted between the screen of Cecil's mobile phone still showing the headline, and her friends' faces. 'So he's really in your house? Right now? Because of this?' She pointed to the screen and they both nodded. What the heck was going on? It was completely bonkers to think that one of the country's best actors was only a few streets away in Gregory and Cecil's gorgeous little cottage. Was he naked? Now that was a nice thought.

'What are you guys gossiping about?' asked Lottie, standing over all three of them. 'We're almost ready to start.'

'Oh, nothing,' Gregory replied, shooting a warning look at Sarah. But Sarah hated the thought of lying to Lottie, they'd become so close. Trying to be subtle, Sarah nodded towards Lottie, widening her eyes at Gregory and Cecil to show they should tell her, but from the sharp shake of his head, Gregory disagreed. Sarah tried again, bobbing her head in Lottie's direction.

'What's the matter with you lot?' asked Lottie, smirking. 'You look like those dolls with tiny bodies and big wobbly heads.'

'We have to tell Lottie,' said Sarah, as the head bobbing and eyebrow wiggling wasn't working.

Gregory took a deep breath and shot it out through his nose. 'Oh, all right.'

'Ooo! Tell me what?' Lottie replied, kneeling in front of them.

'Nathaniel Hardy is staying at our cottage. Incognito. For the next couple of weeks.'

'Are you having me on?' All three slowly shook their heads. 'Yes, you are. Why would he be staying with you?'

'Oh, for heaven's sake,' said Cecil. 'Don't any of you read the papers?' Sarah repressed a smile. 'Because of this.' He showed Lottie the newspaper headline. Lottie's reaction was the same as Sarah's, only Lottie managed to keep her mouth closed.

'I don't believe it,' she said.

Conner's voice sounded from the stage. 'Can we get started everyone, please?' As the play's director, he was keen to begin rehearsing.

'Well, it's true,' said Gregory, standing up and removing his jacket. 'And not a word to anyone. Nothing can appear in the paper.'

'I know,' said Lottie, whose day job was photographer for the local paper, the *Greenley Gazette*. Gregory and Cecil walked past them and began climbing the small set of steps at the front of the stage. Sarah stared at Lottie for a moment, then they both burst out laughing.

'What are you doing later?' she asked Lottie. An idea had occurred to Sarah. A very naughty idea.

'Nothing. Why?'

With a nonchalant shrug she said, 'No reason. I just thought we might take a walk by Gregory and Cecil's house and, you know ...'

'Secretly peer in the windows?' finished Lottie.

'Maybe.'

Lottie grinned. 'Definitely.'

Rehearsals got underway and Sarah, frustrated that the lines just wouldn't stay in her head, read them again from her book. '"I might call him A thing divine, for nothing natural I ever saw so noble."'

'No, dear,' said Gregory kindly. 'You sound like you're on the intercom in the supermarket. "Clean up in aisle five",' he mimicked, holding his nose. 'You need to emote. What's wrong? You played Jasmine so well in the pantomime. I know you can do this.'

He was right. For some reason she was struggling with the part of Miranda, especially the bits where Miranda fell in love. The idea that it was something to do with Vince, her ex, or her general single status, kept flitting around at the back of her mind but she ignored it and ploughed on. She found it much easier to sing. She'd joined the Greenley Players last year by showing off her singing. It had been hard overcoming her vomit-inducing stage fright, but she'd done it, showing them she had a pretty decent voice. Acting had been surprisingly fun in the panto but this was proving hard, hard work.

'Och, leave her be,' said Debbie, their local mad Scottish artist. 'She's doing a fine job.' Sarah smiled at her just as Cecil checked his watch for the eighty-third time, clearly desperate to get back home and see their visitor. Then it was Luke's turn. He was playing Caliban, and had been trying different voices and styles since the beginning of rehearsals. He began his lines, breathing heavily between each word as if he'd just legged it all the way to the theatre. But rather than having the dramatic effect he was hoping for, he was coming across as horribly asthmatic. Sarah stifled a giggle while Gregory bit his lip and looked at Conner, waiting for him to tackle this one.

'Umm ... Luke,' Conner began nervously. 'What, umm, what are you ... doing?' He ran a hand over his long, gelled black fringe.

'Oh,' Luke replied, colouring slightly. 'I thought I'd try something different.'

Mrs Andrews was the first to say, in her usual undiplomatic way, what everyone else was thinking. 'You sound like Darth Vader.'

'With a cold,' offered Gregory. 'I'd try a different technique, dear.'

'I thought you did it brilliantly before,' said Conner. 'Let's stick with that.'

At least it was better than Luke's first attempt, which had involved some sort of lisp and a lot of spit spray. Rehearsals eventually finished for the day with Sarah stumbling over one of her lines again as Mrs Andrews tutted. For some reason she just couldn't get the hang of this damn play. Maybe it was because the Greenley Players had been going for over a year and they were expected to be good – *she* was expected to be good. There was so much more pressure this time around.

'Sarah, darling, you really need to stop mumbling and fudging your lines,' said Mrs Andrews, tottering in her heels down the staircase at the front of the stage. 'You should enunciate, dear, like I do.'

'Yes, I know,' replied Sarah. It just wasn't worth getting into right now. Not only was she too eager to sneak over to Gregory and Cecil's cottage, but her body couldn't seem to decide if it was recovering from her hangover or not. One minute she felt fine, the next nausea swept over her, making her throat close over. She just wanted to get out in the fresh air.

Everyone said goodbye and Sarah watched as Gregory and Cecil raced off mumbling something about extra shopping including champagne and scallops. But from what she'd read she couldn't imagine Nathaniel Hardy would be that interested in eating fancy food. She wouldn't be if she'd had an affair and been found out. Chance would be a fine thing, she mused. The closest she'd ever got to marriage was a drunken proposal from a pervy fiddle player old enough to be her dad when she was at a wedding in Ireland years and years ago. Unsurprisingly she'd said no. Her heart twinged at the memory of her dad and she focused instead on the last time she'd seen Nathaniel Hardy on TV being suave and sexy.

'Ready?' asked Lottie, slinging her bag on her shoulder.

Realising she had been staring into space, Sarah quickly gathered up her copy of *The Tempest* and various multi-coloured pens she used for making notes, shoved them into her handbag and smiled. 'Let's go.' The excitement was bubbling up in her stomach – or the Alka Seltzer was getting to work – she wasn't sure which.

'Where are you two off to?' asked Sid.

'Nowhere that concerns you,' replied Lottie playfully. 'You go home and I'll be back soon. You can peel the potatoes if you like. We're just going for a walk.' Sid shrugged, probably assuming it was girly stuff and nothing he'd be interested in anyway. 'And here, you can lock up today.' Lottie threw the keys and Sid caught them just before they skewered his right eye.

'You're trusting me with the sacred keys?' He gasped and Lottie scowled. She'd always been very protective of the theatre as it was her nan's dying wish that she save it from being sold off. For the last year she'd fought hard to make that happen and amazingly, had succeeded.

As they left the theatre, walking in single file through the small revolving door, the sunshine was blinding. Squinting, Sarah reached into her bag for her sunglasses. The sounds of tinkling crockery and chattering voices escaped from the busy pubs along the seafront where people were enjoying their easy Sunday lunches. The town was more alive at this time of the day and Sarah took a deep breath trying to separate the different smells in her mind: beer, gravy, rich roast beef, and the tangy saltiness of the sea. Suddenly she was hungry. 'I wish my stomach would decide what it's doing. I'm not sure whether it wants me to fill it up or go nil by mouth.'

'I think you should eat something,' replied Lottie as they threaded their way through the pub tables that faced the promenade. 'Are you coming for lunch? I'm doing a big roast today.'

That sounded good, just the thing to fix her. 'Okay. Hey, are you going to tell Sid about Nate?' She was surprised Lottie hadn't said anything earlier.

'I will when we get home. I don't often get to know stuff he doesn't, so I thought I'd tease him for a bit.'

They crossed the main road, past the tiny but surprisingly well-stocked library, and took a left down a side alley into the narrow twisting lanes of the conservation area. For about half a square mile the houses were either small simple fishermen's cottages or larger Georgian houses with shuttered windows, black iron door knobs, and antique boot scrapers. Sarah loved walking through this part of town. In her mind's eye she could see various Jane Austen heroes cleaning their boots before knocking at the door and entering to woo some fine lady. Sarah couldn't afford to live in one of these houses, but Finn could, and did. She wondered if she'd see him today and the thought of that was almost more exciting than the prospect of catching a glimpse of Nate Hardy.

'Keep an eye out for Gregory and Cecil,' warned Sarah. 'Just in case they went to the shop first and are already on their way back. They were talking about getting some champers and expensive shellfish.' Scampering down another side street, Sarah began to sing the theme tune to *Mission Impossible*. Lottie joined in and as they approached the road where Gregory and Cecil lived. They pressed themselves into the wall before ducking down and glancing round the corner. In a final muffled burst of song, they flung themselves round the corner and collapsed into giggles. 'Shhh,' Sarah said, pressing her finger to her lips.

'You shush,' Lottie replied, still laughing. 'You started it.'

Gregory and Cecil lived in the third cottage along. The houses in this part of town didn't have front gardens, the front door opening straight onto the street. From many a drunken dinner party, Sarah knew that the sitting room was at the front of the house with large sash windows that faced the road. Sarah hoped Nate was in there watching telly rather than in the kitchen which was at the back of the house. 'Let's take a slow walk past and see if we spot him,' she said, gently pulling Lottie's arm to bring her level. They strolled as slowly as possible past the window. Sarah peered from the corner of her eye, but a frilly net curtain blocked her view. 'Pants. I can't see anything. Can you?'

'No. Damn their old lady net curtains.'

A man walked past, eyeing them suspiciously and Sarah pretended to be searching for something in her handbag. It was definitely excitement filling her stomach with bubbles now. The adrenaline was surging through her whole body making her feel jittery and giggly. 'It's no good,' Lottie continued. 'We're going to have to get closer, right up to the window. Go on, you first.'

'Why me?' asked Sarah, her eyes wide.

'This was your idea.'

'But you're smaller than me. You should do it.'

'Don't be heightist. Anyway, I'm not going on my own. Come on.' Lottie grabbed Sarah's arm and she had to push down the laughter filling her lungs, threatening to ruin their plan. 'We're the worst spies ever,' whispered Lottie and Sarah spluttered as the laughter forced its way out again. MI5 certainly wouldn't be recruiting them any time soon.

They came level with Gregory and Cecil's house again and bent down before edging towards the window. Sarah placed her fingertips on the sill and slowly lifted her head just high enough to see. Her heart gave a double beat as there, in real life, was Nate Hardy, lying out on the sofa in jeans and a T-shirt, his hands behind his head, eyes closed. He was just as handsome in person – or at least through their friends' window – as he was on-screen. Sarah's mind wandered, picturing what it would be like to wake up, roll over and see that face every morning. He had long dark eyelashes and a manly, rugged sexiness. A hint of toned abs peeked out where his T-shirt rode up. 'He's absolutely bloody gorgeous, isn't he?' she whispered to Lottie.

'He really is. I wish I had my long lens camera.'

'Pervert,' Sarah replied, and they giggled again.

A male voice that Sarah instantly recognised broke into the moment. 'And what do you two think you're doing?' asked Gregory. A shiver of shock ran down her spine. Both Sarah and Lottie looked over to see Gregory glowering at them and Cecil giving them stern looks while holding two shopping bags.

'Run!' Sarah shouted. And like a couple of kids caught stealing sweets, they legged it down the street and around the corner, only pausing when the laughter caused a sharp stitch to pierce Sarah's side.

Chapter 4

Nate's eyes shot open as a loud voice outside shouted something, but he didn't hear exactly what. He stood up and the fat ginger cat leapt off his lap. Nate rubbed his jaw, feeling the stubbly skin beneath his fingers. It always amazed him that women seemed to like his face, he never had. His cheeks were quite square, coming down into a strong chin. As he aged, his dark hair was receding, the hairline gradually moving backwards, though the papers hadn't picked up on that yet. Luckily, he didn't care about ageing. He wasn't worried about crow's feet or the deep-set wrinkles that were forming on his forehead. Nate had always made it a habit to not Google himself, having been told by Robin it wasn't a good idea. It was advice he'd taken. He certainly wasn't going to start doing it now with everything else that was going on. God only knew what they were saying about him. Gritty eyes burned with tiredness, and today Nate Hardy felt much older than his years.

Every alcove in the small, cosy living room was packed with row upon row of books, or photos of his two hosts together. With the low hum of the television in the background the place felt serene. He'd been watching an interior design programme and was sure he'd met the host on some morning chat show once. The front door opened and he heard the two men he was staying with muttering, and carrier bags rustling. Last night they'd been kindness itself if a little star struck, but he was used to that. They must have been in bed when Robin called because when Nate arrived they were in matching striped pyjamas and fluffy navy dressing gowns. He hadn't known what to expect from Robin's description but when they welcomed him in, holding out a cup of tea, it was a strange moment of peace among the chaos of the night.

On the drive down he'd gone over and over things in his head, replaying the scene at the theatre, the faces of his colleagues, the mixture of shock and glee in the audience. Just as he thought his heart was broken and trashed beyond all feeling, Hannah had smashed it even more, taking his pain to a new level. He really needed to call the stage manager and say thank you for handling it so well. If she hadn't taken charge, he didn't know what he'd have done.

After his hosts had settled him in and shown him up to his room with kind, gentle words, he'd slept surprisingly well, exhaustion taking over. This morning he'd enjoyed looking out over the sea when he'd woken up. For a moment it had been like he was on location somewhere, but within seconds the realisation of what was actually happening hit him like a smack in the face and any rest had fled his body, leaving him aching and weary. After getting dressed and using the spare toothbrush laid out for him, Nate had come downstairs. He'd definitely fallen on his feet with these people and he must thank them properly when this was all over. *If* it ended well, that was. If it didn't, he might not have any money to thank them with.

One of the guys poked his head around the living-room door. 'Good morning, Mr Hardy. I'm just making tea if you wanted one?'

'Yes, please, that'd be great. It was Geoffrey, wasn't it?' He followed him through into a large, bright and airy kitchen.

'It's Gregory actually,' he corrected, and Nate felt a flush of embarrassment. 'Come on, Mr Bennett,' Gregory said cheerfully to the cat.

'Right, sorry.' Nate ran his hand through his hair and smoothed it back down, admonishing himself for not getting the name right. The man had taken him in at a moment's notice. It was the least he could do and the height of bad manners to have got it wrong.

'No problem, dear boy. I'm sure with everything else that was going on last night, your poor brain was a whirl. And this is Cecil.'

Nate laughed self-consciously and gave Cecil a small smile to show he'd registered his name. 'Yes, it was all a bit … unexpected, but please call me Nate.' The French doors were open onto a small courtyard garden filled with plants in brightly coloured pots, all flowering and falling into each other in a strange organised chaos. A small wrought-iron table had been laid with a milk jug, sugar and a biscuit barrel in the shape of a pig. Gregory and Cecil went out to the table and sat down facing each other, leaving Nate to sit between them. He followed and absent-mindedly tapped the side of the tea cup set out for him, wondering how much they knew and how much to tell them. He didn't want people to think he was a creep, cheating on his wife, but he had an agreement with Emma he didn't want to break. No one else was to know his marriage was already a wreck. He really needed to speak to her. What had happened last night had changed everything. Maybe once he'd had his tea, he'd call her and talk things through. If she'd answer, that was.

'Tea?' asked Cecil, his kind, bright blue eyes twinkling in his tanned face. He'd either been out in the hot summer sun that had stifled the country these last few weeks, or he had a bottle of instant bronzer in the bathroom. Nate made a mental note to check.

'Yes, please.'

'It's just English breakfast tea. Nothing fancy.'

'That's the best kind,' said Nate. He much preferred a good cup of tea to coffee.

'Help yourself to milk and sugar.'

Mr Bennett strolled lazily out into the garden, flopping down in the sunniest spot, and a strange silence descended. Not uncomfortable, but not easy either. After adding milk to his tea, Nate clasped his hands together in his lap, feeling awkward. Gregory pushed the cheerful porcelain pig towards him. 'Biscuit?'

'No, thank you.'

The two men glanced at each other, clearly unsure what to say next. Nate cleared his throat before speaking. 'I'm very grateful to you both for taking me in at such short notice. Hopefully I won't be here very long.'

Cecil sat backwards. 'I see,' he said after a moment's pause and Nate realised how ungrateful and rude that had sounded. He hadn't meant it as an insult; the cottage was beautiful and the town, from what he had seen last night, seemed sweet and quiet. This was not going well. 'I didn't mean that rudely,' he reassured them. 'I just meant that hopefully I won't be under your feet for too long. I really am very grateful for your help.' Cecil relaxed back into his chair and Gregory smiled at Nate.

After a sip of tea, Nate tried a little harder at starting a conservation. 'You have a beautiful house.'

'Thank you, dear boy,' Gregory replied, clearly warmed by the compliment. 'We moved down here years ago. I used to be on the West End, but when my time was up, we decided to come down and start our little bookshop.'

'Is that how you know Robin?'

'Yes, we were around at the same time. We'd often go for the same roles, though he was far better than me, which is why I decided to give up and hideaway down here, but when his career started to wane, as happens ninety-nine times out of a hundred, he stayed and became an amazingly well-known agent. How do you like him?'

'He's great,' Nate said without hesitation. He trusted Robin implicitly and had been with him since the very early days of his career, when the only roles he got were bit parts in *Midsomer Murders* or three lines on *Casualty*. If anyone could get him out of this scrape it was Robin. 'Did you ever act together? You and Robin?'

Gregory nodded as he drank some more tea. 'A few times. I hate to remember it though, he put me to shame. He really was a very fine actor in his day. I was nearly always relegated to the chorus if we went for the same role. Still, I wouldn't change it for anything. I had a blast and to end up here, with Cecil, well, I couldn't be happier.' He reached out his hand and Cecil gave it a squeeze before returning to their respective cups.

Nate found himself smiling as he listened to Gregory talk of the stage. He hated that he would miss the last few performances of *Of Mice and Men*. It was odd that no matter how tired you became towards the end of a run, you still craved that thrill of stepping out onto the stage. When doing TV Nate missed the stage, and when on the stage he missed doing TV. Silly, really. The thought of losing both struck him again.

'Have you spoken to Robin today?' asked Gregory.

It was the first time they'd referred to what was going on and Nate felt himself stiffen defensively. He drew his arms in closer to his body as if to guard himself, and the muscles of his back tightened. But then he reminded himself that these men were Robin's trusted friends and not reporters. Robin wouldn't have suggested Nate stay with them if there was any risk they'd run to the papers. Nate caught them exchanging glances again at his silence, and felt guilty for being so suspicious. 'No, I haven't,' he replied eventually. 'I might give him a call when we've finished here and just see what's happening. I'm sure it's all over the papers now, but I daren't look.'

'No, dear, I wouldn't if I were you,' said Cecil. Nate looked up, expecting to see a gleeful face. It was what he'd come to expect from Emma and from critics, even fans sometimes. Everyone felt they had a right to judge you when you were in the public eye. But Nate was surprised to see a sympathetic, almost reassuring smile.

'This will all pass, dear boy,' Gregory said, pulling out a biscuit from the porcelain pig. 'If you can be sure of anything, it's that the press will soon find something else to write about and this will be old news.'

Nate's voice was small and shaky, and he cleared his throat again. 'I'm sure you're right.'

'Don't tell him that, Nathaniel,' replied Cecil, smiling. 'He'll only get big-headed.'

'I *am* always right, though.' Gregory grinned, and as they bickered playfully, Nate excused himself from the table and made his way upstairs to the cosy quiet bedroom to call Robin.

On the ninth attempt he finally got through. 'Robin, it's Nate. What's happening, mate?'

'"Good morning, Robin",' his agent said, pretending to be affronted at the lack of civility. '"I realise you've been working for hours and hours, most of the night in fact, trying to clean up my shit-show of a life, but I thought I'd check in and see how *you* are."'

Somehow managing to find a trace of his sense of humour, Nate smiled. 'I should really. You're not as young as you used to be.'

'That's enough of that.'

'But I do appreciate everything you're doing, Robin. You know that, right?'

The fondness in Robin's voice was evident. 'I do. How are you, Nate? Have Greg and Cecil settled you in?' Robin made it sound like this was a hotel, or some kind of wellness retreat for his own good and Nate felt a flare of frustration at the mess he'd created and all the extra work he'd caused Robin. Nate didn't have time to be settled in here, he needed this all sorted so he could get back to London and get his career back on track. He took a deep breath, knowing it was tiredness and stress making him lose control of his emotions.

'They're very nice but I really need to know what's happening there. What's going on with Hannah? Is she gone? And have you talked to Emma yet? She's—'

'Wow, slow down, slow down.' Nate drew back the net curtain and watched the sea shimmer in the light before rubbing his hot eyes with the heel of his hand. 'We're in a difficult situation with her. She's threatening to sell her story to the tabloids. *Hot News* are offering a lot of money for it, but I'm in discussions with her agent.'

'I thought that you paid her before and it was understood that she'd forget about it?' Hearing himself say the words made him feel dirty and a complete scumbag. If only he could wind the clock back and stop himself from making such a stupid mistake.

'We didn't have a contract drawn up and signed, Nate. It was just an understanding. Normally that's enough.'

A lump formed in Nate's throat and he had to work hard to get the words out. 'So what do we do now?'

'I'm negotiating another payment to her. Her agent will make it clear she really has to let this go now.'

'Do you think she will?' He could hear Robin's polished brogues tapping on the floor as he paced.

'Yes, I think so. We don't want to get all legal and make this more complicated than it needs to be. If the press were to pick up on something like that it'd look even worse for you. Has she made contact with you?'

'What? Called?'

'Yeah.'

'No. Nothing yet.' He rubbed his eyes again as the bright sun made them sting.

'If she does, don't answer her. She could record it and go straight to the press.'

'Really?'

'Yes.'

'Okay.' Nate nodded to himself. As horrid as it was to believe, Robin was right. 'Robin, tell me honestly, how bad is this looking?'

'Look, Nate, I know this feels like the end of your career and it is a blip, I won't lie. It's a big one. But you're not the first man to have done this and you won't be the last. It will all die down soon enough, and we'll try and repair the damage. You haven't Googled yourself, have you?'

'No.'

'Good. Don't. Things will get nastier before they get better.'

'Just give me the rundown.' He had to know how the world was seeing him. How his fans were seeing him. It wasn't vanity, it was that, stupidly, their opinion mattered to him. These people he didn't know had sent him nice messages on his birthday. They hadn't known that he'd been alone because Emma was out shagging her lover. Their messages had made him feel less lonely. He knew his actions had disappointed them. He'd let them down and he desperately wanted to say sorry, but he couldn't.

Robin went on, 'The papers are portraying you as a complete dick for cheating on your wife, who's now the nation's sweetheart by default. That's no surprise and we're sending out a press release just asking for privacy while you deal with recent events. We're not saying you did or didn't do anything at this stage. Then there's outrage from those who were hoping to see you in the last few shows. Twitter's gone mental, so turn off your notifications, and you're now a meme thanks to some recording people took on their mobile phones.'

Nate sat down on the side of the bed, his shoulders slumped.

'It's all to be expected though, and within a week this will have calmed down if we keep up with the illness story and you and Emma show a united front. We'll have to do some good PR and you and Emma are going to have to put off your divorce for a bit—'

'Oh, she'll love that.' She'd hate him even more now, if that was possible.

'It can't be helped. An amicable divorce is far more acceptable to the public than something like this. A few public appearances together and then in six to eight months' time you can divorce as planned.' Nate smiled to himself at how Robin had it all figured out. It was why he was one of the best. 'A couple of casting directors have politely withdrawn the offers of roles, but I don't think you were going to do them anyway, so never mind that.'

'Which ones?' Nate asked, feeling a stone settle in his stomach and his intestines wrap around it.

'It doesn't matter.' The fact that Robin didn't want to tell him was worrying. 'There'll be more though, so be prepared.'

'Have you spoken to Emma again?' Nate asked cautiously. Though Emma didn't love him and hadn't for a while, his heart still ached. They'd been together for so long. A part of him still cared for her and wanted her to be okay. Robin didn't answer. 'Have you?'

'Sort of.'

'Sort of?'

'I've made sure she's okay, but I think you should talk to her about the plan to put off the divorce. It isn't my place to go into that sort of thing.'

A wry smile pulled at Nate's mouth. 'You mean you're scared of Emma blowing her top?'

'Terrified.'

'Don't worry, I'll call her in a minute.' Nate sighed.

'Good luck,' Robin replied. 'Let me know what she says, especially if it changes things. I've got to get back to Hannah's agent. She wants quite a lot of money this time. But, Nate, this will all be okay in the end, okay? Just give it time.'

'All right. But I'll pay anything, Robin. I just need this to end for mine and Emma's sakes.'

'I don't know why you're worrying about her after the way

she's treated you, but I'll do my best. It's all I can do.

'I know, and I appreciate it. Truly.'

'Just chill out there and stay out of sight. We don't want the papers getting wind of where you are. Okay? Oh, and some clothes will be delivered to you shortly. I've sent them via courier.'

'Okay, I'll speak to you later.' As the call ended Nate realised he was shaking. His hands trembled and his head pounded as he pressed the button to call Emma. It rang a few times before she answered. When she finally spoke, her voice was cold and harsh.

'You've got a bloody cheek ringing me.'

'Emma, look, I'm really sorry for all of it, but we need to discuss how we're going to get through this. I've been speaking to Robin and he suggests we put off the divorce—'

'What? For God's sake, Nate, really? You know how serious things are between me and Stewart now.' Christ, she was selfish sometimes. And cold. She'd always had an ice queen quality about her that, in the beginning, he'd found attractive. Her cool good looks – pale skin, blue eyes and light blonde hair – had set her apart from all the other girls. But as time had gone on, the coolness had become an impenetrable coldness freezing him out of her life. At first, she'd been happy to stay with him as he was getting more famous, hoping there'd be a knock-on to her career. But then she'd become jealous, jealousy had turned to anger, and anger had turned into affairs. Since things had got serious with her latest fling, divorce was suddenly on the cards. 'Why shouldn't I just do it now?' she asked spitefully. 'The world's on my side remember, Nate. Every woman in the country is going to sympathise with me. Do you know how humiliating this is for me? A glamour model. I mean, how corny can you get? Every little detail of your sordid affair is going to come out if we're not careful. Do you realise you're dragging our name through the mud?'

Nate felt the heat of shame rise up his spine. 'I'm sorry,' he said again. 'But I think we can come out of this with some dignity though if we do what Robin says. He's concerned that if we split now and the press go digging, they'll find out …' He searched for the right words, not wanting to openly mention her affairs and settled on 'more'. Nate lowered his head, placing his thumb and index finger on his temples. Applying some gentle pressure, he tried to ignore the pounding at the back of his eyes. 'I made a mistake, Emma, just like you did.' He didn't want to remind her that she'd begged him not to end their marriage when he'd discovered her first affair. The memory still stung. She'd asked him to keep it quiet, and he'd agreed to turn a blind eye for months now. 'Please? All I'm asking for is a little … understanding.' She scoffed. Emma loved to throw salt onto the wound and he was fed up of being a doormat, all for the sake of public image. 'Listen, Robin is trying to speak to Hannah's agent, offering her some money to keep this private. He thinks we should put off the divorce for another six to eight months and let this die down—'

'Six to eight months? Are you fucking joking? I was thinking two at the most.'

'I wish I was.' The line went quiet while she considered it. She must know it was best. Making a bigger deal of things now with a messy split would only encourage the press to dig into their lives and see if he'd done it before, which would risk them uncovering her affairs and ruining her reputation. Her big-wig producer daddy would ruin his career forever if that happened. He'd already threatened that after one of her early affairs. They both needed this. He could picture Emma thinking, pushing her hand through her long, blonde hair. She was more likely to listen to a suggestion of Robin's.

'Fine,' Emma agreed with a huff. 'But, Nate—'

'Yes?'

'Get this sorted. Now.' She hung up.

'I will,' he said to himself, placing his phone down on the bed. He had to. If he didn't, he'd lose everything.

Chapter 5

Thank God it was Wednesday, Sarah thought, checking the work diary on her desk. The start of the week was always ridiculously busy at the doctor's surgery where she worked as a receptionist. Somehow the townsfolk became super sick over the weekend and so, at eight-thirty each Monday morning, when the phone line switched from voicemail, the entire population of Greenley-On-Sea called up to see the doctor. Sarah loved her job, but she was always surprised at how open people were about their problems, even though she never asked. The things she'd heard had created frightening mental pictures. Pictures she could never un-see. She also suspected some of the more menopausal women had a crush on Finn too, because they insisted on seeing only him. Sarah couldn't imagine anything more embarrassing than discussing hot flushes, dry lady bits, and hormone replacement therapy while Finn looked at you with his gorgeous brown eyes and smiled reassuringly with his lovely kissable lips. Realising she was chewing her pen lid and ignoring Mandy, the other receptionist, Sarah quickly pulled her attention back to the conversation.

'So then,' Mandy continued, 'Harry says to me, "Don't you think you should cut down, you'll only moan about being fat later." Bloody cheeky sod. So do you know what I did?'

'What did you do?' asked Sarah, smiling and switching on her desk fan. It was getting hot already. When the doors opened for the day their location on the seafront meant a cooler breeze would let some air in, but it was going to be another scorcher.

'Well, I hit him over the head with my family bar of choccy and told him if he ever said anything like that to me again, I'd divorce him.' Sarah could well believe it. She didn't want to get on the wrong side of Mandy, as some of their more pushy patients had found out. Though a little bit scary she was an absolute joy to work with. She'd started at the surgery six months ago and was both scarily efficient and hilariously funny. They both liked Wednesdays best. The crazy Monday morning rush of emergency appointments had passed and it was all a little more relaxed come the middle of the week, which meant they could actually enjoy their jobs and catch up on the gossip. Even moody Dr Stephanie Shepherd was a little bit less horrible. Unlike Finn, Dr Shepherd didn't like to take extra appointments, and from Monday through to Wednesday had a face like a constipated bear.

While Mandy regaled Sarah with a detailed account of the subsequent argument between husband and wife, a figure approached the automatic door and held up his hand in greeting. It was Dr Finn MacDonald and Sarah could feel the smile lighting up her face. She got up to go and open it, smoothing down her dress. Her favourite striped summer dress that stopped at just the right place, making her legs look long and lean. She reached down behind the fake plastic pot plant to switch the automatic door to open and let him in. He was in his normal black suit with a grey shirt, undone at the collar and no tie. His slightly curly strawberry blond hair fell onto his face and Sarah tried to play it cool. As soon as the gap was wide enough, Finn squeezed his tall, rangy frame through the doors. 'Thanks. Morning, Sarah.' He smiled and his eyes sparkled.

'Morning, Dr MacDonald.'

'Morning, Mandy.'

She broke off mid-sentence. 'Morning, Doc.'

'Nice weekend?' he called over his shoulder as he strode towards the office.

Sarah's mouth opened, ready to tell him all about Nathaniel Hardy but remembering it was a secret, closed it again. 'Not bad, thanks.' She tidied some magazines on the small coffee table next to a bank of chairs. 'I didn't really do much. You?' He turned to answer her, walking backwards.

'Oh, I met some friends but otherwise no, pretty quiet actually.' The corners of his mouth lifted causing creases to form in his cheeks, then he spun back and went into his office. Sarah took her seat at the reception desk and tried to stop fantasising about kissing him, by tidying up her in-tray. About ten minutes later Finn came back out carrying a file and Sarah concentrated on her screen. The next thing she felt was him leaning down, his arm resting on the back of her chair as he placed the file beside her keyboard. His naturally husky voice sent a shiver down her spine. 'Could you chase up Mr Robinson's MRI results for me please? I need to call him today and they're taking ages at the hospital.'

A husky voice asking her to chase up a crotchety old man's MRI results shouldn't make her leg twitch and get her all hot and bothered, but something about Finn MacDonald's voice did that to her. She swallowed. 'Yes, of course. I'll do it first thing.'

'Thanks. I'll tell you what, I'll make you a cup of tea in return.' He picked up her cup emblazoned with the phrase, 'There's a fairly good chance this is gin', and disappeared. It took every fibre of her being not to turn around and watch him go. Mandy teased her enough already.

In fact, Mandy was already holding her cup in the air, waving it madly and saying, 'Oi, what about me?' to which Finn came back and grabbed it.

'How could I forget you, Mandy, hey?'

When he'd gone to the kitchen, Mandy looked over and gave Sarah a wink. 'He likes you.'

'Only as his receptionist,' Sarah replied with an ache in her chest. Finn was the perfect man as far as she was concerned. She'd known him for a year so if anything happened it wouldn't be a whirlwind romance. She wasn't making that mistake again. People always said the best relationships begin at work but there wasn't much chance of anything happening as far as she could see. 'I don't think he sees me as anything more. He's been here for a year and hasn't made a move yet.'

'Well, he never flirts with *me* like that.'

'He wasn't flirting!' *Was he?* 'He was making tea and asking for MRI results.'

Mandy shrugged. 'Maybe he's not sure how you feel about him?'

'How can he not be?' As much as Sarah hated to admit it, she knew she sometimes went bright pink when Finn spoke to her, and he must know, from the way she looked at him. But it wasn't just his body she was attracted to. He was kind, caring, charismatic, and good with kids. You only had to see him with the young ones who were scared that something was really wrong with them. He always had them laughing and joking before they even entered his consulting room.

Oh, this was ridiculous. She could pretty much feel herself ovulating at the thought of having kids with Finn. They'd be bloody gorgeous.

Mandy gave her a knowing smile. 'You wait,' she said sagely. 'Just you wait.'

Finn delivered them both cups of tea, pausing by Sarah's desk. 'It's not gin, I'm afraid.'

'That's okay,' Sarah replied. 'I've got a hip flask in my top drawer.'

Much to her delight, Finn laughed at her joke. Making him laugh was one of the highlights of Sarah's day. The way he lifted his head and tipped it backwards did something to Sarah's heart. And the way his Adam's apple bobbed up and down made her want to reach up and kiss him. She felt her cheeks grow hot.

'I know where to come when I need a drop then,' Finn replied. For a moment their eyes stayed on each other, as the gentlest of smiles played on his lips. If Helen's face launched a thousand ships, then Finn MacDonald's launched a thousand twitches, all filling Sarah's body with such an intense heat she was actually relieved when he went back to his room. Goodness, she was worse than the menopausal posse.

* * *

Every day the surgery closed for an hour during lunch and once the last patient had gone, all the staff had lunch together in the staffroom. They were lucky that it was quite modern and airy with comfortable seats. Sarah had worked in some places where the staffroom was more like a dungeon designed to torture the good humour out of you. Mandy was always ready to start a conversation with whoever was near her and today she'd turned her attention to Finn.

Meanwhile, Sarah flicked through the weekly gossip mag that someone had left on the table. The front page was full of the Nathaniel Hardy scandal. Sarah still couldn't quite believe he was in town, staying with Gregory and Cecil. The picture in the magazine had been taken as Nathaniel had left the theatre after his disastrous last performance. The poor man looked completely shell-shocked and Sarah wondered what she would say if she ever met him. There was no excuse for cheating in her book. The memory of the night she'd decided to surprise her ex, Vince, at his house, only to find him in bed with someone else, flitted through her mind before she could stop it. Could this be why she was struggling with playing Miranda in *The Tempest*, perhaps? Miranda fell in love for the first time in the play, and when Sarah had fallen for Vince she'd fallen hard, thinking it was the real deal. Remembering his betrayal still stung her heart.

To distract herself from the memory, Sarah tuned back in to Mandy's conversation with Finn.

'So, Dr Mac, who were these friends you met up with, hey? Was it a naughty weekend away?' Sarah felt a slight flush at the innuendo and hoped it hadn't been.

'Just some guys I knew at medical school,' Finn answered and smiled at the memory.

Maybe it *had* been a dirty weekend away. The way he was smiling, it seemed he was remembering something nice, but then he'd said, 'guys'. Not girls, or women, or ladies.

'They work in Nottingham so I went up to see them on Saturday, came back yesterday. Good thing, really. I needed yesterday to recover.' Finn turned to Sarah, clearly eager to head off Mandy's line of questioning. 'How are rehearsals going, Sarah?'

'Urgh, rubbish,' Sarah replied, resting her sandwich in her lap. 'I'm really struggling with *The Tempest*. I just can't seem to get the hang of Miranda's speech and I find it all a bit confusing.' She felt a bit silly saying it, but at least if they knew now how much she hated it, they might excuse a bad performance later, which was undoubtedly what she'd give unless she could crack it. Finn chewed thoughtfully on a mouthful of crisps.

'*The Tempest* is the one on an island isn't it, with Caliban and Prospero?'

She nodded. 'Do you remember it?'

'Vaguely.' He shrugged. 'I'm not great on Shakespeare and I know nothing about acting. I wish I could help.'

Sarah smiled. 'Don't worry, there's a while to go yet. I'm sure I'll get it eventually.' Though it might mean facing up to feelings about Vince that she'd hoped had faded.

'Of course you will,' Mandy reassured her. 'I'm sure you'll be brilliant. Better than that Mrs Andrews, she's a right old handful, isn't she?'

'She definitely has her moments,' said Sarah, remembering the first time she'd met the MP's terrifying wife. Mrs Andrews had wanted to play Beatrice in the Greenley Players' first attempt at Shakespeare last year. They'd performed *Much Ado About Nothing* and it had been so bad it had nearly spelt the end of the Greenley Players and the theatre. It was only thanks to Lottie that things had kept going. A sudden hard knock on the door out in the reception area caught their attention. 'Who can that be?' said Sarah, checking her watch. 'The guy who collects all the gross stuff doesn't normally come till three and the town know we close for lunch. I hope it isn't an emergency.'

The knocking continued.

'If it's a patient demanding to be seen,' said Mandy, adjusting her posture as if she was readying for a fight, 'I'll be giving them what-for. We've got another fifteen minutes till we re-open. Everyone knows we close from one till two. Not a moment before or less.' Three more decisive knocks echoed through the empty surgery. 'Are they actually trying to break the bloody door down?' Mandy asked.

They all made their way out of the staffroom, down the corridor and into the reception area. Everyone knew that the surgery closed for lunch; no one would bang on the door like this unless it was an emergency. Images flashed through Sarah's mind of someone holding a child in desperate need of a doctor, or of someone bent double having run to get help for a road accident, but there'd been no sirens, no sign of trouble. When Sarah saw the figure outside the glass door, fist raised, ready to knock again, her heart stopped beating. Every muscle paused. No air filled her lungs, and she didn't dare breathe. In that instant she knew that everything would be different from now on. That the life she had begun to love was about to change, and not for the better.

Finn carried on towards the door, his shoulders squared, carrying an air of authority. Mandy stopped when she realised

54

Sarah was lagging behind. 'What's wrong, love? Christ, you've gone white as a sheet. What's the matter?'

The man at the door had stopped banging and stood back with his hands in his trouser pockets. Clearly there was no medical emergency. The only emergency was the one suddenly happening in Sarah's own life. The man looked like any normal customer they might see. Blond hair cut short, greying at the temples, wrinkled features.

'Do you know him?' asked Mandy, placing her hand on Sarah's forearm. Sarah's hands were covering her mouth. Finn turned around and waited for Sarah's reply. His eyes were full of concern and a small line had formed where his eyebrows pulled together in confusion. 'Sarah?' Mandy asked again, giving her a gentle shake. Stuck in a moment of suspended animation, Sarah looked first at Mandy and then at Finn, knowing that if there had ever been any hope of something happening between them, that hope was about to be snuffed out like a lit match caught in a breeze. Everyone would know her secret soon, and she had no idea how to deal with it.

Under their concerned gaze, Sarah forced the words out of her dry mouth. 'It's my dad.'

* * *

'Do you want me to open the door?' asked Finn. 'Or should I tell him to go away?'

A shiver ran down Sarah's spine, carrying all the way to the tips of her fingers as she balled her hands into fists. Did she want to go out there and talk to him, or would it be better to speak in here? Should she speak to him at all? If he came inside everyone would know what he'd done. But then, if he was back, they were bound to find out sooner or later anyway. Her mind whirled with a million and one things as all the while Finn watched her.

'You can speak to him in my room if you want,' he said gently, and Sarah found herself nodding. Finn moved forwards and opened the door. Ben, Sarah's dad, stepped forwards in his tatty brown suede shoes. He'd always worn shoes like that. Had he been allowed to wear them in prison? she wondered. Every sound was muffled but she heard Ben politely thank Finn for letting him in and say something about wanting to speak to her. Finn walked back towards the staffroom. As he passed Sarah he reached out and took her arm. 'I'll be in the staffroom if you need anything.'

Mandy followed him out, casting a concerned glance at Sarah. Though she tried to respond with a smile to show she would be okay, Sarah couldn't seem to move her face. Her features were frozen in a mask of startled panic.

'Hello, sugarplum,' Ben said in a hoarse voice she barely recognised. But by calling her sugarplum she was suddenly six years old again, her dad reading her bedtime stories, or a teenager, and he was picking up the pieces after a boy had broken her heart. Sarah's frozen body began to thaw but before it could her brain replayed one of the last times they had spoken. It had been on the phone because he was in prison. She was alone, dealing with her mother's rapid decline from cancer. A sudden surge of anger hardened her jaw and made her teeth clench. How could he have left them to deal with everything alone? Left her? And even worse, how could he come back now?

Straightening up, she said, 'We can speak in Dr MacDonald's room.'

At her coldness Ben's face fell, but she had no sympathy for him. He couldn't have expected a warm welcome, and if he did, he was a fool. With a brisk turn on her heel Sarah marched into Finn's room, leaving Ben to close the door behind him. He had barely taken his hand off the handle when she asked, 'What are you doing here?'

Ben pushed his glasses back up the bridge of his nose. He'd always done that when he was nervous or thinking. 'I was released from prison last week. I … I wanted to see you.'

'Why?' Her voice was harsh, with a hardness she hadn't known herself capable of. The question shocked him and his head shot up, eyes full of hurt.

'Because you're my daughter.'

'I've got nothing to say to you.' Sarah crossed her arms firmly over her chest, unwavering.

'Sugarplum, please—'

'Don't call me sugarplum. I'm not a child. And I have nothing to say to you. You're not my father anymore.'

The wrinkles of Ben's forehead collided as he knitted his brows together. 'You don't mean that.'

'Yes, I do. You selfishly stole money from your job and got yourself slung into prison leaving me to deal with Mum dying all on my own.' There was so much more to mention but she couldn't bring herself to say it. She'd locked those things away, too much to deal with at the time and too scared to try now.

'I know.' He dropped his eyes and kept them on the ground. 'I'm sorry. I—'

'Sorry isn't enough, Dad. Sorry can never erase my memories of watching Mum wither away. Of having to sort out the funeral all on my own, of having to pretend you'd left us to work abroad because it was easier than telling everyone you'd been sent to prison. Sorting out all of Mum's clothes when she'd gone—' Sarah's voice cracked and tears pooled in her eyes. She squeezed them shut, willing the tears away. She'd vowed long ago not to cry over her dad anymore. Taking a quick breath in, she said, 'How dare you come back.'

Ben hung his head in what Sarah hoped was shame and shoved his glasses back up. 'I had nowhere else to go.'

'Then find somewhere, because I never want to see you again.' The room felt suddenly oppressive, like the world was shrinking, threatening to crush her. She needed to get out. To get away from him. Hurrying to the door, she flung it open and marched off.

Finn must have heard her raised voice, as he was waiting for her at the staffroom door. 'He's leaving,' Sarah said without looking back. 'Can you make sure he goes – please?' He opened his mouth to speak but she headed him off, worried what he would think of her now. 'I'll be okay, I just need him to go.'

Whilst Finn escorted Ben out of the building, Mandy slid back into the staffroom.

'Jesus Christ on a bike, that was intense,' said Mandy. 'What was all that about?' Sarah turned but couldn't speak. If she was going to tell anyone it would be Lottie and she hated the fact she was going to have to wait till tonight to do it. 'Sarah?'

'I'm sorry, Mandy. I can't.' A fierce heat burned her cheeks. 'I just can't right now.'

'All right, love. But do you really have a hip flask in your top drawer? Because I could do with a drop now and I don't even drink gin.'

'No,' Sarah replied, trying to smile and pretend everything was okay. She smoothed down her brown hair, her heart beating rapidly. 'But I bloody wish I did.'

Chapter 6

Sarah stood in front of the theatre's revolving doors wondering whether to go in or not. The theatre had become a safe, happy place for her and, as cheesy as it sounded, a home from home – a place full of friends. Well mostly, if you excluded Mrs Andrews. But even she wasn't that bad underneath it all. Sarah took a deep breath and rubbed her forehead. She wasn't sure if she wanted to go in after all that had happened today. She'd been supremely angry all afternoon, and as that had begun to fade, she felt nothing but tired and exhausted.

Somehow, she had managed to hold it together that afternoon at the surgery, smiling at the patients and answering the phone. She'd even managed to laugh with Mandy about the soap opera they both watched. Mandy had questions, but they were ones Sarah wasn't prepared to answer yet. Finn had grabbed her once during a quick tea-making round to see if she was okay. As they stood together by the boiling kettle, a part of her had wanted to tell him everything. She just knew that he'd understand how angry she was and not judge her for it. But she couldn't bring herself to tell him anything at all. The risk of lowering his opinion of her made her shy away from opening up. But she was sure that when she left that day, saying goodbye to him across the empty surgery, there'd been something between them. He'd kept his eyes on her a moment too long and there'd been a spark in the air, something new that hadn't been there before.

'Are you coming in, Sarah?' It was Luke, the guy playing Caliban. Without thinking Sarah took a step forward; it seemed she was going in after all. Besides, she still needed to tell Lottie what had happened. It was strange that after being so secretive for so long, she actually wanted to tell someone. She couldn't imagine not telling her best friend and bottling everything back up. Lottie would know what to say to make her feel better. She always did. 'Are you all right?' Luke asked, giving her a concerned look when she didn't move any further inside.

Sarah plastered on a smile. It was time to act normal, even if she didn't feel it. 'Yes, I'm fine thanks, Luke. Just a busy day at work.' They entered together, making polite conversation about the weather and how the play was going, to see most of the main cast had already arrived. Sid and Lottie were setting the stage with a circle of chairs ready to have another read-through, whilst the other players stood around chatting or muttering their lines to themselves.

Sarah approached her best friend. 'Hey.'

Lottie's high blonde ponytail swished as she turned. 'Hey, you.' Her smile quickly faded. 'Are you okay? You look like you've been crying.'

'I'm fine,' said Sarah as Mrs Andrews waltzed in, waving to everyone like the Queen on a state visit. 'Can we catch up later, though?'

'Yeah, of course,' Lottie replied, gently rubbing Sarah's arm. Sarah gave a weak smile and forced down the anger and hurt still pushing up from her chest. Diverting her attention, she fumbled in her bag for her copy of *The Tempest* and climbed onto the stage to find a seat. She would have preferred talking to Lottie before the rehearsal, but they only had just under four weeks till showtime and there was a lot still to learn in that time.

The stagehands were busy painting the large jagged boards of wood at the back of the stage that were being made to look like rocks. Debbie McCray had already sketched out what they were to look like and two of the guys were painting them as instructed. It was like painting by numbers, just bigger. As a local artist Debbie was proving amazingly useful in designing sets. In the middle, between the boards, stood an MDF cut-out of a sparse, leafless tree. It was yet to be painted but even in this half-decorated state the theatre was coming together and that always sent a thrill down Sarah's spine.

Debbie had just arrived herself, and her strong Scottish tones echoed around the theatre. 'Sorry I'm late, everyone,' she called, eyeing the work being done on stage. 'I had a wee accident in the gallery.' She lifted bright red hands, stained with paint, but her smile was wide and cheery. She was wearing a green tie-dye dress that clashed wildly with her newly dyed cherry-red hair. Quite possibly, it was this that was all over her hands.

'Whatever happened?' asked Mrs Andrews. Since last year Mrs Andrews had softened somewhat towards her fellow players, but that didn't stop her being a right old snooty boots when it suited her, or trying to take over. She looked at Debbie as if she was a knife-wielding lunatic smothered in blood.

'Och, I didn't realise a tube of cadmium had a split in it until I squeezed some out onto my palette and the whole bloody thing exploded onto my hands. Now look.' Debbie wiggled her fingers. 'Never mind though, it'll fade in a week or two.'

Mrs Andrews shook her head. There was no way she would have waited that long. She liked everything to be spotless; her housekeeper was working overtime dealing with the dust and debris from the kitchen extension.

Gregory and Cecil were the next to arrive in matching bright white loafers and long tailored shorts. They looked like they were on the Riviera rather than in Greenley; all they lacked were straw boaters. From the way they fidgeted, they were still incredibly excited about their little secret and took a seat either side of Sarah, grinning at each other like pantomime dames.

'How's your visitor?' whispered Sarah.

'Oh my gosh,' said Gregory, 'he is completely adorable, isn't he Cecil?'

'Ad-or-a-ble,' Cecil confirmed, before sitting back and running a hand through his short brownish-grey hair.

'Did he appreciate your spare pants?' Cecil gave her his we-are-not-amused look.

'Obviously he's kept himself to himself being under house arrest but, do you know,' Gregory said in a hurried whisper, 'the other night while I was making spag bol he came in and offered to help chop the mushrooms.' Gregory sat back as if he'd just said Nate had offered to pay off the rest of his mortgage. Sarah opened her mouth into a wide circle of mock surprise.

'Oh my gosh! He did not. What a gent!' she teased, but her tone soon sharpened as she recalled why he was there. 'Well, we'd best forget all about him being a cheating scumbag then, hadn't we? He clearly isn't an absolute grade A knob cheese if he offered to chop mushrooms for the spag bol.'

Cecil straightened up defensively. 'All right, Sarky Sue. What's the matter with you?'

The back of Sarah's neck prickled. She was being horribly unfair to Gregory and Cecil, plus downright rude. Of course they were excited about having a gorgeous TV star come to stay with them in secret. They didn't deserve her grumpiness just because she'd had the worst day in history. It was all her stupid dad's fault. She had to get a grip on the anger still pulsing around her system. Lowering her head, Sarah softened. 'I'm really sorry, guys. I just had a really shitty day, that's all.' Looking imploringly at them both, she wished she could tell them, but as there was a chance that after today her dad wouldn't come back, she chose not to. If he didn't come back, no one need ever know what had happened.

Gregory leaned over and rested his hand on hers. 'Do you want to talk about it?'

Seeing his kind face made her throat tighten as she tried to control her emotions. 'No thanks, it's fine. Best to just forget about it, I think. I really need to concentrate on this anyway.' She shook her copy of *The Tempest* at them and began thumbing through the pages.

'Right, everyone,' said Conner, bringing the meeting to order. He'd changed his lip ring for a long bar and his hair was gelled up into a Mohican. If you didn't know him you'd think he was a thug but he was actually quite shy and sweet. Only in his second year at university, he was still working with the Greenley Players to gain some more experience. Sarah hadn't had any idea what she wanted to do at Conner's age and found his focus remarkable. 'I thought we'd begin with the scene where—' They heard the door revolve and looked up.

'Coo-eee! Wait for me,' called Kathryn, another new member of the players. She came in with a long baggy cardigan hanging off one shoulder, her handbag dangling from her forearm and her unbrushed hair falling out of its bun. 'Sorry, I had to wait for Steve to get home so he could give me a lift.' Conner smiled. No one could be mad at Kathryn even though she was always late. She was like an insanely cheerful mother hen.

After a moment he began again. 'Okay then, everyone, we really need to get started. I wanted to work on act one, scene two. It's one of the key scenes in the play where we first meet Prospero, Miranda, Caliban and the spirits. But before we do, can I just remind you all that *The Tempest* has some singing in it too.'

Everybody groaned. Even Sarah. Though she was known as the singer of the group, with a voice often compared to Adele's, singing weird Shakespearean rhymes was proving incredibly difficult for everyone. The last time they'd tried they sounded like a bunch of drunks making their way up the High Street after a few too many. 'We all need to practise,' reminded Conner. 'So please do the exercises Gregory gave you last time.' Gregory glowed at the reference to him.

'Also,' interrupted Lottie, 'we'll need an accompaniment for the song. I've been through the storeroom and all I could find was one maraca, a triangle, and a tambourine with a hole in. Does anyone play a musical instrument?' Everyone gazed around at everyone else, but all heads were shaking.

'I played the clarinet at school,' offered Mrs Andrews, 'and though I was very good, I haven't played for years.' Gregory and Cecil rolled their eyes at Mrs Andrews' modesty.

'I used to play the drums,' said Luke. Sarah had a mental image of Luke sitting in front of upturned saucepans using wooden spoons as drumsticks because suffice to say, the Greenley Players didn't own a drum kit.

'Okay,' replied Lottie with a disappointed shrug. 'I guess I'll have to figure something out.'

'Thanks, Lottie,' said Conner and he turned back to Sarah. 'Right, Sarah, why don't you start us off.'

Sarah took a deep breath and began to read, thankful she wasn't expected to know this by heart yet. '"If by your art, my dearest father"...' Her voice trailed away, the day's intense feelings flooding back in a second. Her dad had come back. Today. His sad, worn face at the surgery doors suddenly flashed into her mind. She'd managed not to think about him for so long and she hated that he was forcing her to do it now. He'd been a dear father during her childhood. It had been perfect. He'd called her sugarplum, stroked her head when she was ill, even grabbed her fizzy drinks and chocolate when she was hungover. Her face tensed as tears unexpectedly threatened and she recalled the day they found out he'd been stealing from his bosses' firm. And then her mum was diagnosed with cancer and it was only because of that the firm agreed to keep everything quiet, but her dad was still prosecuted. He still went to prison and left them. It destroyed her mother and made it harder for her to fight the cancer that ultimately consumed her. It was all his fault. She would never forgive him because things might have been different, if only he'd been there.

'Sarah?' asked Conner gently. She looked up to see everyone staring at her. Even Mrs Andrews had a flicker of concern on her Botoxed face. Lottie's brow was wrinkled in worry and Sarah averted her eyes.

'Sorry,' she muttered. 'I think I've got hay fever.' Sarah wiped at her cheek making sure there were no tears, then cleared her throat and began from where she'd left off. '"You have put the wild waters in this roar, allay them."' Her voice lacked any sort of emotion, aware that if she did tap into her feelings there'd be no telling what would come out.

Rehearsals continued but every time Sarah spoke she felt everyone's eyes on her again and was grateful when her scene ended and Mrs Andrews began as Ariel. Her strong, powerful voice filled the theatre. Halfway through a line, Conner interrupted. 'Mrs Andrews, that was great but you're still playing Ariel as if Ariel is the one in charge of the relationship. Try and remember that Prospero holds all the cards here and is the dominant one.'

Mrs Andrews couldn't have looked more disgusted if Conner had sat in her lap and farted. Sarah suppressed a grin, grateful for the distraction. Last year, Conner had been so quiet and shy, his role as director was a bit of a joke – not surprising as he was only 18 then and spent most of his time hiding under his long gelled black fringe. Since then, the change in his confidence was incredible. They began again and despite the banging of nails being driven in to the scenery, and the swish of paintbrushes, they seemed to make some progress.

'Thanks, everyone,' said Conner. 'Before we finish, I was thinking about a little game we could play to get to know the characters a little more. I'd like you to tell me three things about a character. It can be anything at all, so it could be about their appearance, personality, or their actions.'

'Does it have to be about the character we're playing?' asked Luke.

'No. It can be any character. Just name them, then tell us the three things. I'll give you all a minute to think and then, Gregory, we'll start with you. Okay? I just thought it'd be a great way to get to understand the play better.'

Gregory nodded, closed his eyes to think, then lifted his head. 'Prospero: powerful.' Mrs Andrews curled her lip. 'Fatherly. And ... manipulative.'

A pang of pain pierced Sarah as he said this, thinking of her own father's manipulations.

'Very good,' said Conner. 'Luke?' He was really enjoying playing Caliban, the deformed child of a witch, and slave to Prospero, and he was very, very good, not that he knew it. Gregory always called him a natural and that meant a lot coming from him.

'Umm, I'll go for Prospero too. He's magical—'

'Why, thank you very much,' replied Gregory with a teasing grin.

'Umm ... old—'

'Steady on now,' Gregory replied again, and embarrassment forced Luke to look away.

'And ...' Luke shrugged, unable to think of anything else.

'Let's go for handsome, shall we?' teased Gregory and everyone laughed.

They continued with the game until everyone had had a turn. Finally, Conner called it a day.

'And don't forget,' said Lottie, 'drinks for Sarah's birthday on Saturday the fourth of August. Here's your little reminder card.' She handed the cards round, giving one to an embarrassed Sarah who tucked it into her book. After a final flurry of activity, the theatre was empty once again, and Lottie and Sarah sat down in the front row.

'What's going on, honey?' Lottie asked. She crossed her slightly plump legs and Sarah noticed for the first time that evening that she was wearing a skirt and her legs were bare. This was virtually unheard of for Lottie whose confidence wavered when it came to her weight. Though she'd been so much more content about it this summer.

'I like your skirt,' Sarah said, admiring the floaty material and pale-blue colour. Lottie brushed it down and a tinge of red came to her cheeks.

'Thank you, but don't change the subject. What's the matter?'

Despite the warmth of the theatre, Sarah shivered. She cocked her head wondering where exactly to begin. Every part of her wanted her friendship with Lottie to remain as it was, yet another wanted to tell her everything, or as near to it as she could manage. But she worried about being judged. When Sarah's words came out, they were punctuated by long, unhappy pauses. 'So, you know when my mum had cancer my dad left us to work away?' Lottie nodded. 'Well, he didn't exactly leave, he went to prison for false accounting.'

Lottie's eyes widened. 'But I thought … You never said.'

Sarah dipped her eyes. 'I was embarrassed. Dad got greedy and took some money. By the time it all came out, Mum was ill, but we didn't know then she was terminal.' She inhaled, steadying her breathing. 'Because Mum was sick, the company he stole from agreed to keep everything quiet, but Dad was still prosecuted and went to prison. Now he's been released and is kind of … back. He turned up at the surgery today. Out of the blue.'

Lottie gasped. 'Shit. What did you do?'

'I told him to go, and that I never wanted to see him again. I told him he wasn't my dad anymore.' As the words finally came out, Sarah found they wouldn't stop. Everything she had imagined saying to a friend all the time she didn't have one was flowing out. All except that one thing: the worst thing of all. 'And I'm just so bloody angry.' Sarah balled her hands into fists. 'He wasn't there when it was awful. Horrible. When Mum was sick, all I could do was watch her fade away. Literally shrinking before my eyes as the cancer ate away at her. I always wondered if she'd have been able to fight if Dad was around, you know? Would things have been different?' Sarah forced out the memories of her mum on the night she'd said goodbye. The body in the bed at the hospice was just a shell and she'd known then that her mum's soul had already left. But Sarah had kissed the soft skin of her cheek and told her she loved her all the same. 'Then afterwards when I had to sort through all her things and Dad wasn't there – I hated him.' Lottie took her hand and suddenly Sarah's cheeks were wet, tears streaming down her face. She hadn't cried like this for years, she had trained herself not to, but she couldn't control it now. Sarah sucked in a big breath of air but before she could say anything she shivered and folded in her chair, dry sobs shaking her body.

Lottie held her for a long time, not speaking, just making gentle shushing noises until the intense emotion began to subside. When Sarah finally lifted her head, Lottie asked, 'Stupid question, but are you going to see him again?'

'I don't even know where he is. I didn't get his number or anything. I just told him to never speak to me again.'

'Oh, honey, what will you do now?' Sarah shrugged. Lottie smiled, her eyes full of sympathy. 'I really think you should come and stay with me tonight. You shouldn't be on your own. Sid can go back to his own flat for a night and we can have a girly night. If I can sleep in this heat, that is.'

Sarah smiled and found a tissue in her handbag. 'Thanks, but I'm okay. I'm just so tired I think I'll go home and have an early night.'

'Okay. If you're sure.'

'I might take a walk along the beach first though. I could do with some fresh air.'

'Do you want me to come?'

'No, thanks. I think I'd prefer to be on my own right now. My head's a mess.'

Lottie nodded. 'You did really well tonight, by the way. I think you're getting there with Miranda now.'

'No I'm not, you bloody awful liar.' Sarah laughed, standing up and readying to leave. 'But at least I had an excuse today.' She wiped her face with her hands. 'I really need to up my game before the next rehearsal on Sunday. Maybe I'll do some research if I feel up to it, see what I can find on the internet. It might be nice to be someone else for a while. I'm not really enjoying being me at the moment.'

'You're amazing,' replied Lottie in true best friend fashion, giving her a hug. 'I think you're incredible.'

'Incredible? I don't know about that. The Incredible Hulk maybe, if Dad turns up again.'

Lottie laughed. 'Then for his sake, I hope he doesn't.'

'Me too,' replied Sarah, and it hurt her how much she actually meant it.

Chapter 7

There was no getting away from it, Nate was bored. Really, really bored. It was Wednesday evening and he'd been here for a few days, inside all the time. He hadn't been this inactive since breaking his leg trying to leap off a building. He'd landed half on, half off the inflatable stunt bag and it had really, really hurt. At least he wouldn't be out for as long as that. Hopefully.

Robin had given strict instructions to stay indoors and out of sight. If the papers found out where he was, they'd be there like a shot. Nate stretched and strode around the living room. The mantelshelf was filled with photos of Gregory and Cecil together, but over on the bookcase he spied pictures of Gregory with famous actors, some of whom had been idols of his own. And they weren't just fan photos, they were photos of colleagues, smiling and laughing together. Impressive. Picking up his phone he wandered to the kitchen and switched on the kettle for yet another cup of tea.

His hand reached for his mobile phone, temptation niggling at him. It was taking all Nate's resolve to not find out what the world was saying about him. It wasn't the world, of course, he reminded himself. He wasn't an A-list Hollywood celeb. But still, curiosity was gnawing at him. He sat down at the kitchen table and tapped a rhythm with his index finger. Gregory and Cecil had gone out to their amateur dramatics group and Nate smiled as he remembered his first acting experiences with the local am dram when he was 15. It had started him on this career path, sowing the seeds of his love of theatre. Then onto RADA. His eyes glanced down towards his phone again and he wondered what his old teachers would be thinking about this mess.

Nate studied the kitchen decor to distract himself. He really quite liked Gregory and Cecil's cottage. The kitchen units were painted in pale blue or sea green, and a powder-blue range cooker took centre stage. There was even a porcelain butler's sink. The place was bigger than he'd imagined it would be too, and the period fireplaces and unique seaside touches like rope banisters were stylish. From sitting out in the garden he'd noticed the air smelt different down here too. Not just when the tide was high or the breeze picked up carrying the smell of the sea, but in general the air was clearer and lighter than it was in London. It was just too hot to stay inside the whole time.

A sudden ringing broke the peacefulness of his thoughts and Nate answered it, glad it was Marcus, his best friend. He hoped Marcus wasn't blaming himself because it had been at his stagdo he'd met Hannah.

'Nate? Where the hell are you, man?'

'Hey, Marcus—'

'You've disappeared off the face of the earth. Are you okay? Unsurprisingly, Emma isn't accepting any of my calls and when I went round your place there was a pack of reporters outside. I legged it before they saw me and started asking questions. Are you in lockdown? Do you need anything?' Marcus was always so concerned for everyone else. Nate smiled, glad that the wedding was over and done with and not being tainted by all this mess. Marcus and his new wife didn't deserve that. 'Nate?'

'It's okay, Marcus. I'm not there. I'm ...' He almost gave himself away but pulled back just in time. He could trust Marcus, that wasn't in question, he just didn't want to put him in a difficult situation. 'I'm away somewhere, out of the spotlight, somewhere the press won't find me. It's probably best you don't know.'

'Blimey, it's that bad?'

'It is.'

'I'm so sorry, Nate. It's my fault, I should have stopped you—'

Nate stood up and began pacing. 'No way, man. This was one hundred percent my fault. You didn't force me into getting drunk.'

'No but I know Big Stan can be quite persuasive. I knew I shouldn't have invited him but—'

Nate sat again and rested his elbow on the table. 'Marcus, listen to me. This is my fault, no one else's. I misjudged the situation with Hannah. I didn't think she even knew who I was at first.' He gave a resigned chuckle. 'I was so drunk *I* didn't know who I was.'

'I hope you don't feel guilty about Emma. Nate, she's cheated on you for ages.'

'I know, but the ring is still on my finger.' He decided not to mention that his heart was a jigsaw of broken pieces. 'I should have stopped myself.' Nate's voice croaked as if someone had their hands around his throat, which was just what Hannah Salgado was doing to his career. God, he'd been so stupid. He should have been stronger instead of letting his vanity be flattered and following his urges into bed.

'What are you going to do now?'

Nate shrugged even though Marcus couldn't see him. 'Ride it out. It's all I can do.'

'There must be something we can do?'

'There's nothing really. We just have to wait and see. Emma doesn't want the press digging around in case they find out about her affairs so she's agreed we just wait for the story to die and then I come back. We'll announce the divorce later.'

'It sounds pretty unfair to me. You're already being painted as the bad guy. Don't you think the world should know the truth?'

'No, I don't,' he said emphatically. 'I made Emma a promise not to expose her affairs. Plus you know her dad could ruin my career permanently if he chose to. This really is the best way.' Marcus went quiet. 'Come on, I've thought about this enough, believe me. Tell me some good news.'

They chatted about Marcus' work and other people they knew while he watched another glorious evening sun paint the sky. Finally, Nate ended the call and tapped the corner of his phone down on the linen table cloth. The French doors were open again and the plants rustled as a few birds hopped and fluttered about. A seagull landed in the garden searching for food and Nate pulled a biscuit from the barrel, broke off a piece and threw it out into the garden. The sky above the tall stone walls of the courtyard garden was turning a crazy mix of orange and pink. He'd never paid that much attention to the sky in London. He was always too busy, head down, thinking about the next job.

Walking outside, Nate paused at the garden table. His muscles were tense from the constant anxiety and he felt a twitch in his legs. They wanted to move, to run. He hadn't been out for a run in over a week now and felt like his lungs hadn't taken a full, deep breath since before that night at the theatre. Bugger it, he was going out. Surely he'd be okay to take a quick walk along the seafront. No one was expecting to see him there, so he probably wouldn't be noticed. Mr Bennett rubbed his fat ginger tummy against Nate's legs and Nate reached down and gave him a fuss behind his ears.

In their meticulously tidy hallway, Nate found his trainers placed neatly in line with Gregory and Cecil's slippers. An old-fashioned coat stand stood in the corner next to an umbrella stand in the shape of a lighthouse. Neither had been needed in weeks. Though he didn't have a key, Gregory and Cecil would surely be back before him. They'd been gone a long time already. Nate opened the door, and stepped out into the world, the evening light still bright and the air fresh on his skin. Although it was still warm, goosebumps rose on his forearms where the breeze swept over him, a reaction to his days inside. He turned right, as the road seemed to lead away from the centre of town, and following the winding streets, he admired the beautiful houses. It was like being on the set of a costume drama. By pure chance the lane he walked down opened out onto a busy main road running all the way along the seafront. Nate crossed, hopping over a small concrete wall that must have been to stop the tide when it rose too high, and stepped down onto the pebble beach. As he hastened towards the sea, the shingle crunching under foot, the sound of the road receded to be replaced by the rhythmic hum of the tide.

Seagulls swooped overhead and Nate stopped with his hands in his pockets. The muscles of his neck and shoulders dropped down, the tightness shifting from his chest, and he took a deep steadying breath. For a second, he closed his eyes, enjoying the feeling of breathing in and out, keeping time with the sea, content in a moment of utter peace and quiet. When he slowly opened his eyes again a strange sight caught his eye. Down the beach, at the very edge of the water, stood a woman gazing out to sea. The skirt of her dress floated gently on the breeze and stray strands of dark brown hair drifted onto her face. She pushed them back, but as the light caught them, a myriad of different tones appeared from deep espresso to hints of pillar box red. Despite the heat of the sun, her skin was pale with only a hint of bronze on her legs. From her stance she seemed incredibly troubled, like him.

Unable to move closer for fear of disturbing her, Nate sat down where he was and though he tried to keep his eyes on the waves as they rose higher and higher up the beach, he found his head pulling to the side, watching her. At one point he thought she wiped at her face as though she was crying, but her features were hidden behind her hair, so he couldn't know for sure. Something about her, like a siren in old mariners' tales, seemed to call to him. He was tempted to go over and speak to her and see if she was all right, but he couldn't. He couldn't risk being recognised anymore than he had already and that made him unutterably sad, so he ignored the tugging at his soul and kept his eyes on the horizon. For half an hour she gazed out, standing all the time, lost in her own world until, at last, she turned and headed back the other way, away from him.

Nate wondered who she was, and what was troubling her. There'd been something almost ethereal about her as she'd stood there. Something ghostly. From the dipping of the sun it was time to head back to the cottage. He'd left a note but still, he couldn't be much longer. Gregory and Cecil would be wondering where he was. The last thing he needed was them phoning Robin and getting him into even more trouble. Though it wasn't as if things could get any worse. With one last look, trying to find a glimpse of the woman again, he got to his feet and brushed down his jeans, all the while wondering what it was about her that had intrigued him so. Probably boredom and his penchant for drama creeping out.

As he came back to the concrete sea defence he spotted Gregory and Cecil over the other side of the road, looking like a couple of worried mothers. When they spotted him, they waved, clearly relieved. He waited for a car to pass then crossed the road, watching Gregory's face harden into an expression of disapproval. He was going to have to do the washing-up tonight to make up for his naughtiness. Taking one last look behind him at the brightest of suns setting slowly, and the black shapes of the gulls cawing in the sky, he filled his lungs with fresh air, not knowing when he'd get to do this again. With heavy legs he followed Gregory and Cecil back to the cottage, and back to his solitary confinement.

Chapter 8

After a long week at work, Sarah opened the door to her house and headed in. Leaning on the banister she forced off her pretty sandals. Her feet had swollen in the oppressive heat and were criss-crossed with little red lines from the straps. She wiggled her toes and a horrible smell rose up. Oh God, did they stink? Might Finn have smelt them when he approached her desk? Still resting on the balustrade, she picked up her foot, brought it as near to her face as possible, which wasn't that easy as she wasn't very flexible, and tried to smell it, causing a muscle to cramp in her side. 'Aarrgh.' She let go of her foot, wobbled, and then fell to the right, stopping herself just before she hit the Jane Austen book cover framed on her wall. *Pride and Prejudice*, her favourite. 'I'm such an idiot,' she said to herself. But at least if she hadn't smelt anything, that probably meant Finn hadn't either.

After opening the windows in the living room and kitchen, she filled a glass of water at the sink to quench her thirst. Today had been hotter than Satan's underpants and she was parched after the drive home.

Friday had taken a long time coming after a tough and eventful week. And she wasn't sure, but it felt like Finn was talking to her more. It seemed like they'd spoken more in the last three days than they had in the whole of the last year. A couple of times he'd even touched her arm or her shoulder, and once, when they'd been passing in the corridor his hand had brushed hers, sending a tingle through her fingers and up into her heart.

Sarah looked around the kitchen and thought about how much she loved being at home. She loved her house and the little estate it sat on. It wasn't the most expensive part of town and the houses were quite ugly – aesthetics weren't a priority in Seventies' architecture apparently – but it was just the right size and she had lovely, if somewhat mad, neighbours.

On her way home, Sarah had stopped at the corner-shop and bought some ingredients for dinner. After coming across a recipe for moussaka in one of the magazines they kept in the surgery's reception, she'd had a weird craving that hadn't shifted all afternoon. She'd found it by accident after one of the horrid old gents had shouted at her because Finn was running late, which was apparently her fault; and then the tiny desk fan she and Mandy shared had broken. Seeing Sarah's face, Mandy had suggested a few minutes away from her desk might help keep her sane.

In her perfectly tidy kitchen, Sarah turned on the radio and emptied her carrier bag before grabbing a knife and the chopping board to begin slicing the various vegetables and making the béchamel sauce. Her mum had taught her how to cook. From a young age she'd stand on a chair, mixing, stirring, tasting, and of course, licking the bowl. Sarah's eyes darted up to the photograph she kept on the kitchen windowsill. Photos of her mum were everywhere, except the bedroom. No one wanted their dearly departed mother watching on while they got down and dirty. Not that Sarah had much chance of that lately, but still, on the rare occasions it did happen she didn't want to have to spend ten minutes hiding photos like a weirdo. It kind of killed the mood.

The radio played one of her favourite songs and Sarah found herself singing along when there was a knock at the door.

Frowning, she wiped her hands on a tea towel and went to answer it. Lottie and Sid were having a date night so it couldn't be them. It could conceivably be Mandy come to cheer her up, but she didn't tend to be spontaneous because she was always super organised with her kids going here, there and everywhere. A bubble of excitement fizzed in her stomach. Was it Finn? Maybe he'd come to see if she was okay after her week from hell and brought a bottle of wine with him. Maybe he'd brought a DVD. Some silly movie to cheer her up. He seemed like that sort of guy. They could order a takeaway or she could cook as she had all the ingredients. Sarah smoothed down her dress, checked she hadn't splashed anything on herself and flicked her hair back over her shoulder. A smile was just forming on her face as she turned the handle and pulled the door to, when it fell away to be replaced by an angry frown.

Her heart stopped beating and the fizz of excitement gave way to a heavy dread. A sudden chill washed over her and as she forced the words out, she ensured her tone was flat and bereft of emotion. 'What are you doing here?'

'Sugarplum, please?' said Ben. He was wearing the same clothes he had the other day at the surgery. He'd been allowed to take a set or two with him, then she'd given away most of his things, apart from a few bags that were stowed in the loft. The sun reflected off the lenses of his glasses.

'I'm not your sugarplum anymore.' Despite her efforts to control it, her voice was rising already and she tried to bring it back down. 'What do you want?' It amazed Sarah that she had this angry, hard side to her personality that had only come out with her dad. But then, he shouldn't have done what he'd done.

'Sarah, please. I wanted to see you.' A spike of anger surged through her as he used her name. It was hard to know which was worse, sugarplum or Sarah.

'Just go away, Dad. I've got nothing to say to you.'

'Can we talk, please? I'm so sorry. I just want to explain.' Behind

Ben's head, a curtain twitched in the house opposite and Sarah knew people were watching. If she closed the door on him, would he go away or stand there knocking? As if in answer Ben said, 'I won't give up, Sarah. Not until we've talked. I've waited years for this moment.' His voice began to crack. 'Imagined it hundreds of times. Please, I just want to talk.'

'Why?'

The question threw him and he didn't answer straight away. 'Because it's too late for me to apologise to your mum, but I can apologise to you.' If his eyes hadn't misted with tears, she'd have closed the door in his face, but the pain and anguish were evident in the set of his mouth. The coldness that consumed her whenever she thought of her dad thawed a little.

Hesitantly, Sarah met his gaze and his lips quivered as he bit back his emotions. 'You'd better come in.' She left the door open for him and walked into the living room. He followed her in and she perched on the edge of the sofa, rubbing her hands on the soft fabric for comfort. Ben sat down in the seat opposite and her copy of *The Tempest* that was resting on the arm of the chair fell to the floor. A piece of paper fluttered out and Sarah realised what it was. The save-the-date card for her birthday drinks. Ben picked it up and tucked it back inside. Relieved he hadn't noticed what it was, Sarah relaxed a little. Her birthday was the last thing she wanted to talk to him about. Ben studied the book, his eyebrows raising almost imperceptibly before he placed it on the coffee table between them. Clasping his hands in his lap he looked like a lost little boy and Sarah found the role reversal unsettling. Her brain began to whirl as they sat in silence. Should she speak first or let him? Ben cleared his throat.

'I know what I did was wrong, sugar – Sarah,' he corrected, with a small shake of his head. 'I got greedy. Stupid. When Arthur turned me down for a pay rise, after all the work I'd done helping him set up the business, I just ...' He lowered his head into his hands and stayed there. 'I'd been with him since the beginning and never asked for anything. I didn't know then your mum was sick. You have to believe me. We just thought it was indigestion. I had no idea it was stomach cancer. You have to believe that I'd never have let anything take me away from her like that. I loved her.'

Sarah desperately wanted to believe him but if that was true then why had he … She still couldn't bring herself to think about the other thing – the worst thing of all. Her mum's diagnosis had been such a shock and her decline so rapid, when she tried to remember, it was a blur. She'd forgotten Ben had supported Arthur from the beginning and how angry he'd been when he requested a pay rise and was turned down. It was no excuse for what he'd done, but her brain had wiped out that particular memory focusing instead on everything that had happened after. But he hadn't had to deal with her mum's broken heart when he got sent to prison. Or how it had made her sicker when she could have been putting her energy into getting better. A flash of white-hot anger stiffened her.

Ben pushed his glasses up and continued, his voice wavering. 'I'll never forgive myself for not being there at the end, Sarah. Never. I loved your mum so much. And I love you.' He broke down and tears flowed, tracing the line of his sallow cheeks. The words echoed around her head like a gale force wind, swirling up her emotions. She was angry but she had missed having a father in her life. Just as quickly, the strength of her resentment pushed down any sympathy and her jaw tightened again. How could he say he'd loved her mum? Sarah had been rubbing the soft fabric with her fingertips so fiercely she could have started a fire. She made an effort to still her fingers.

'Why did you do it? We had enough.' She'd wanted to know for a long time but refused to visit or write to him in prison.

'I wanted us to have more than just enough. I was so angry seeing Arthur drive about in his flash car, and hearing about their expensive holidays when all we could do when you were little was go to Butlins every other year. It just wasn't fair. I wanted to give you and your mum something special. Just once.' His cheeks reddened with what Sarah assumed was shame. 'I knew that if I only took what I'd hoped for as a bonus it would look suspicious, so I took a big round figure. It was easier to hide and I thought we could all have a posh holiday.'

Sarah stared. 'A holiday? To where?' The idea was almost laughable. As a little girl, she'd adored their trips to Butlins. For an only child it was a perfect opportunity to have her parents to herself for a whole weekend. And although they hadn't had any holidays in years, it hadn't mattered one bit. She'd never asked for posh holidays away and neither had her mum.

Ben nodded without speaking, then said, 'I know it was stupid.'

'It was,' Sarah added, 'and selfish.' He nodded again. Seeing her dad's eyes so filled with sadness was both heartbreaking and infuriating. A whole lifetime of love and memories had been wiped out, not only by that stupid action and its terrifyingly far-reaching consequences but by the news that had followed his departure. News she'd tried hard to forget but she knew now she couldn't repress any longer. News of an affair with a co-worker. The ultimate betrayal of her mother and it was this more than anything else she couldn't forgive. After a long, dreadful silence she said, 'So ...' but the sentence trailed away as she had no idea what else to add. The hurt was overwhelming her brain, stopping all functions.

Ben said, 'I thought about writing to you to let you know I was being released but I didn't think you'd answer my letter. All the others had been sent back.' He was right. She wouldn't have answered. There was no way she'd even have read them. She had nothing to say to him and was surprised that he had anything to say to her. He'd written every week for the first year of his incarceration, but she'd returned each and every letter unopened without a second thought. Her mum had died within a few weeks of his imprisonment and the letters did nothing but remind her of how selfish he'd been. With a heavy sigh he rubbed his forehead. 'I'm trying to put my life back together.'

She couldn't bear to look at him and the preciousness of her mum's memory forced her to say, 'No one knows you went to prison. And I want to keep it that way. Arthur agreed to keep things quiet as Mum was sick. It was all dealt with very quietly. I don't want the town knowing. They think you left to work away.'

He nodded in recognition, keeping his eyes on the carpet, and silence descended. Even when that had come out, they'd still had more than their fair share of sympathetic looks and, worst of all, pity. Remembering it, Sarah had a sudden urge to push him away. 'I don't want you in Greenley.'

Ben's face registered shock, guilt and hurt all in one go. His eyebrows pulled together and his eyes darted to hers then away again.

At the hospice, at the end, before her mum had finally drifted into unconsciousness she'd begged Sarah to forgive her dad for the theft – Sarah had kept the rumours of an affair from her – and Sarah had agreed but only for her mother's sake, to assuage her suffering and the agony it was causing. But when it had been time to ring the prison and tell Ben her beloved mum had died, trying her hardest to get the words out among the sobbing and howling, all he could do was cry and repeat the word, 'Sorry,' over and over again. In her fury, Sarah couldn't bring herself to say the words her mum had wanted from her. Instead, she'd hung up and that had been the last she'd said to him before this week. However much she'd missed having Ben around, she wasn't ready to forgive him and didn't know if she ever would be.

Ben pulled a handkerchief from his pocket and wiped his face. Sarah could hear her own sharp breathing and knew there was nothing more to say. She couldn't give him what he wanted. She couldn't forgive. Unsure how to end the meeting she said, 'Is there anything else?' and Ben winced. She didn't sound angry anymore, which would be understandable; no, she sounded cruel and it disgusted her.

'No. Nothing.' With his shoulders sagging in defeat he handed her a scrap of paper on which he'd written a mobile phone number in a shaky, sprawling hand. 'If you do decide you want to see me, here's my number.' Sarah took it without meeting his eye and hurried to the front door. As she closed the door behind him, he tried to look at her, but it took all her self-control to keep the tears inside, even though her nose was stinging with the effort.

When Ben had gone, she fastened the chain lock and went back to the kitchen on autopilot. Staring at the mix of half-chopped vegetables Sarah realised she wasn't in the least bit hungry now. The pulsing in her chest refused to subside and a horrible wail erupted from her mouth. She couldn't shake the image of her mum in the hospice bed. A pathetic shrunken husk of the strong woman Sarah had always looked up to. Angrily, and with the scrap of paper still in her hand, she swept all the vegetables into the sink and bent double, hanging onto the counter with white knuckles. The emotions she'd kept under control for the last few days burst out but her face remained dry. She was too angry to cry.

'Damn it,' Sarah shouted to the worktop, hot with anger. It was ironic that she finally had friends but couldn't go and see them. Lottie and Sid were out. If she couldn't see them, she normally went to Gregory and Cecil but they had superstar Nathaniel Hardy with them. The weirdness of that statement made her laugh and it was a strange, almost hysterical screech that escaped. The idea of swinging by and catching a glimpse of him was tempting, but she didn't want to go through all of this with the UK's hottest, most gorgeous man watching on.

With no other option she grabbed her bag and car keys from their place on the kitchen counter. Darting into the living room she took her copy of *The Tempest* from the coffee table and headed to the car. What she needed was her favourite spot on the seafront.

The exact spot her mum used to bring her to as a child. Somewhere quiet where she could think of something else, maybe read a little, and the gentle flowing rhythm of the sea might calm the tempest raging inside her.

Shakespeare would've been proud. If she could recite it.

Chapter 9

'We're just off out to rehearsals, Nate,' said Cecil, as he adjusted his hair in the hall mirror.

Nate loped down the stairs in the old T-shirt and shorts he wore to bed, smoothing down the random tuft of hair that always stuck up. Robin had done quite well with the packing and remembered pretty much everything. Anna, Robin's wife, must have had a hand in it. Though it was already ten o'clock on Sunday morning, he'd only just woken up. Having nothing to do was really playing havoc with his body clock. The only trouble was, no matter how inactive he was at the moment, he didn't feel rested, he just felt more and more tired, his body drained of energy. Robin had sent a few scripts down and he'd been reading them but the short note that came with it had filled him with dread. 'Might be worth a try' was a far cry from the 'Dead cert' he'd written previously. Seeing Cecil's smiling face, he said, 'How long have you got to go?'

'Just over three weeks.'

The idea of the theatre and performing again lifted Nate's spirits for a moment before they plummeted again like an elevator in a horror movie. 'Whereabouts?'

'Have you not seen our gorgeous little theatre down on the seafront?'

Nate shook his head. 'No. It was so dark when I arrived last week, and I didn't pay much attention when I nipped out the other day.' Gregory came out of the kitchen, passing Nate a cup of coffee. Nate smiled in thanks, but Gregory didn't return it. He tutted instead. 'You really shouldn't have done that, you naughty boy. I could have got into all sorts of trouble with Robin if you'd been spotted. Though wouldn't it be lovely if he popped by rehearsals when this was all over.' He nodded at Nate. 'You could give us a masterclass.'

'I'd be delighted.' Nate felt himself brightening. It was the least he could do to repay Gregory and Cecil's generosity and he actually enjoyed teaching. He'd gone back to RADA a few times to talk to the students and they always ended up running some scenes together. He felt privileged to be able to come back as a success.

'Gregory, we really must go,' Cecil said, taking his arm and leading him to the door. 'We've left you out some pains au chocolat and croissants, or there's eggs and bacon in the fridge.'

'Thank you,' Nate replied, holding his mug up in acknowledgement, and they headed out of the door with a grin. Nate went in to the sitting room and watched from the window as they hurried away. He might have to take a wander down towards the sea again if he didn't get out of here soon. Before he could think about anything else, his stomach rumbled. He needed some breakfast.

After dressing quickly, Nate came back downstairs. Thankfully the French windows had been left open and the kitchen was cool. The breeze was stronger today, ruffling the table cloth and Nate ate in the garden, watching the small fluffy clouds drift across the sky edged forwards by the wind. Aeroplanes left vapour trails in vertical stripes and he wondered where they were headed and if he could go there too. The sweet smell of melting, gooey chocolate hit his nose as he broke apart the pain au chocolat. It wasn't a bad way to start a Sunday, or a bad place to be starting it in.

He took his mobile phone from his pocket and checked his emails. Nothing new from Robin but then, it was a Sunday. And absolutely no contact from Emma. There was a rather odd email from Marcus, asking about one of Emma's first lovers. Nate remembered him well from the hurt it had caused him. Emma had been playing with fire; the guy was married. He'd worked on a show Emma had done – sound or lighting or something technical like that – but the guy hadn't been particularly thrilled when Emma had moved on. There'd been phone calls to the house trying to make sure his wife wouldn't find out and even Emma's dad had got involved through an assistant. Nate was pretty sure the guy had been told he'd never work again if he kept it up because not long after, the calls stopped. Clearly, Marcus was trying to justify Nate's actions but he couldn't. Nate knew it was his own fault. He was just grateful for Marcus' friendship. All his other so-called friends, especially the fair-weather celeb types, had disappeared into the ether not wanting to associate with him. It made him feel even more alone, worthless and stupid.

Boredom began to settle and a restless impatience made him jiggle in his seat. If only he didn't have to stay indoors. He quite fancied a little trip down to the beach again and a breath of fresh air. That woman might be there. She'd seemed so worried. So far away. Beautiful too. Like something from a dream, or a film. She'd popped into his head a few times since that day. There'd just been something about her, he didn't really know what, but her profile had imprinted itself on his brain. Or perhaps it was just that her troubled soul matched his own. Perhaps he was just looking for the dramatic or romantic, missing acting out these types of scenes. Whatever it was, he needed a diversion from it.

Then the rational side of Nate's brain took over. No, he couldn't go out again and risk being found out, no matter how much he wanted to see the sea again. If the press discovered him, Gregory and Cecil would be hounded. A small smile played on his lips because they'd probably enjoy that, for a while at least. He and Emma had in the beginning. The way the press walked backwards in front of them, camera lights flashing in their faces, constantly calling their names, had been exciting at first. They used to play a game, walking at angles, trying to get the reporters to walk into bins. It had been funny. But they soon got tired of it, and so would Gregory and Cecil. Nate gathered up the crumbs from his croissant and scattered them for the birds before heading into the living room.

Outside on the windowsill he could see Mr Bennett sitting in the sun, hopping down as something drew his attention. Nate picked up a script and studied it but a moment later the sound of tyres screeching to a halt in the road outside tightened his throat. Had Mr Bennett been hit? He'd grown quite fond of the lardy ginger cat who had taken to sleeping on his bed. Rushing outside, Nate checked around. The car had moved on and there was no evidence of anything having happened in the empty street. Mr Bennett toddled out from around a neighbour's house and relief brought a smile to Nate's face.

Unfortunately, he didn't notice the front door creeping slowly closed until it was too late. He leapt back hoping to catch it, but the strong breeze carried it forward and it closed firmly, leaving him standing outside staring at the house. Nate rested his hands on his hips and let his head fall against the door as a mild panic rose up. He tried his best to stay calm by taking deep breaths. At least he had shoes on and wasn't standing there barefoot. Checking again that there was no one around, he tried the door handle but it wouldn't budge. The mild panic turned to annoyance and he rattled the handle violently. 'Fuck,' Nate shouted at the door, frightening an old lady walking past with her poodle. The old dear jumped, then tutted at him as she hobbled on. Even the angry puffball of a dog raised its head in disgust before snootily turning away. Nate had never liked poodles, they clearly thought too much of themselves. 'Shit,' he muttered again.

The town was getting busier. He had to find a way back inside and quickly. Focusing his mind with a deep breath he remembered that the French doors were open. If he could just climb the six-foot walls of the courtyard garden, he could hop over the top and be back inside in no time.

Following the cobbled street, Nate dashed around to the back of the house, counting along until he was standing outside the high stone walls that edged Gregory and Cecil's backyard. On tiptoe, Nate attempted to peer over the top, trying to find a spot to climb up that wouldn't end with him trampling the gorgeous flowers or smashing the pots as he landed. More and more people were ambling by now, enjoying a leisurely Sunday morning stroll, and his mild panic was descending into a full-on meltdown. Anxiety rocked his body making his hands tremble and his chest tighten. He needed to get back inside quickly and without fright-ening anymore old ladies or their miserable looking dogs.

Nate found a small gap between the overabundant honeysuckle and some kind of huge plant that reached up and over the wall. If he stood on tiptoe, he could reach the top and if he jumped, he might be able to pull himself up. He'd been working out – he had pecs, for goodness' sake. Surely he could do this.

Closing his eyes and waiting for a young man to pass who was eyeing him suspiciously, he made a jump for it. His toes scraped the stones as he scrabbled, trying to find purchase and help lift him up, his legs moving in a running motion. But after less than a minute he had to admit his upper body strength wasn't quite what he thought and he fell back to the ground with an ungainly thump, sending a shockwave up his spine. 'Crap,' he mouthed.

Would a run-up help? Nate stood up and surveyed the wall again. Stepping back to the other side of the road, he was just about to sprint forwards when a tubby cyclist in skintight Lycra pulled up and put a hand on his shoulder. ''Ere, what do you think you're doing?'

'Oh, nothing,' said Nate, smoothing down his T-shirt and

trying to smile. 'I'm a friend of the owners and I accidentally locked myself out.'

'Hmm.' Fat Bradley Wiggins didn't believe him. 'So if I ask Gregory who you are, he'll be able to tell me, will he?'

'Yes. Yes. I'm not a burglar,' Nate replied with a laugh. The man narrowed his eyes and studied him.

'Don't I know you from somewhere?'

No! thought Nate. He'd be in so much trouble if he got found out now. Not to mention that he'd look like a complete moron for locking himself out. 'Umm, I don't think so,' he replied quickly. 'I've just got one of those faces. Don't worry, I'll go and find Gregory at the theatre.' Nate pointed the way Gregory and Cecil had set off earlier, hoping they hadn't taken a detour first. 'Bye.' And striding away before the man could stop him, Nate took a deep breath and searched for the little theatre on the seafront.

The cool sea breeze dried the beads of sweat on his brow. Realising his shoe laces were still undone, Nate bent down and quickly tied them. He crossed the busy main road onto the promenade and gazed around. There, further down the seafront he spied what looked like the theatre. It was a large, grey, majestic building with wonderful old-fashioned revolving doors. Somehow, it fitted in with its surroundings being perfectly situated on the seafront. It must be lovely to come and see a play here, then stroll along the beach afterwards, stopping in at one of the pubs for a quick drink before heading home. Nate found his pace had slowed and his shoulders had relaxed, though there was a small ache in his right arm. He must have strained a muscle. He'd have to cobble together some sort of exercise routine to keep himself in shape; one that he could do in Gregory and Cecil's garden.

After waiting for a bus to pass that was full of people he hoped hadn't recognised him, Nate crossed to the theatre and the grand revolving doors. It brought a smile to his face and reminded him of some of the older theatres on the West End. A strange feeling flooded his body as he reached out his hand to push the door.

Trepidation mixed with anxiety and a touch of sadness. Would he ever get to step foot in a West End theatre again? And if he did, would it be as the leading man? He felt a pang in his chest. It was important not to get ahead of himself or be overly dramatic. He just had to wait for this to pass. And anyway, first things first. He had to speak to Gregory and explain how he'd managed to lock himself out. The trouble was, his mobile was still in the house and he hadn't quite considered how he was going to get inside without attracting the attention of the rest of the players. He was going to have to sneak in.

Nate crouched down and slowly entered through the revolving doors. When his eyes adjusted to the slightly dimmer light inside, the sight before him made his breath hitch in his throat. He'd expected a certain level of shabbiness, but the deep red carpet was fluffy and plush, the chairs clean and comfy, and the stage – well, the well-built stage, framed by a fine, deep red velvet curtain, was full of random people sitting in a circle, staring at him. The inside of the theatre was the most unusual set-up he'd ever seen. The doors opened straight into the body of the theatre. There was no foyer, no entrance area, just a small square landing that had a small set of stairs leading down on either side, meaning everyone could see him. Damn.

Cecil got to his feet first, followed swiftly by Gregory who shot up out of his chair like his bum was on fire. They climbed down the steps at the front of the stage and made their way towards him, walking quickly, whispering to each other. Cecil's face was softer and more concerned, but Gregory's was stuck in an angry frown. Nate felt like a naughty schoolboy about to be told off. He scanned the rest of the Greenley Players. Among the shocked faces he recognised one and something strange happened to his tummy. The woman with the dark hair who had been standing on the beach was watching him. She'd looked so different then, worried and weighed down, but now her eyes were bright, and her sweet pink mouth was lifting at the corners into a really quite attractive and cheeky grin. He pulled his eyes away as Gregory and Cecil drew level.

'What on earth are you doing here?' asked Gregory, his tone matching the stern look on his face. 'You shouldn't be here.' Nate was taken aback and shuffled.

'I got locked out. Sorry. I thought something had happened to Mr Bennett—'

'Mr Bennett?' asked Cecil, concern marring his fine features.

'I heard a car screech and worried he'd been hit. But he's fine,' he reassured them.

'Awww,' replied Cecil, pressing a hand to his chest. 'You are such a sweetie.'

Having grown accustomed to their fondness over the last week, Nate smiled. 'The silly thing came waddling out absolutely fine but before I knew it the front door was swinging shut and I couldn't reach it in time.'

Cecil patted Nate's arm. 'Was the back door open? The wind does take it sometimes.'

'It was,' Nate confirmed.

'It creates a through-draft,' Cecil continued as Gregory watched on, still frowning.

'Are you two finished?' he asked crossly.

'Yes. It is still open though,' said Nate, now wondering if the place could have been robbed. If it had, whoever burgled it had to have the upper body strength of a stuntman to get over that wall, or a very long ladder, so the chances were probably not.

'Not to worry, dear, it'll be fine. We don't really get much crime around here, do we, Gregory? And anyway, we have lovely neighbours who'd let us know of anything suspicious.'

Nate wasn't sure that was true; it didn't seem podgy Lance Armstrong had called them after he'd spotted Nate scaring old ladies and trying to scale the back wall, and that must have looked incredibly suspicious. Perhaps he'd call tonight! 'Anyway, I wondered if I could grab your keys to let myself back in?'

'If Robin finds out Nate left the house,' said Gregory, 'he'll be furious with me. And you,' he said, staring at Nate. 'You've already done it once and now, walking all the way through town. How long do you think it'll be before someone recognises you? People here do watch telly, you know. It might be the countryside but you haven't gone back in time and people here aren't stupid.'

'I know,' Nate replied, his tone coming out sharper than intended. 'I'm sorry. It was an accident.'

'Oh, dear one, don't be so grumpy,' said Cecil. 'No one's noticed.' Gregory stared at Cecil like he'd gone mad, his eyebrows lifted so high they almost hit his hairline.

'Look behind you. Everyone knows who he is.'

Nate turned to see the Greenley Players were up out of their seats, chattering in little groups, staring at them. A plump middle-aged woman was searching in her bag and came out a few minutes later with a notepad and pen, clearly hoping for an autograph. A young man with jet-black hair gelled into a spike stood in the middle with his mouth hanging slightly open. And the woman from the beach was speaking to a pretty, short blonde who was talking animatedly. Her own brown hair fell backwards as she laughed and Nate didn't quite know why he kept looking at her, but he couldn't bring himself to turn away.

'You have to leave,' said Gregory, turning back to them. 'We need to pretend you're not you, even though you look like you. You know, that you just look a lot like you. We can say you're our nephew.'

'But they know you haven't got a nephew, dear,' Cecil answered. 'And my sister's 52 with the mothering instinct of an army sergeant. It just won't work.'

'What do you suggest then, Cecil? They clearly know who he is.'

Nate knew he should say something helpful, but he wasn't really sure what. Gregory was a bit frightening when he was cross. He'd had no choice but to come, and now he could have ruined everything. There was absolutely no reason why someone here couldn't take a snap of him and send it to the press. Yet again he'd been stupid.

Cecil shifted his weight. 'I have an idea. Why don't we tell them the truth and ask them not to tell anyone.'

'I'm sorry, what?' asked Nate. It sounded utterly preposterous. Like asking the press nicely to leave them alone. Whenever he and Emma did that it resulted in twice as many being camped at their door.

'We'll just ask them not to tell anyone,' said Cecil, speaking slowly. 'They're our friends. I'm sure they'll help us.'

'Do you really think that'll work?' asked Nate, half in hope, half astonishment. Cecil and Gregory exchanged glances and after an almost imperceptible raise of his left eyebrow, Gregory nodded agreement.

'I don't think we've got any other option,' said Cecil.

'Follow on, then, dear boy,' said Gregory, resignedly leading the way to the stage. The players' chattering died away and they mounted the steps. Everyone sat down again except for Gregory, who directed Nate into an empty seat next to the pretty brown-haired woman, and then stood in the middle of the circle. Nate sat, feeling a frisson of tension being next to her. Gregory began speaking. 'Okay, everyone, this is, as you probably all know, Nate Hardy.' There were a few gasps and the middle-aged woman with the notepad wriggled in her seat in excitement. Nate smiled at her, glad he still had one fan at least, and waved. He immediately regretted it because it looked rather creepy instead of friendly. 'And you probably all know the papers have been after Nate for the last week or so. Well, as a favour to a dear friend, Nate's agent, who I used to act with, he's been staying with me, out of the limelight.'

Nate watched on as Gregory surveyed the group before speaking again. He may not have acted professionally for a while, but he still had good timing. 'I need to ask you all, as our dear friends, to please keep this a secret. If the press find out, they'll arrive here in droves and hound the poor fellow. Not to mention myself and Cecil too. I'm asking you all as a friend. We both are.' He turned to Cecil and the look of affection that passed between them was a timely reminder to Nate that there was still love in the world and that some relationships did stand the test of time. 'Nate, would you like to say a few words?'

An unexpected flush of embarrassment prickled his skin. He was used to playing parts, speaking in front of hundreds of people; why was he feeling like this now in this small little group? It was like his first am dram performance all over again. He cleared his throat to dislodge the tightness growing inside it. 'Hi, everyone. Umm, yeah, you've probably seen the papers and you know why I'm here.' From the corner of his eye he spied a disapproving look on the brown-haired woman's face and it saddened him. 'Firstly, I'd like you to know that it isn't all as it seems. I can't go into details, but I'm not the man the papers are making me out to be. I've made some mistakes, but I'm not the devil either.' A few of the players exchanged glances and a posh-looking woman in her forties pinned him with her eyes. Nate leaned forwards in his seat, resting his elbows on his knees and clenching his hands together. 'I know it's a lot to ask and I've no right to ask it, but I'd really appreciate it if you could keep my being here quiet. I'm trying to deal with things and I don't want anyone to get hurt any more than they have already, so ... please?' The players nodded with solemn faces. 'Thank you.'

Gregory rifled in his pocket for his keys and held them out. Nate stood to take them.

'You're not going, are you?' asked the middle-aged motherly woman.

'Kathryn, he has to,' Gregory replied.

'I really should be getting back out of sight,' Nate said kindly.

Disappointment registered on the woman's face. 'Oh. Hang on, why doesn't he stay and watch the rehearsal and give us some tips? It's not every day you get a real proper actor here, is it? You've done some Shakespeare, haven't you?'

Nate smiled and drew his hand back from Gregory's outstretched one. He knew he should go but something inside him wanted to stay. Not because of the pretty woman, he told himself, but because he wanted to help if he could. 'Yes, I have.'

'And you don't mind, do you?'

'Umm, no. No, I don't mind,' Nate said. He could feel Gregory's disapproving stare, but Cecil was smiling.

'Well, wouldn't it be a waste if he went without helping us a bit?' Kathryn continued. 'We're not doing that well, are we?' There were murmurs of approval. Nate glanced over at the brunette woman, but her expression was unreadable. She still had an ethereal quality about her he couldn't describe. 'Let's have a vote,' said Kathryn, standing up and taking control.

'Kathryn, please, he really should be getting back.' Gregory stepped between them.

'All those in favour?' There was a unanimous show of hands, except for Gregory and Cecil. Kathryn smiled triumphantly.

'Oh fine,' Gregory huffed. 'I suppose then we can all walk back together.'

'Conner, what should we do now?' Kathryn asked with a satisfied grin.

So the young man with dark hair was named Conner and was directing them. That was cool. He seemed suddenly shy and, avoiding Nate's eye, he said, 'Let's continue with the scene we were reading shall we? Mrs Andrews ...' He gestured for the posh-looking woman to continue and the rehearsal began again, this time with Nate a part of it and the peaceful, fulfilled feeling that ran through him was like a balm over the troubles of the last week. A gangly man who spent most of his time making goo-goo eyes at the short blonde grabbed an extra chair for Gregory and they all shuffled around making room for him.

'I'll explain who's who as we go,' whispered Cecil, leaning over the pretty brunette. She didn't look in Nate's direction and acted like he was just another colleague, but Nate admired the shape of her face from the corner of his eye. She had a small nose that turned up slightly at the end and soft, full lips. A sudden wailing screech made his head spin back to the rest of the group.

'Umm, what was that, Mrs Andrews?' asked Conner, looking confused and possibly a little afraid.

'Well, I was being a sprite and you know … mystical.' Mrs Andrews was turning very pink as Cecil leaned in and whispered, 'Mrs Andrews: thinks she's good, has the acting talent of a cardboard box and is a horrid, horrid snob. It's true, isn't it, Sarah?'

Ah, Sarah. So that was her name. Nate rolled it around his brain. It was an ordinary name but when he said it with her pictured in his mind it seemed different, special. 'Hi, Sarah, I'm Nate,' he whispered.

'Yes, I know,' she replied with a small smile and self-consciously tucked her hair behind her ear. 'Do you normally sneak around theatres on a Sunday morning?'

'I wasn't sneaking.' Sarah's humour brought a lightness to his life for the first time in what felt like ages. 'I was inspecting the floor.'

She giggled. 'And did you find anything?'

He felt a grin lift the corners of his mouth. 'No, it's a very fine floor. Well done.' Hearing her suppress a laugh was a bright and cheerful sound perforating the cloud of doom that had been hanging over him. In the background, Conner was explaining that they didn't need Mrs Andrews to make strange noises that would frighten small children because they had sound effects they could use that were neither terrifying nor ear-piercing. It wasn't going down well.

A woman with bright red hair wearing a baggy dress and a huge ugly brown cardigan said, 'Och, you sounded like a broken bagpipe.' It took Nate a moment to decipher what she'd said but once he'd mastered the accent, he got it.

'Debbie McCray,' whispered Cecil. 'Mad as a box of frogs, but lovely. She's very good at doing the scenery isn't she, Sarah?'

'Yes, very good but she struggles a bit with faces.'

'That's true,' Cecil agreed. 'Oh, dear, it seems Mrs Andrews is taking direction as well as she normally does.' At that moment Mrs Andrews was berating Conner and making her case for the weird sounds she'd made before. Conner was doing his best to hold his ground.

'Why don't you say something?' Sarah said, leaning in to Nate. He could feel her breath on his face and when she realised how close she was, a tide of pinkness rose over the apples of her cheeks. She pulled back slightly but their eyes met for a moment and Nate admired the deep brown colour. 'Can't you help?'

'I'd like to, I really would, but quite frankly I'm terrified.'

Sarah smiled. 'Haven't you worked with people like Mrs Andrews before? You must have done.'

'Awkward people? Yes, but Mrs Andrews isn't awkward she's …'

'Scary?'

'Forceful. I'm too scared to insult her, she might hear me.' Sarah giggled and Mrs Andrews' eyes shot to her, then Nate.

'Someone should really help Conner,' Sarah said, and Nate knew he had to.

'Can I suggest, Mrs Andrews,' he said, standing up, 'that you let the sound effects do that for you? You don't want to detract from your excellent performance. That's what we want people to remember.' The compliment puffed Mrs Andrews up and she nodded at Conner. Nate sat back down feeling satisfied. He'd helped the boy and Sarah approved.

'Well done,' said Cecil. 'Didn't he do well, Sarah?'

'Yes he did.' Her head tipped slightly towards him. 'Thanks for saving Conner.'

'My pleasure.' He tried to ignore the happy feelings her thanks had earned him.

'Shall we move onto the scene with Prospero, Miranda and Caliban?'Conner said. Gregory shifted in his seat, plumping out his chest. So, he was playing Prospero. He began reading and Nate could see the years of experience in his read-through. His performance was subtle, confident and Nate admired him more and more as the speech went on. But when it came to Miranda, played by Sarah, she read the words but didn't infuse them with any emotion. There was raw talent there though. It just needed some training. As she read, she glanced towards him once or twice, each time her cheeks growing redder with embarrassment and Nate shuddered at making her feel uncomfortable. The young guy playing Caliban was exceptional. A raw talent as well, rather than the polished performance of Gregory, but it was surprising how accomplished so many of them were.

Cecil continued his helpful descriptions. 'Luke Wheeler, completely gorgeous, very good we think. Single.' Nate wasn't sure why Cecil mentioned this last bit and wondered if it was for Sarah's benefit. Did that mean she was single too? He banished the thought. It didn't matter anyway.

At the end of the rehearsal Conner stood up. 'Thanks, everyone. Don't forget. It won't be long and you'll need to have it memorised.' Nate was impressed. This young guy was really good. He certainly hadn't been that confident at his age.

Kathryn, the woman who had instigated everything, turned to Nate and said, 'What d'ya think then?' He paused, his brow furrowed as he thought. 'Oh, no, he thinks we're crap—'

'No, no I don't,' Nate said quickly, stepping forward towards her. Everyone stopped gathering their stuff and stared at him. 'I thought it was brilliant, you've got a lot of talent here. Umm ...' he scratched his forehead, trying to think how to explain what he meant. He should be more erudite, but he was so worried about something coming out wrong and people getting upset, he needed to choose the right words. 'I really think it would help if you got to the very bottom of the play.' Instinctively, he grabbed

Cecil's copy of *The Tempest* from the seat of his chair, and pressed his hand against the cover. 'A lot of the characters' motivations come from being powerful, or powerless. I think if you can understand which camp your character is in, you'll better understand their motivations and that'll make your performance much more believable.' The Greenley Players were nodding at him, all except for Sarah who was staring at something, her face hard. Nate followed her gaze to see an older man walking down the central aisle between the banks of chairs. In the noise and chatter no one had heard the door.

When he turned back, Sarah's expression changed to one of anger and pain as she walked to the front of the stage and down the steps. She met the man a few rows back. Behind him, Nate heard Gregory whisper, 'Who's that?'

Cecil beckoned over the short blonde. 'Lottie, do you know who that is? I've never seen him before and I didn't think Sarah was in to older men.' The blonde bent her head to one side, considering her response.

'I think it's her dad,' she said quietly. Gregory and Cecil gasped melodramatically.

Nate desperately wanted to ask what was going on. What was the big deal? From Sarah's body language and hand movements, she wasn't pleased to see her father. After a few angry gestures she sent him away, watching him until he left the building. All was quiet in the theatre. When she turned, tears were pooling in her eyes, making them glisten, but with a dignity that Nate had never seen in anyone before, she came back, calmly picked up her things and walked out. Lottie threw her keys at the gangly bloke. 'Sid, can you lock up, please? I'll see if she's okay.' Then she grabbed her stuff and followed Sarah out.

'Bloody hell's bells,' said Gregory. 'She's never mentioned him, has she, Cecil?'

'No, not to me. A no-go area whenever we've tried. He went away, didn't he? Just before her mum died?'

'Yes, well. I don't know about you, my darling, but I need a drink after that.'

Nate nodded. 'Sounds like a good idea.' You didn't have to be a genius to know that whatever had just happened wasn't good.

For a moment Gregory was silent. 'I was actually talking to Cecil, but you can be my darling too, young man, if you like.' Nate laughed at his mistake and trailed them out of the theatre, all the while listening to their gossip, trying to figure out what the big deal was. The rehearsal had made him forget his own situation but as reality came crashing back, he hoped the players would stick to their word and keep his being there a secret. It seemed there was enough drama going on in Greenley-On-Sea without him making the situation worse.

Chapter 10

'Sarah, wait! Sarah?' Sarah slowed her pace and Lottie's footsteps grew louder as she caught up. Though her body still throbbed with anger, she stopped. Panting a little, Lottie rested her hands on her hips. 'What happened back there?'

The breeze blew Sarah's hair all over her face. She hadn't minded at first; it hid the tears misting her vision, as she held back sobs. She didn't want to cry over her dad. He didn't deserve it. Angrily, she pushed the strands back and held the ends down with her hand. Lottie watched her, her clear eyes kind and under-standing. 'That was my dad.'

'I guessed.'

'He just keeps showing up asking me to forgive him but it's not that easy.' She threw her hands in the air. 'All I want is for him to leave. Why can't he just go?' They began walking again, Sarah needing to move to release the tension in her muscles. 'I can't believe he thinks it's all so easy to fix. Like just saying sorry is enough.'

Now level with the pier, Lottie threaded her arm through Sarah's. 'Come on, let's go for a walk down here.' Turning right they headed up the long curving ramp that led to the gated entrance. A large wooden sign, battered and bruised by the weather, read, 'Bait and rods available'. Sarah had a sudden flashback to the one and only time her dad had taken her fishing. She'd hated it. It was cold and boring and took hours and hours. As a little girl she'd spent most of the time making up dance routines and getting in the way of other fishermen, but they'd still had fun. She'd loved performing to everyone; her dad had cheered and clapped, and she'd received a few pound coins in recompense. Ben had jovially conceded that maybe fishing just wasn't as much fun for girls and they'd stopped at the shops on the way home, where she'd bought a new outfit for her Barbie doll with the money she'd earned. Why did these memories keep popping up to complicate things? Stirring up old feelings and causing confusion.

The wind was stronger on the pier and though they had to stop now and again for a fisherman to cast his line, the walk was pleasant, calming Sarah's temper so she could finally speak, rather than shout, at Lottie. 'He came to my house on Friday night.'

Her head turned. 'What did he say?'

'He said he was sorry. That he was ashamed of himself. That it was too late for him to apologise to Mum, but he could still apologise to me.'

'And what did you say?' Her voice was calm and soothing. Enquiring, rather than judgemental. For so long Sarah had never imagined having a friend like Lottie and she found herself profoundly grateful she was here now.

'I said I didn't care.' At this Lottie looked into Sarah's face. 'I know it's harsh,' Sarah replied. 'But when Dad's around it's like there's this monster inside me and every time I open my mouth this cruel horrible thing speaks for me. To be honest, he's been out of my life for so long I didn't know I felt like this about him and it scares me. I'm the worst version of myself when he's around.' She gazed at the horizon. 'I thought I'd dealt with everything and moved on but ... I didn't tell you everything the other night.' Sarah took another breath, readying herself to let out the worst bit. The bit she'd kept shut inside, the hurt was just too much. 'Just as Mum moved to the hospice near the end, rumours started about Dad having an affair with a colleague. That's what I can't forgive more than anything, Lottie.'

'God, that's horrible.'

'As naive as it sounds, I honestly didn't expect him to ever try and see me again. I made it very clear I never wanted to see him.' She turned to Lottie. 'And now it's brought it all back – the pain and hurt – like no time had passed at all. Please don't think I'm a bad person.'

'I don't,' Lottie replied, gently, her eyes kind. 'Did he have an affair?'

Sarah had thought about it a lot at the time until it had torn her apart and for the sake of her health she'd locked it all away. 'The woman worked with Dad, and afterwards I realised he'd been working late a bit more and he'd been distant at times with Mum. At first I thought it was because he was scared. Men do that, don't they? Close down or back off. When they don't know what to say they say nothing.' She scoffed at her own foolishness. 'But when I thought back, the woman had called a few times too. Dad said it was about work but all I remember is he'd laugh when he'd speak to her. When I found out that Dad had stolen, I realised he wasn't the man I thought he was. Before I'd never have thought him capable but I got him wrong once …' The wind whipped her hair onto her face. Now she'd unburdened herself there was a weightlessness in her mind. Lottie had listened so patiently and Sarah laughed at herself for bottling it up for so long. 'So, in short, yeah, I believe he did have an affair.'

'Did you ever confront the woman?'

Sarah shook her head. 'Her marriage broke up not long after Dad went inside, and she moved away. It pretty much put the tin lid on it for me. There was no doubt after that.'

'I'm so sorry, honey.' Lottie took her arm. 'I can't believe you've had to deal with so much, but do you think he means it when he says sorry?'

Sarah nodded. 'Yes, I think he does.' That Ben was genuinely sorry had never been in doubt. His expression, his words, everything showed Sarah that he meant what he said. 'I do think he means it, which makes it worse. When it all came out about what he'd done it was like I was dealing with a different version of my dad because the one I'd known would never steal or cheat.' Out at sea, the vast expanse of water shimmered and glittered under the midday sun. 'The anger inside made it easy for me to not see him as my dad anymore, but now ...' Her voice faded, unsure how to finish the sentence. 'But now he's back it's like – sometimes it's like he's my dad again and I keep thinking about all the things we did when I was a kid.'

'I'd have loved memories like that,' said Lottie and Sarah felt selfish. Lottie's parents had upped and left when she was a teenager and hadn't been particularly great before that. She'd lived with her nan who had sadly died the year before. Elsie had been chairman of the committee to save the theatre before Lottie and was a wonderful, if somewhat formidable, old woman. Lottie was exactly like her. 'Do you think you'll ever be able to forgive him?' Lottie asked.

Sarah sighed, feeling the weight of her emotions pressing on her chest. 'I don't know. I really, really don't know. It just feels too much to forgive.'

'It is a lot,' Lottie agreed. 'But you do need to think about how you'd feel if something happened to him.'

'What do you mean?' A jolt of fear broke through the anger and she looked up.

'If he left again, as you've asked him to, and you never saw him again, how would you feel? Do you think you'll feel the same when the anger's worn off?' Sarah stared at the ground then walked to the edge, peering over to see the waves roll up the legs of the pier, driving the salty smell into the air. She'd never thought of it like that. 'Do you think you'll wish you'd forgiven him or at least talked to him calmly about what happened? You know, tried to sort it out?'

Sarah's mouth opened to automatically protest but the burning anger hadn't flared as much this time. 'I don't know. I guess I'd need to think about it.' Sarah squeezed Lottie's arm. 'I'm so glad I've got you. Thank you for listening to me.'

'That's what friends are for,' Lottie said with a grin.

'Shall we have a coffee at the café? My treat?'

'As long as it's an iced one. That breeze is nice, but it's still bloody hot. And I'm sweating like a pig from running after you.'

Sarah smiled, and arm in arm they made their way to the café at the end of the pier. The walls were made of glass with views over the English Channel. The day was so clear you could see France on the horizon and ships travelling from the nearby port. The sea sparkled in the bright sunlight and a pale-blue sky was peppered here and there with big fluffy clouds like bubbles scooped up from the bath. A very sullen waitress came over and they ordered their drinks.

'So what did you think of Nate Hardy turning up at rehearsals then?' asked Lottie, a twinkle in her eye.

'It was horrible.'

'Horrible?' Lottie couldn't have looked more surprised.

Sarah ran her hands over the plastic table top. 'Yes! Horrible! You didn't have to sit next to him and recite lines. It was like taking my driving test all over again. I was sick in the footwell the first time, I was so nervous.'

Lottie giggled. 'Bet that was nice for your examiner.'

'He wasn't best pleased. I think that's partly why he failed me.'

'You think?' The waitress delivered their drinks and they both took a big glug of their iced frappucinos. 'Did he smell nice?'

'My examiner?'

'You know perfectly well I mean Nathaniel Hunky Hardy.'

Sarah smiled. 'He did actually. He smelt of Gregory and Cecil's washing powder and something citrusy.'

'Gin and tonic?' asked Lottie and Sarah narrowed her eyes.

'He didn't seem like a drinker to me.'

'Who could blame him though? Poor man.'

'Don't you think he's in the wrong for cheating on his wife?' asked Sarah, scowling.

'Yeah, but …' Lottie gave a half shrug. 'Haven't you been reading the papers? Apparently, they've been on the verge of splitting for months.'

'You can't believe the papers, Lottie.'

'Hey!'

'Sorry,' Sarah replied, stirring her drink with the straw. Lottie and Sid worked on the local paper, Lottie as the photographer and Sid as the one and only reporter. Though there wasn't much in the way of scandal in Greenley-On-Sea.

'If you can't believe the papers,' Lottie countered, 'then how do you know it's true about him shagging the model?'

'Why would he be hiding out here, alone, if it wasn't true?'

Lottie considered for a moment. 'Okay, I'll give you that one. I'm just saying that there might be more to it than we think, that's all. He even said as much, didn't he?'

'Maybe.' Life was rarely simple, as Sarah herself was finding out.

'Anyway, did you actually sniff him, or did he just waft near you?' asked Lottie, leaning forwards over the table.

Sarah felt her cheeks begin to burn but happy to share the secret, she leaned in too. 'Might have done.'

'When?'

'When Cecil was whispering to him, he leaned over to whisper back and I had a little sniff. You should try it if we ever see him again.' Sarah couldn't help the grin spreading across her face. She couldn't believe she'd actually sat next to Nathaniel Hardy. 'He's really bloody handsome. I almost couldn't look him in the face.'

'He kept looking at you, you know.'

'No he didn't,' Sarah replied, shaking her head.

'He did, when you were reading your lines.'

'He was probably thinking how shit I was.' Sarah almost shuddered. It had been incredibly embarrassing but the chances were she wouldn't see him again. Gregory said he had only come there as he'd locked himself out. He should be under house arrest.

'I bet he thought you were good. I did.' Sarah raised her eyebrows, sure Lottie was only trying to make her feel better. 'I found it hard to look at him too though.'

'Did you? Why? You were over the over side of the circle.'

'Because,' said Lottie, already grinning, 'every time I did, I kept remembering when we watched that BBC thing he was in and he did that semi-nude scene.'

Sarah spluttered her drink just as she was tipping it to her mouth. 'Oh my gosh, I remember now. That shower scene! We kept rewinding it and watching it over because we thought—'

'We thought we could see his bits!' Lottie and Sarah descended into hysterics. They'd been at Lottie's – Sid was out teaching at the adult education centre – and there was a scene where Nate came out of the shower. They'd rewound it, watching it again, leaning forwards, tipping their heads as if that would help them see better. Then they'd missed a crucial plot twist because they were too busy laughing. 'He gave us some good advice though,' said Lottie once they'd calmed down. 'I thought what he said was very helpful.'

Sarah nodded. 'Me too. I'm going to re-read my lines tonight with that in mind.'

'Did he give you any other tips? You were getting quite chatty at one point.' Lottie was mischievously wiggling her eyebrows.

Thinking back, Sarah couldn't believe how easily they'd talked together. Even though he was so handsome it was almost intimidating, he'd been kind and funny, and Sarah had felt strangely at ease. His eyes had softened when he'd laughed or whispered with Cecil and he was so normal. She felt a weird bubbling in her chest and admonished herself for her schoolgirl crush. She was 31, for crying out loud. 'He was just commenting on Mrs Andrews,' she said to distract Lottie. 'She was on top form today.'

'She certainly was. And what the hell was that noise she made? I thought the fire alarm had gone off.'

Sarah toyed with her straw. 'I thought we had a ghost.'

'Some sort of banshee?'

'Yeah. If she does that on the night, we'll get complaints from parents with terrified children or old people who've had heart attacks.'

Lottie suddenly perked up. 'I've just had a great idea. I can tap him for some funding before he goes. If *The Tempest* doesn't make enough money we're going to struggle. Nate could really help and we *are* doing him a massive favour keeping schtum.'

'Are we still applying for charity status?'

'If I can get the paperwork done,' said Lottie, rubbing her forehead. 'There's so much to do and the mayor's being his usual helpful self. But if Nate could be our patron it would really help. Oh, and I wanted to show you these.' From her huge handbag Lottie pulled out a programme and an A5 flyer. 'There'd also be big posters for the frames out the front of the theatre and this is a mock-up of the programme. What do you think?'

Sarah took the flyer and studied it. She and Gregory were photographed in costume. 'What size will this be out front?'

'A0.'

'Urgh, my face will be absolutely enormous.'

'Then it's a good job it's such a pretty face.' Sarah eyed Lottie over the top of the flyer.

'Can't we be in silhouette?'

'No, it'll look crap.'

'Oh. Okay then,' she agreed reluctantly, not relishing the prospect of a blow-up of her face being on a huge poster for everyone to see. 'I love the programmes though.'

'Great. I'll get these off to the printers then.'

Sarah's phone beeped with a message and she checked it,

109

worried that somehow her dad had got her number. He was being quite persistent, and she wouldn't have put it past him. But she was surprised and pleased to see it was from Finn.

'Who is it?' asked Lottie in concern.

'It's Finn,' she said, smiling as a warm feeling replaced the depression that had settled before.

'The sexy doc?'

'Yeah.' Sarah tried to read the message and keep calm but an image of his gorgeous face and curly strawberry blond hair kept popping up.

'He is lovely,' agreed Lottie. 'He treated Sid's ingrown toenail.'

Sarah scrunched up her face. 'Eww, too much information.'

'Sorry.'

'He is lovely though. We've been chatting a lot more recently.' Sarah read the screen one more time just to be sure she hadn't imagined it.

Hey, Sarah, would you like to go to dinner with me Friday night? Please say yes!

Sarah felt her heart squeeze. She'd imagined this moment time and time again, though in her head it had been face to face. Still a text invitation was better than none at all. 'Finn's just asked me out for dinner!' She giggled and waved her phone screen at Lottie, knowing full well she was beaming from ear to ear.

'Yay! When?'

'Friday.' Lottie pulled a face. 'What?'

'Why not ask you tomorrow at work if it's for the end of the week?'

Sarah shook her head. 'He's off this week coming. Got a conference in Newcastle. He's back Friday morning.' Sarah wiggled in her seat with pleasure. 'He is so lush. In the past week he's brushed past me a few times and the other day I had something in my hair and he got it out for me. I thought I was going to swoon! Or just straight out launch myself at him.'

'I'm so pleased. I know how much Vince hurt you.'

'Yep, but Finn's different. I've known him for ages. In fact, I feel like I know a lot about him already. Though the other day some random woman came into the surgery demanding to see him – she didn't have an appointment or anything – and she was quite pissed off. She started shouting and saying she had to see him, no one else would do, but Mandy went and got him, and he came and calmed her down.'

Lottie's jaw dropped. 'What did she want?'

Sarah shrugged. 'She's registered as a patient with us, but Finn didn't say. He just squeezed her in between appointments and didn't say anything more. He wouldn't though, would he – patient confidentiality. She left after he'd seen her, she seemed fine.'

'Weird.'

'Yeah. Weird. But that's what I mean about him being lovely. He could see she was in distress and even though he had to have a shorter lunch, he still saw her. He's such a great doctor.'

'So apart from crazy ladies shouting in the surgery, things are looking up?' asked Lottie tentatively and Sarah's grin widened.

'I think they are.'

Chapter 11

The phone rang, and rang, and rang. Nate hung up again. The worry in the pit of his stomach that had begun as a faint fluttering was now an ever-tightening knot. Robin wasn't answering his calls and hadn't been for two whole days, since Monday morning. Nate had called, left messages, emailed, but nothing. Was he being frozen out? A lump formed in his throat as he thought about how he'd completely ruined his career, all because of one stupid action. Nate tried once more and this time Robin answered. 'Hey, Nate, how are you holding up?'

'Fine, fine.' He wasn't fine but the relief spreading through his veins made him say it. 'Where've you been? I've been calling since Monday.'

'I know, I'm sorry.'

'Have you been avoiding me?' Nate asked, jokingly, but the pause at the other end made him stiffen. He stood up and paced around his room.

'Not exactly, but I have been trying to sort things out for you. Nate …' Robin sighed and Nate clenched his jaw. 'Hannah's saying she's pregnant.'

Everything went quiet. All the noise coming in through his open bedroom window receded and there was only the blood pumping in his ears. The birds stopped their chirping and the chatter of passers-by disappeared. As the walls of his bedroom closed in, all he could think to say was, 'How?'

'How?' Robin scoffed. 'Do I really need to explain that to you?' Nate failed to see the funny side. His whole life was falling apart. This just wasn't the time. Robin read his silence. 'Sorry, that wasn't appropriate.'

'Does Emma know?' Nate managed to croak. His mouth and the back of his throat were dry and sticky.

'Yes. I'm sorry, but I had to tell her and her agent.'

'Before you told me?' He was hurt and a little offended. Somehow, it felt like a betrayal.

Down the line he could hear the scraping of Robin's chair as he stood up. No doubt he'd be pacing around his office or looking out of the huge windows at the skyline of London. Nate could picture it himself, brilliant in the bright sunlight. 'Hey, listen, don't be like that. It's going to hit the papers tomorrow. I've been doing everything I can to control the story. I was hoping if I could get her agent on board, convince them it'd be best to work together, we might be able to do something, but it's not looking good.'

In his mind, Nate listed all the expletives he knew and took a deep breath. But among the chaos of his thoughts, one thing kept popping up. He was going to be a dad. His brain pictured tiny fingers and toes, gummy smiles and large eyes, and for some reason, he wanted to smile. He'd never thought of becoming a father. Emma was focused on her career and Nate had discovered early on in their marriage it wasn't on the cards for her and therefore for him too, so he'd ploughed all his energy into his career pushing down the yearning whenever it arose. But now, in these less than ideal circumstances, the idea of fatherhood had an unexpected effect: he was pleased. 'What did Emma say?'

'Do you really want me to repeat it?'

Oh God. Was she hurt? He'd screwed everything up so much

and changed their life together immeasurably. He'd never meant to hurt anyone. And Hannah? How was she feeling? They'd have to sort things out somehow. Christ, what a mess. 'No. Not really.'

'Needless to say, she doesn't want you coming back to the house anytime soon. She said she's bringing forward the divorce. I think it's her dad's idea. As one of the UK's top producers he probably thinks she can walk away now and everyone will be sympathetic. And he's right. Even if her affairs are discovered they'll be able to spin it in her favour. You'll have been neglectful, forcing her to it. He must be confident it's the right move. Either you're majorly damaged goods now, or he thinks the chances of them even discovering her little trysts is slim. I've heard she's up for a big presenting job, she'll be guaranteed it as the wronged wife.' Robin gave a mirthful laugh. 'Her dad should have been an agent not a producer. But your reputation is going to take one hell of a battering. Especially with big guns Daddy involved. We had a chance with Emma sticking by you, but now …' His voice tailed off. 'I'm sorry, Nate. It's not that she's particularly hurt by what you did, she's just trying to save her own reputation.'

Nate closed his eyes, imagining Emma's angry face when Robin told her the pregnancy news. He wished he'd known first. He'd have told her. It would have been hard, but the decent thing to do. But there was no point dwelling on that now. 'I understand. I just can't believe that after everything I've done, sticking by her, she's throwing me to the wolves now.' A sharp pain shot through his heart. 'So what do we do now?'

'Do you want her to keep it?' Robin asked.

'What?' Bile rose up in this throat. 'The baby? Yes, of course I do. Why? Doesn't she want to?'

'I don't know. I'm trying to find out.' His deep voice was matter-of-fact. 'You're going to have to release a statement or something. We'll send it from the office and you can remain hidden. We've done quite well so far. They haven't been able to twist your words because you haven't said anything, so you're not looking as bad as some have. Believe me, I've seen much, much worse.'

'How is my pneumonia anyway?' Nate asked sarcastically.

'Terrible.' Nate could hear the more cheerful lilt to Robin's voice. 'You've got worse but are slowly on the mend. We're hinting you're recovering in Scotland so hopefully if they go looking for you, they'll be at the other end of the country.'

'That's something at least. Have we any work to discuss?'

Another ominous pause. 'Things aren't great at the moment, Nate. There's some work in the US that looks promising, you know how they love a bad boy, especially a British one, but the wholesome period drama stuff is off the table. They're not going to want you in those roles until this has been forgotten.' That had been his bread and butter for a while now. It was how he'd made his name. That and a bit of British espionage.

'What about theatre stuff?' Nate flopped onto the edge of the bed.

'Unless you fancy being Widow Twankey in some town on the arse end of humanity, I wouldn't go there if I were you.'

Great, thought Nate, swallowing down his disappointment. It was all crashing down. But the idea of a child, an innocent victim in all of this, changed things. Something stirred within Nate and the shame that had kept him paralysed began to fall away, replaced by something more positive. He had to stand up and apologise for his actions. He respected Robin's expertise but Nate realised he'd been hiding behind it, letting him run the show because it was easier than standing up and taking the criticism. It was time to take action. 'Okay. I want to come back.'

'What?' Robin screeched. Nate had never heard his voice so high. Except for that time Anna had made Robin go on a get fit campaign when he'd first been prescribed blood pressure tablets and during a game of squash Nate had accidentally hit the ball right into Robin's gentleman's area. He'd collapsed like a sack of shit shouting expletives and calling Nate every name under the sun. Nate could tell Robin was shaking his head from the noise of the phone brushing his ear. 'No, not yet.'

'Why not? Isn't it about time I did something?'

'No, definitely not.'

'Why?' The heaviness of disappointment weighed in on him and he felt the need to move, pacing around the small bedroom again. He could only take a few strides one way before having to turn and head back, but he had to keep moving.

'Because things are going to get a lot worse before they get better. Look, I know you want to do the right thing, but trust me, now isn't the time. Just stay where you are and hang on in there, please?'

'But Robin, I really think—'

'Nate, trust me on this. I've seen false pregnancy claims before. I know you don't want to believe it, but it could be the case. You could demand to see the results of a pregnancy test – a proper one at a doctor's, not just weeing on a stick. If she's got a pregnant friend, she could get them to do that for her.'

'No, I won't do that.'

'Then take my advice and hold out there. It's what you pay me for, after all. There's a lot to get through yet. When the time's right I'll bring you back straight away.'

Nate sagged down. 'All right, but soon, yeah?'

'Soon.'

'Can you draft a statement for me then, please? You've always been better at that than me. Apologise to Emma. Apologise to Hannah if I did anything to lead her on, and say that we'll work together for the sake of the child to make everything right.'

'That sounds pretty good already,' Robin replied. 'I'll get back to you.'

Robin hung up and a horrible dizziness hit Nate as he stood up. His head was pounding and he flopped back onto the bed with a thud. Squeezing his eyes shut and taking long deep breaths, Nate tried to make sense of this latest development. He knew he had to speak to Emma. He had to talk things through, but he couldn't do that until he was sure of things himself. A light tapping at the door told Nate it was Cecil rather than Gregory. 'Come in,' he called out.

'We're just off to rehear … cripes, are you okay, sweetie?'

Nate lifted his head and swallowed. His head wasn't spinning anymore but he still felt giddy. 'Yes, just some more developments.' He needed time to figure this out himself first before he said anything. Gregory appeared from behind Cecil, his head popping into view above Cecil's left shoulder. They really were quite an eccentric pair, but Nate was grateful for their genuine care, and now they'd got to know him better, they were treating him like a real person. 'It's all such a mess and things just keep getting more and more complicated.' Gregory and Cecil exchanged worried glances.

'Why don't you come with us to rehearsals?' said Gregory. 'Take your mind off things?'

'Isn't it too risky?' Nate asked.

'Well, we're only an hour from London and the players have known for what … four days now. In the absence of any reporters I'm guessing no one's blabbed.'

It was a miracle, but Gregory was right.

'Okay then.' Nate nodded. It would take his mind off things for a while if nothing else and if he could help with the production, so much the better. 'I best put on a hoodie or something and hide my face just in case. Though I'm not sure Robin's packed me one.' Nate searched through his suitcase that lay open on the bedroom floor, but couldn't find one. Turning back to Gregory and Cecil he said, 'Do either of you have one I can borrow?'

Gregory stared at him distinctly unimpressed. 'Do either of us look like we own a hoodie, dear boy?' Even Mr Bennett, who had followed them upstairs and was sitting at his feet, glared in dismay.

Nate smiled. 'Umm, no. I don't suppose you do.'

'But I do have a marvellous trilby and a stick-on beard you

can borrow.' And with that he nipped off to find it. Nate contemplated asking why Gregory owned a stick-on beard but decided not to. He wasn't a hundred percent sure he wanted to know the answer. When Gregory raced back and proudly presented it, Nate was pleased to see it was still un-used and in the packaging. He hesitated, but seeing Gregory's face, took it and squeezed past him to the bathroom to stick it on. Staring in the mirror Nate laughed to himself. He looked like Brian Blessed and was even tempted to mimic his booming voice, but didn't in case he scared his hosts. When he came out, Cecil made a sound somewhere between a laugh and a hiccup while Gregory hurried them on their way.

As they strolled to the theatre, Nate took the time to admire the town. A strange mixture of calm and vibrancy rang through the air. It was incredibly hot again today and the sweat forming on his brow caused the stick-on beard to start sliding down his face. Luckily, before long they were at the theatre. It really was a beautiful building. There was something quite peaceful about it, but Nate could also see it full of people and abuzz with excitement. *Every town should have a theatre like this*, he thought, as he followed Gregory and Cecil down to the stage where the Greenley Players were gathering.

The Scottish woman with bright red hands and matching hair – Debbie, Nate remembered – was shouting something he couldn't quite make out to one of the stagehands.

Next to him, Cecil sighed. 'Ah, Debbie. Lovely, but you know …' He held his hand up near his ear and made circular motions with his finger to show she was mental. Nate held back a laugh. Cecil then pointed out a few more people he hadn't met before. When his eyes rested on Sarah, he found that seeing her again calmed his angst a little. She looked even prettier today in a plain white T-shirt and denim shorts with long, toned legs underneath. Her brown hair glowed with hints of gold under the lights and her eyes sparkled as she laughed with Lottie. He could just make out a constellation of freckles over her nose and, realising he was staring, pulled his gaze away.

They were soon ready to begin. The circle of chairs was now absent as the actors were expected to start inhabiting the roles, moving about the stage and getting a feel for how their characters would react. He loved this part of the process – really getting to know the person you were playing, letting them take over a small part of you, like you were a puppet and they were in control. Everyone was taking a seat and small groups clumped together here and there.

'Don't forget,' said Conner, from the centre of the stage. 'You can have your scripts today, but they'll be gone next week. If you get stuck, Joan will be acting as prompt.'

There was a subdued groan and Nate looked to Cecil and Gregory who were sitting with him in the second row back. 'What's the problem?'

'Joan,' said Gregory.

'Why?'

Cecil pointed to the other side of the theatre where, about halfway back, sat an ancient white-haired woman, knitting. Even with her enormous spectacles she was squinting at the needles that moved with frightening speed. 'She's deaf as a post,' said Cecil. 'Unless her hearing aid's turned up full blast, and even then she's so busy with knit one, purl one, she gets her timing wrong. Lottie's tried to convince her to do something else but alas, to no avail. You see, Joan can't do the stagehand stuff because she's virtually dead and any kind of physical effort would probably kill her, and she can't do make-up or wardrobe because she's got the speed of a knackered tortoise. Bless her heart, she just so desperately wants to be involved and we can't really stop her.' Joan glanced up and waved at them all. Cecil waved back. 'Evening, Joany, all right, love? How's the bunion?' shouted Cecil. Joan simply grinned, almost dislodging her dentures, and turned her gaze back down to the ball of pink wool in her lap.

This was the best thing about local theatre as far as Nate was concerned. No one was excluded no matter what. Everyone worked together. Sarah and Lottie were smiling, watching the conversation, and Nate noticed how Sarah's face had lightened since the last time he'd seen her.

'Shall we get started?' asked Conner, looking out from the stage. 'Right then. Let's start at the beginning. Act one, scene one.' A number of players climbed onto the stage and acted out the scene. Some were pretty awful, but a couple were okay. They were supposed to be acting like they were on a boat, staggering across the stage but unfortunately looked more like a bunch of happy drunks messing about. Nate was just about to open his mouth and suggest they add more fear to their performance when Conner shouted, 'Don't forget you think you're in a storm and that you're going to die, you're not on a heavy night out! You need to be terrified.' This young man was quite impressive.

'He's doing really well for someone so young,' said Nate to Gregory.

'Yes, he's very good,' Gregory replied. 'We're very fond of him. He sees all this as "building his career" or something like that.'

'Maybe I could get him an internship somewhere?'

'Oh, that would be brilliant,' said Cecil, clasping Nate's arm. 'You sweetie. He'd love that.' As soon as this was all over, he'd sort that out for him.

They then moved on to the next scene which was Miranda and Prospero. Gregory and Sarah walked onto the stage. As she moved to the middle, Nate noticed how her eyes flitted to his and away again. He hoped he wasn't making her feel uncomfortable and smiled to put her at ease which only seemed to make her more terrified. Her speech was still stilted and wooden and he noticed a slight tremble in the tips of her fingers.

'Poor Sarah,' whispered Cecil and Nate leaned in. 'She's actually getting worse. I don't know why but she just can't seem to get Miranda going. I thought she'd be great. We did *Much Ado*

About Nothing last year and it was horrendous but—'

'Oh, I'm sure it wasn't.'

'No, really. It was,' said Cecil. 'Even the birds didn't bother watching. We were performing in the bandstand in the park and it was so bad people left halfway through.'

'Why weren't you here in the theatre?'

'Because this was all a decrepit mess. It was our dear Lottie who got it back to this state. She's a good girl. We were all terrible but by the time we did the pantomime last Christmas we were so much better. Sarah particularly was fabulous as Jasmine. She's always got such terrible stage fright, but she seemed to really be coming out of her shell then. Oh, here we go. This should be good.' Cecil nodded to the stage and Nate followed his gaze to see Mrs Andrews had come out from the wings in some kind of strange voluminous green hooded kaftan. She looked like Yoda. And with arms outstretched, she wafted towards Gregory and Sarah who were biting back a laugh. Mrs Andrews began her lines as Ariel. Cecil smiled and crossed his arms over his chest. 'I think she's taking this sprite thing a bit too far, if you ask me.'

'Is it supposed to be a dress rehearsal?' Nate asked. Cecil slowly shook his head and soon they too were suppressing their laughter.

'Umm,' said Conner. 'Okay ...'

'I think she's throwing herself into this because she's having trouble with the builders. And that isn't a euphemism. She's having an enormous extension built on her already enormous house and it isn't going very well. Even the Botox isn't stopping the frown lines this time. And I haven't seen Mrs Andrews' face move in the last five years.'

'Right, let's pause there,' said Conner, walking to the centre of the stage. He cast a bemused glance at Mrs Andrews before moving on. 'Well done, everyone. Now the next part is the singing.' Another groan echoed around the theatre and two middle-aged burly men stepped out from behind the scenery, wearing overalls splattered with paint. One had a huge bushy moustache and the other a wiry beard, but it was what they were carrying that had Nate stifling a giggle. The moustached man was holding a triangle and a teaspoon – they clearly hadn't been able to find the wand to hit it with. The bearded man was holding a single maraca and grinning.

'Oh, sweet Jesus,' mumbled Cecil. 'Close your ears, this is going to be nasty.'

Mrs Andrews started singing in an ear-piercing soprano note and Nate closed one eye, wincing. The bearded man was shaking the maraca with such vigour Nate wondered if he was going to shout, 'Tequila' at some point, and the poor fellow with the triangle was randomly whacking it whenever the mood took him. Music, it certainly wasn't. Sarah and Gregory regarded them quizzically and Nate was surprised to see how Sarah was even more beautiful when she relaxed. Her cheeks were pushed up by the force of her smile and her eyes were shining. Gregory's shoulders were shaking with laughter.

After the cacophony had died down, Cecil said, 'Right, it's my turn in a minute,' and squeezed past to the end of the row.

'Who are you playing?' asked Nate.

'Ferdinand. I get the fun of being in love with Sarah. And she's a doll, so it's always fun.' A funny feeling squirmed in Nate's chest. It was almost like jealousy. No, it couldn't be. It was probably just his wish to be acting again pushing back up.

The rehearsal continued and they got through almost half the play. Things would get a little more difficult once they were negotiating props, but apart from Prospero's staff there wasn't much to worry about at present.

'What's the verdict today, then?' Kathryn asked Nate once the rehearsal had finished.

'I thought you were all fantastic,' he replied. Mrs Andrews beamed and removed the hood of her kaftan. He wasn't sure, but had she just pouted at him? She came towards him shaking it off her shoulders and jutting out her chest.

122

'So, Nate. How long are you staying here for?' She slipped her arm through his, making him feel like he was caught in a spider's web.

'I, umm, I don't really ...'

Sarah had paired off with Gregory and Cecil, and Nate overheard her sadly saying how difficult she was finding the role of Miranda. He wanted to hear more but Mrs Andrews was talking nineteen to the dozen, clinging to his arm like a barnacle.

Nate caught Cecil's eye and flashed him a 'help me' look.

Cecil got the message and, taking Nate's other arm, guided him gently away. 'I just need to borrow Nathaniel for a moment, Mrs Andrews, if you don't mind.'

'Well I—'

'Thank you *so* much.' Cecil steered Nate towards Sarah and Gregory. Mrs Andrews, her mouth set in an angry little line, turned on her heel and marched off. 'Now,' Cecil said to Sarah, 'what were you saying, dear?'

A flash of bright red rose on her cheeks covering the bridge of her nose. 'Just that I'm finding Miranda quite hard.'

'I thought you did very well,' Nate replied, trying to ease her mind, and she caught his eye which sent a pulse through him. He didn't know why he was saying it, he knew it was important to be honest with actors and let them know when things weren't going so well, but for some reason he didn't want to hurt her feelings.

Surprisingly, Sarah smiled. 'No, I'm really not getting it at the moment. I don't know why.'

Nate had no idea why he said what he said next. His life was complicated enough at the moment but before he could stop himself, he heard words coming out of his mouth. 'Well, why don't I give you some coaching while I'm here?'

Sarah's head shot up at the suggestion. Nate expected her to pull her gaze away but she didn't. Her cool stare pierced right through to his core and he found he was the one looking away hoping her answer would be yes.

'What a fabulous idea,' said Cecil, excitedly.

Sarah fidgeted, putting her hands in her pockets and rocking from side to side. 'I'm not sure. I couldn't take up your time like that. It must be the last thing you want to think about right now.'

'We haven't got long until opening night, dearest,' Gregory said gently. 'It's only about three weeks to go. I think it would be a good idea.' His words seemed to really hit home and she nodded.

'Okay, then. Thank you.'

Cecil clapped. 'Fantastic. Why don't you start tomorrow night?'

'Tomorrow?' Sarah's face was a mixture of panic and shock that Nate also felt himself. What had he got himself into now?

'Well, we don't know how long we've got him for, do we, sweetie?'

Reluctantly, Sarah agreed. 'Okay then.'

'I promise it won't be painful,' Nate offered in an attempt to bring the smile back to her face. A weak one came and went just as quickly.

'I guess I'll see you tomorrow then,' she said.

'Yeah, see you tomorrow.' It was strange how much he was looking forward to it.

Chapter 12

The next evening, Sarah knocked on Gregory's door and stepped back, placing her hands in the pockets of her skirt. Why was it that skirts and dresses hardly ever had pockets? Trousers always did. Men's shorts always did. Did designers not realise that women needed pockets too? Smiling at the thought, Sarah ran her hands through her hair. The natural kink she'd hated as a kid had been hard to tame, but now she'd stopped trying, it gave her hair a gentle curl that she liked. Not that she was thinking about looking nice for Nate. The bright blue Fifties-style skirt flowed out gently and teamed with a simple pale-blue T-shirt made Sarah feel stylish and confident. She needed to feel confident if she was to be in the same room as Nathaniel Hardy.

A slight breeze blew over her face and she adjusted her bag. Finn lived in this part of town. The posh part, as Sarah knew it. Glancing around, every house shouted 'money' from the large black front doors and sash windows. She wondered if she'd see him tonight. Maybe run into each other after this and go for a drink. Her date was tomorrow night and just thinking about it caused her stomach to flutter in anticipation. She'd really missed Finn this week. Missed the banter in the office, missed his smile and the general air of fun he brought with him. So far, Sarah had planned and dismissed several outfits for her date. And at work she couldn't concentrate. She'd even misfiled someone's medical records, her mind too filled with what they would talk about, and if it would end in a kiss. Mandy had pointed out her mistake and put the file in the right place, but not before teasing Sarah, causing her to deeply regret mentioning it.

'Hello, darling,' said Gregory, pulling the door wide and letting her through. He had a full wine glass in one hand, waving it around flamboyantly as he spoke. Luckily, none spilled onto the beautiful tiles of the hallway floor. 'All ready for some one-on-one time with our resident hunk?' He wiggled his eyebrows suggestively and Sarah rolled her eyes.

'This is going to be agony,' she replied. 'It'd better work.'

'Why is it going to be agony? Honestly, darling, he's an absolute sweetheart. You just have to forget he looks like hot sex on a stick.' He paused, thinking. 'And that you've seen him pretend to have sex for that matter. Oh' – he fanned himself with his spare hand – 'I'm coming over all funny. Those smouldering take-me-to-bed eyes he did on that spy thing with the Ukrainian gypsy woman – if he'd have looked at me like that I'd have simply melted. Anyway ...' Sarah shook her head in mock reproach. 'Cecil and I thought you might want to work in the living room. We'll be in the kitchen or the garden if you need us. Do you want a drink or something? I've got a bottle open.'

'Oh, God, yes, please.' She was going to need a large one, or two, to get through this. The nerves in her stomach were bouncing around and she wished she'd eaten before coming over, only she couldn't face it. Sarah followed Gregory through to the kitchen to see Nate and Cecil laughing and chatting like old friends. Nate was looking ridiculously handsome in a pair of old, battered jeans, the frayed ends catching under his well-worn trainers. Not the horrid skinny jeans that were the fashion at the moment, but normal jeans. His pale cream T-shirt revealed strong forearms that were crossed over his chest, and there was a hint of a tan line at the end of his sleeve. Nate looked up from under his eyelashes and Sarah felt a strange stirring in her heart. It was the smouldering look Gregory had been talking about at the door but more natural and unintended. It didn't seem real that he was there in her friends' kitchen. She'd been there so many times before but tonight the place felt different. The relaxed atmosphere she'd grown used to was gone and in its place was a hum of anticipation.

Nate gave her a wide, welcoming smile, his eyes crinkling. His hair was slightly fluffy and Sarah repressed the urge to run her hands through it. *Stop it*, she told herself. *He's not one of his characters now. He's an actual proper person and you can't go around rummaging through people's hair in real life. And remember, he cheated on his wife so he's not a very nice man anyway.* Finn was a nice man and with any luck she could rummage through his hair tomorrow night. Again, the thought of her date overwhelmed all other feelings. 'Hi,' Nate said, lifting up his hand in greeting.

'Here you go.' Gregory shoved a scarily full glass of white wine towards her.

'Hi,' she replied to Nate before taking her wine and leaning back against the counter. There wasn't really enough space for the four of them in the small kitchen, but Sarah didn't know what to do with herself. It was like some awful double date. Although she had to stop herself using words like 'date' when she was around Nate Hardy – it did something she didn't like to her body and would definitely put her off her lines. She normally only got that tingly sensation around Finn but her upcoming date was ever present in her mind so it was probably caused by that. What was even more off-putting was that Cecil was grinning at Gregory like they were up to something. No one had started a conversation yet and as Nate seemed to be finding his shoes endlessly fascinating, Sarah took a large swig of her wine. At least you could rely on Gregory and Cecil to buy the good stuff. They didn't hold with cheap wine and the taste of it was amazing, the light, crisp, fruity flavours refreshing in the evening heat.

Just as an uncomfortable silence was forming, Nate said, 'Shall we get started?' in his smooth, slightly gravelly voice and Sarah began to think again how this was all a really terrible idea. How on earth was she going to do anything with those sexy blue eyes staring at her? The thought that he might judge her and she'd come up short made her wince. Sarah reminded herself how she'd got over her fear of the whole town judging her last year at the showcase when they were trying to prove how talented they were. But her nerves were always so crippling. At the showcase she'd thrown up in a bin backstage. If she could get over herself and perform then, she could do this now, she had to. If something didn't click soon, she'd bring the whole performance down. Realising she hadn't answered, and that Nate was watching her with slightly raised eyebrows, she nodded.

Gregory began to usher them out of the kitchen. 'Right, you two into the living room. We'll be out here if you need us.' She couldn't think why she might need them, but you never knew. If that tingling didn't stop soon, she might need to make a quick escape to the garden and cool down. They went into the living room, Nate pulled the door closed behind them and Sarah sat down, placing her wine on the coffee table. She took her script from her bag and a pen, ready to make notes.

'So,' said Nate, perching on the edge of the chair opposite her and leaning slightly forwards. 'I've heard great things about you, Sarah – about your acting, I mean. From what I've seen you're getting to grips with the play, but why do you think you're struggling with Miranda?'

'I don't know,' Sarah replied. 'I just don't seem to be clicking with her, if that makes sense?' He nodded. 'I'm remembering the lines, but I don't really know how she feels, so when I say the words, they're just words.'

'Do you understand her meaning when she's speaking?' he

asked, his hands gently clasped together. He was still wearing his wedding ring and Sarah shuffled uncomfortably. She didn't approve of cheating. Not a surprise really, after her dad. There was no excuse for it as far as she was concerned. Marriages might fail – that was life. But regardless, you didn't go hopping into bed with someone else until you'd both officially separated. Vince had cheated and it had broken her. 'Sarah?'

'Sorry?' Her head shot up but he must have noticed her eyes flit back down to his wedding ring because he moved his hands so one covered the other, hiding it. Perhaps that was why she'd been struggling with Miranda. Did it somehow remind her of being with Vince? Miranda fell in love in the play. Was Sarah's own heart still too sore? No, that didn't sit quite right. She had feelings for Finn, after all. It must be something else.

'Do you like Miranda?'

The question threw her. 'What do you mean?'

Nate shrugged. 'Do you like her? What do you think of her?'

Sarah thought for a moment, twisting the pen in her fingers, unsure why this was relevant. She'd assumed he was going to tell her how to recite the lines and that was it. Advise her on where to place the intonation, where to pause. Sarah repressed a huff, not seeing the point of all this personal analysis. 'She's nice enough.' *What a stupid and dull response*, she thought. 'She's a bit naive maybe but she's lived on an island her whole life. She's—'

There was a kerfuffle in the hallway, followed by the screeching of Mr Bennett. A whispered voice said, 'Shoo! Mr Bennett, you silly cat.' And Nate stood up and went to the door. Sarah chewed her lip, half smiling but with an idea of what had happened. When Nate opened the door Gregory and Cecil were heaped on the floor having fallen over one another, and an indignant Mr Bennett sat by the shoe rack, cleaning a paw. 'Everything all right?' Nate asked, as they tried to straighten up without falling over the hall table.

'Oh, yes,' Gregory began. 'We were just trying to … umm—'

'Stop the cat from scratching at the door,' Cecil finished. 'We didn't want him disturbing you.'

Nate glanced backwards at Sarah, then nodded at Gregory and Cecil. 'That was very kind of you, thanks.' He closed the door on the smiling pair and resumed his seat. 'Sorry, you were saying about Miranda.'

Sarah re-focused. 'She's quite sweet and it's nice that she falls in love.' Her voice trailed away as she ran out of things to say. When nothing else came to her, she shrugged.

'And what don't you like about her?' Nate asked. Another question Sarah didn't really see the point of. All she wanted was to know how to say Miranda's bloody lines. Why couldn't Nate just tell her how to do that?

'Why does it matter?' she asked. 'Sorry, but I don't really understand why you're asking me all this.'

Nate smiled. 'I know it might seem a bit over the top but it's important to understand everything about your character so you can tap into their emotions. I've seen you, Sarah, you're a good actress, all the movement stuff will come once you've unlocked Miranda's feelings and motivations. There must be something you don't like about her. What are her faults?'

Sarah rubbed her forehead feeling hot and sweaty. Her desk fan was still not working and she'd been forced to make an old-fashioned one out of paper. She must have got dehydrated in the heat and it was affecting her body temperature. 'I don't know.'

'Just think about it for a moment.'

But Sarah was struggling to think. She'd had a long day at work with angry patients shouting at her and giving her more intimate information than she needed. She was never going to get the image Mrs Williams had described of her husband's abscessed scrotum out of her mind. What she wanted was to go home and prepare for her date. The one she'd dreamed of for ages, and every time she did, her heart thumped in her chest. She wanted to paint her nails, do a facemask, that sort of thing.

'There's no rush,' Nate said again. 'It'll give Gregory and Cecil time to think of another way of interrupting us.' This genuinely made her smile and Nate grinned back at her. Crikey, that smile was a killer.

'I'm surprised they're not listening at the door now, or out the front, peering through the window.' She glanced over just in case they were.

'Maybe they'll ask if we need some more wine,' he said, taking his glass and a large sip.

'It'll take me all evening to finish this one. They don't do half portions.' She picked up her own glass.

'No, they don't, do they?' After they'd taken a sip, Nate began again. 'Let's try a different approach. What do you think of her relationship with Prospero?'

God, it was like being in a job interview. Sarah was sure her T-shirt was beginning to stain from the damp sweat patches forming under her arms. She really didn't need this tonight. All she wanted was to relax. She didn't need this ... this ... homework club.

'Sarah?'

This had gone on long enough. 'Look, I know you're trying to help me and I really appreciate it, but honestly, I just need to know how to say the lines.'

Nate reached out and his hand lightly rested on hers sending a shockwave through her. She must have been sweaty or something because he balked and pulled back. Standing up, Nate paced the room. 'I know it may seem pointless but please trust me. Come on, what do you think of Miranda and Prospero. Is she a good daughter? Is he a good dad?'

'Well,' she said slowly, 'Miranda's a horrible, snotty daddy's girl, isn't she?' And as the words came out of her mouth, uncontrolled, she paused. That was the crux of her problem. That was why she couldn't play Miranda well. Miranda was a daddy's girl and Prospero a devoted father. He'd raised her alone, protected her, been her everything. Just as her father had been to her when she was young. But unlike Prospero, Sarah's father had given up the right to be a dad when he'd been greedy and stupid and got himself sent to prison, abandoning her. Sarah realised now she'd kept Miranda at arm's length, not wanting to tap into her emotions and open herself up to having to love a father when the relationship with her own was so difficult. All this time she'd thought it was a sore heart over Vince and her single status holding her back, but it was something entirely different.

The pen dropped from Sarah's fingers and she focused on the script, but the words didn't register. Ben was back now and sorry for what he'd done. She had a choice to make, and a chance to rebuild their relationship to that of a loving father and daughter. With a click, like a lock being undone, Sarah's body and mind flooded with anger and sorrow all at once. It must have registered in her expression because Nate reached out and his fingers barely touched hers. 'Sarah, are you okay?'

His light blue eyes scanned her face and she shot up out of the chair. She had to go home. She had to get out of the hot stuffy room. She squeezed past Nate and opened the living-room door, knocking over Cecil, who held a plate of artistically displayed Twiglets that went flying into the air as he screeched and fell backwards into Gregory.

'I was just coming to see if you wanted any nibbles,' he said, regaining his composure. They'd obviously been ear-wigging at the door again but there was no stopping to tell them off. 'What's the matter?' Cecil asked, concern written over his wrinkled forehead.

'Nothing,' she breathed out quickly. 'I have to go, that's all.' Sarah made for the door, pulling it open with such force she nearly ripped the handle off. Without saying goodbye, she stepped into the street, the air weighing heavily on her chest. She needed the sea. It was always cooler on the beach, on her spot on the seafront where she could watch the waves roll in and out.

Through the window, she saw Gregory, Nate, and Cecil in an animated discussion with Nate clearly confused at what he'd done to necessitate such an exit. Sarah wanted to tell him it wasn't his fault but worried if she opened her mouth she might cry. She sped down the road towards the beach.

The main road was busy as she checked left and right, but with the swirling thoughts in her head she didn't hear anything as she crossed. It was only as she approached the sea that the cadence of the waves began to soothe her. The pebbles scrunched under foot, some forcing their way into her sandals, hurting the bottoms of her feet but, ignoring the pain, she strode on. Finally at her spot, Sarah sat down, closing her eyes and listening to the sea. She matched her breathing to the in-out rhythm of the water, inhaling and exhaling slowly in perfect symmetry. Hungry gulls dived and squawked, children laughed and screeched away in the distance. Focusing on anything and everything, she repressed the voice in her head shouting at her to be kinder to her dad, to listen to Ben and forgive him. A small pile of stones fell down the brow behind her and she looked up to see Nate had followed her onto the beach.

Shit. She must have frightened the life out of him, acting like a complete nut job and legging it like that. He sat down, drawing his knees up and resting his arms on top. Sarah tried to think of something to say, to explain without explaining everything, but when she opened her mouth she couldn't think of how to begin. Turning her eyes back to the sea, she watched the sun setting on the horizon and the pale shimmer of the water under its heavy rays.

Nate took a deep breath. 'I'm sorry if I said something to upset you.'

From the corner of her eye, Sarah watched for a second. He clearly had no idea why she'd reacted that way, but it was sweet of him to apologise. She couldn't quite match up the man in front of her with the one she'd read about in the papers, the one at the heart of the scandal. Maybe there was more to his story, there was more to hers. 'It wasn't you,' Sarah said at last. 'It was Miranda.' A small laugh escaped at how silly that sounded. Her emotions were churning inside her, making her hot as the anger surged, then cold as sadness took over. She couldn't perform the play feeling like this, she'd have to pull out. There was no other way around it. Better to do it now when there was still time to cast someone else than keep pretending she could get over this and let everyone down at the last minute. 'I don't think I can play her.'

'Yes you can. You're very good,' Nate said, reassuringly. 'You've got a lot of talent, it's just figuring out—'

'No.' Sarah shook her head. 'I don't think I can bring myself to do it.'

'Why not?' Nate's voice was soft and quiet and almost floated towards her on the breeze.

'Because it reminds me too much of my dad.'

'The man who came to the theatre the other day?'

She nodded, surprised he remembered. She was even more surprised when, under his gentle gaze, she opened up to him, telling him the truth. 'He's just come out of prison. He was sent down for stealing from his firm, he was an accountant. False accounting, if you want to get technical. Just before my mum got diagnosed with terminal cancer. He was inside when she died.' She might as well tell him, he wasn't exactly in a position to judge her; his life was just as much of a mess, if not more. Plus he'd be gone soon anyway so it didn't matter if he knew.

'Sarah, I'm so sorry. That's ...' He shook his head. 'I can't even imagine dealing with something like that.'

'And you call yourself an actor?' His head spun towards her and seeing her smile, he mirrored it.

'Do you have any brothers or sisters?'

'No, it was just the three of us. Then the two of us.' She gasped in a breath. 'Then just me.'

'So you had to deal with everything?' Nate asked gently. Sarah nodded. To her relief, her eyes weren't welling with tears and the raging sea of emotion was calming to a gentle ebb. 'Did you want him to come back?'

'I didn't at first. But now …' The sun shone onto her face, warming her up. 'Lottie said I should think about how I'd feel if I lost him too. Before we'd managed to sort things out.'

'That's good advice.'

'She's a good friend.' Sarah picked up a plain white pebble, rolling it around in her fingers, feeling its perfect smoothness. 'It's just all so complicated. Sometimes it feels like there's too much to forgive.'

Nate's voice was small and wavered slightly. 'We all make mistakes.'

Sarah glanced over. Deep lines of concern were etched into his forehead and there was a sad droop to his mouth. Nate's eyes were fixed on his feet, where he was moving the stones with his scruffy trainers. Was that what he'd done? Just made a mistake? There seemed to be more to it than that and Sarah wanted to ask what it was. Not out of nosiness, and she wouldn't even consider going to the papers, but he was burdened with something and she wanted to help him if she could. 'I'm sorry, this is the last thing you need at the moment.'

'It doesn't matter, I'm happy to listen. But I'm not …' He kept his eyes away. 'I'd like you to know that I'm not …'

'What?'

Their eyes met and she studied his face. There was an unexpected softness to the angular features she hadn't seen at first. A deeply unhappy soul lurked beneath the surface and she had the feeling that not many people saw that side of him. He didn't seem the type to have lots of friends or be that gregarious and show-offy.

'I'm just – I'm not the man I appear to be in the papers. It's …' He sighed.

'Complicated?' Their lives couldn't be more different, but sitting here on the beach they were the same. Both trapped in complicated situations, both hurting.

'Yes,' he replied with a sad laugh. 'Very, very complicated.'

Chapter 13

That evening Nate sipped his wine, sat with Gregory and Cecil in their glorious back garden. Calming birdsong filled the air and Nate reflected that never, in all the places he'd travelled, had he heard anything more glorious. The sky above was still a bright blue and clear of clouds. Gregory and Cecil were chatting about their day spent at the bookshop, gossiping good-naturedly about the customers while Mr Bennett lay out on the warm paving stones, soaking up the last of the day's sun. It was a rare moment of serenity, but his mind kept wandering back to the earlier coaching session with Sarah, and the bolt of electricity that had shot through him when he'd touched her fingers. It had raced down his spine, powerful and significant, like nothing he'd ever experienced before. But he'd sworn off love, sworn off women. Love hadn't worked out for him and neither had a one-night stand with no emotional involvement. He was better off playing it safe and closing off his heart, protecting it from any further damage. But still Sarah's voice, honey-warm yet with a strength he admired, played in his head. Even thinking of it now lifted the hairs on his arms. Nate rubbed his right arm self-consciously, but stopped when his phone beeped with a short, simple message from Robin. Story breaking tomorrow. You got bumped today.

Nate stood up from the table. 'Would you excuse me a moment, please?' An image of Sarah's brown eyes floated across his mind but he ignored it.

Going into the living room and taking a seat on the sofa, he wondered what to do. Could he tell Gregory and Cecil? Should he? Nate felt so alone, he needed someone to turn to. Friends to turn to. Now he thought of it, Gregory and Cecil were friends, not just people helping him out of a tight spot. They'd been better friends than a lot of his own who hadn't even texted or called. Marcus was the only one reaching out. He was still reminding Nate of one of Emma's first lovers and asking some more questions. It was a heavy-handed way of justifying Nate's actions and it wouldn't work. He'd have to gently ask Marcus to stop because it was having the opposite effect to the one he intended, only serving to make him feel even more of a fool.

Was Sarah a friend? Something strange had passed between them on the beach earlier that afternoon. Something he could only describe as significant. Some kind of connection between them. She'd been so honest with him, he'd really wanted to be honest with her but a frisson of fear stopped him. He didn't want her to think badly of him, which she would, of course. Their meeting had made him think about coming clean to the world, just apologising for everything and hoping they'd leave him alone after that. It was unlikely, but his conscience was telling him to do something, not just bury his head in the sand and let someone else clear up his mess. Robin was better equipped to handle these things, but it still felt cheap.

Being in a self-imposed media blackout, he wondered what had bumped him and, risking seeing something he didn't want to see, he quickly checked the tabloid gossip pages on his phone. One of those female reality TV stars had fallen out of The Ivy and into the bins then punched a photographer in a drunken rage. Flashing your knickers then lumping a paparazzi was always going to trump him, he thought, ruefully.

For a moment Nate let his head fall backwards to rest on the cushions. He closed his eyes and tried to listen to the birdsong again, but the predominant sound was of Mr Bennett purring. The fat lazy cat had been curled up on the sofa fast asleep, but after a stretch, and looking up to see his friend, he'd begun to purr in contentment. Nate liked cats. He could get one if he wanted, now Emma wouldn't object.

It had been just under two weeks since Hannah had come to the theatre, but it seemed like so much longer. Everything had changed. His whole life had been turned on its head. Being bumped from the front pages today showed that things would be forgotten eventually, but there would always be fall-out – mentions in the media whenever he was caught out and about, false rumours about co-stars – that sort of thing. Nate tapped his phone against his chin. He and Sarah had swapped numbers to arrange the next coaching session and he wondered if he should let her know what would be happening in tomorrow's press. She probably wouldn't care, it wasn't like they'd known each other long, and she had her own troubles to deal with right now. He didn't envy her. But he wanted to hear her voice, and he couldn't hide in the living room forever. Standing, he went back to the kitchen.

Gregory and Cecil were still in the garden, a newly opened bottle of white sat between them on the garden table in a wine cooler, complete with folded tea towel. 'Everything all right, dear boy?' asked Gregory as Nate approached and sat down.

'Not really, I'm afraid. I'll be staying a bit longer if that's okay.'

'Of course,' Gregory replied, his brow furrowed in concern.

'We're happy to have you,' said Cecil, tapping his arm gently. Nate managed a small smile.

'And you should know things are about to get ...' He was going to say worse, and in a way it was, but he couldn't bring himself to call his child that and decided on 'more complicated'.

'Can you tell us?' asked Gregory.

To which Cecil added, 'If you can't, it's no problem, we won't pry.'

'It's fine, I can tell you. It'll all be out tomorrow anyway.' He looked at Gregory. 'Robin said you were a good friend and you'd help me through this.'

'Oh, sweet, sweet Robin. How kind. And yes, we'll help if we can.' He turned to Cecil and they both nodded.

Nate's heart swelled. How lucky he'd been to meet them, even though it wasn't in the best of circumstances. He'd begun to feel so very much at home here in Greenley and could see why they had settled down here. A large mouthful of wine helped relax him a little. 'Before I begin, you should know that my marriage to Emma completely fell apart about eighteen months ago. She'd had some affairs and we'd grown into different people. She didn't want kids …' He paused, pushing down the mass in his throat. 'I did, but the thing is, she doesn't love me anymore.'

'Did you still love her?' asked Cecil, quietly.

'Yes, for a long time after she stopped loving me, but …' He realised now he was speaking of Emma and his marriage without an ache in his heart. Despite the situation, the physical distance between them was clearly helping, giving him space to see things clearly. 'But I'm getting over it. We decided to stay married for the sake of our careers. Her father's a top producer and I knew he could ruin my reputation if I ruined Emma's. He wanted us to stay married too. It looked better. I know it sounds bad. But then one of her affairs started getting serious and she asked for a divorce. We were just starting to sort it all out, prepping for the media scrutiny when this happened. God, I sound so mercenary.'

'Not at all, dear boy,' Gregory replied. 'Don't forget I was in the West End at a time when some men preferred to be a in a loveless marriage than admit to themselves, and the world, they were gay. Needs must sometimes.' A flicker of sadness passed over his face and Nate wondered who he was thinking of. Cecil reached out and took his hand, stroking it gently with his thumb.

'It sounds like I'm making excuses for myself but I'm not. I still cheated and that was wrong, but I want you to know that it wasn't that I cheated on a loving, caring wife. We'd grown very distant. Anyway, the divorce was planned for a month's time. We were going to do it amicably, well, fairly amicably, you know, try and keep some dignity. Like that guy from Coldplay and Gwyneth Paltrow. I didn't want to seem the bad guy and at the time there was nothing to throw at me. But when I met Hannah on my friend's stag do, I was feeling really low and—'

'Drunk?' asked Gregory, smiling.

'Yes, drunk.' He managed a laugh. 'She flattered me, and stupidly I fell for it. She made me feel important and I hadn't felt important to anyone in a long time. One thing just led to another, as they say. She was never really that interested in me though. It was all just about getting her name in the papers.'

'Oh, you poor thing,' said Cecil. For a moment they sat quietly in the evening breeze and Nate wished that was the end of the story. Though it had seemed like the end of his career at the time, things were now even tougher.

'There's one more thing.' Having had a day to deal with it and figure out his own feelings he now felt ready to tell them. 'Hannah's saying she's pregnant.' They gasped and Nate twisted the stem of his wine glass round and round in his fingers.

Gregory sat up indignantly. 'So is that the part coming out tomorrow?'

Nate nodded. 'Emma said she's bringing forward the divorce.'

'Is that a bad thing?' asked Cecil. 'You'll be free.'

'Free to do what? If her father wants, he can stop me getting a lot of work and the media will make me out to be a demon love rat. Even though Emma cheated first I'll be the one painted badly. That's if her affairs are discovered. Her dad will protect her. I've heard on the grapevine she's up for a big presenting job now. It'll be a long time before I get the quality roles I've been getting. Do you think you could forewarn the rest of the players?' asked Nate.

'They won't give you up now, dear boy, don't worry about that. They've kept it quiet for this long. We can rely on them.'

'It's not that,' he said, frowning. 'I hoped you could explain a little without going into all the details. Let them know that I'm not quite the bad guy I'm going to be painted as.' He ran a hand through his hair. 'I just don't want them thinking badly of me.'

'Of course,' Gregory replied, and he and Cecil exchanged glances before regarding him like he was a wounded puppy. Mr Bennett, who had followed them into the garden, rubbed against Nate's leg then jumped up and made himself comfortable, ready to sleep. Nate envied him – there was no way he'd be sleeping well tonight.

Chapter 14

Sarah looked around the beautiful new Italian restaurant recently opened in Greenley and then across at her gorgeous date. Her heart pounded with excitement. There was no Szechuan Palace for her tonight, no terrible first date with a bloke like Dean. She smoothed down her black wrap dress feeling confident and excited.

Bella Napoli was swanky with a shiny bar, a gin menu, and thick wooden tables. The waiter had seated them and delivered their drinks order, and now Finn sat opposite her talking about the conference he'd attended. Without thinking he pushed back his strawberry blond hair before reaching for his glass, and the movement made her heart flutter. She could imagine him instantly making friends with the other attendants then holding forth in the bar all evening. He was funny, quick-witted, and charismatic. Even more disconcerting was that he was looking effortlessly handsome in black jeans and open necked shirt. Sarah was finding it very hard not to stare at the smooth skin where his neck met his chest, or reach over and try to undo the rest of his buttons. She wondered if Nate wore a shirt open like that and quickly shunted the image from her mind. She didn't want to think about Nate Hardy and wished he'd stop randomly appearing in her head. Their moment last night kept playing in her mind. It was like she'd seen the real him, but she didn't want to think about that right now. She wanted to think about Finn MacDonald, preferably naked – no not naked, now she was getting all red and sweaty, and a bit tingly. It had been a while since she'd had sex but that was no reason to lose control. Still, it was somewhat reassuring to know those bits still worked. Sarah hid behind her menu for a moment to regain her composure thinking about something completely un-sexy like Donald Trump.

'Sorry, I'm rambling on about some boring conference and you're—'

She popped her head back up and stopped picturing Trump's strange wig-like hair and Oompa Loompa face. 'No, you're not rambling at all. It sounded interesting. I was just trying to decide what to have. It all sounds so good.'

'It does, doesn't it?' He picked up the other menu and perused. 'Have you been here before?'

'No, never.' They both watched two plates being taken to a nearby table. The food was beautifully presented in neat little piles and smelled delicious. 'That looks good.'

'I was just thinking that,' replied Finn, smiling. 'I'd better decide quickly or I'll be here all night. It always takes me ages.' A slight self-conscious blush hit his cheeks, and Sarah's heart pulsed. She'd only ever seen him being cool and calm at work, that flash of vulnerability aided her nerves in calming down; he was clearly feeling a bit nervous too.

Sarah made her decision and after placing the menu on the table popped an olive into her mouth. She quickly wished she hadn't as her teeth hit the stone. Now she had to try and spit it out without looking gross. Manoeuvring it around her mouth she managed to grip the stone between her teeth and grab it before popping it down on her plate. 'Did you learn anything new at the conference?'

'A few new things but I won't bore you with them. It was quite dull. I drew a lot of matchstick men on my notes.'

'Were they doctors too?' she asked with a grin, enjoying the flirtatious banter. There'd been no banter with Dean, only endless chomping on plate after plate of greasy food. Everything was going so well.

'Some were, with little matchstick stethoscopes and scalpels.'

'They sound a little bit scary now.'

'They do,' he said with a laugh. 'Sorry about that. How are things going with the play?'

Having been on quite a few dates, this one simple question meant a massive thumbs up for Sarah. So often she had sat opposite good-looking, respectable guys who only wanted to talk about themselves. The fact that he'd asked her about something she was interested in was a very good sign and she had to work to keep the smile from her face. 'I've been having some coaching with …' She stopped herself just in time. 'With Gregory and I think it's really helped. I was really struggling with my character, but I think I'm getting somewhere now.' She didn't go into details about why she was struggling. No one else needed to know about her dad. Or that the reason she was making progress was because of one-on-one coaching with Nate Hardy. She pictured his face on the beach and thought about how strange it was that they should both be here at this time, both wounded, then seeing Finn she shook it from her mind. She'd wanted this date with Finn for so long, nothing else would come close. Not even Nathaniel sex-on-legs Hardy.

'I think you're amazing. I've heard you sing, you're exceptional.' He took a sip of his beer and smiled.

Sarah's eyes widened and she brushed her hair back. 'Oh, no. I must remember not to sing at work. It's a bad habit I have.'

Finn shook his head. 'I haven't heard you sing there. I saw you at the showcase last year.'

'Really?' She'd had no idea Finn had been there.

'I don't think I'd ever heard anything so beautiful.'

145

Sarah felt herself colour, her cheeks growing hot under his gaze. She'd imagined sitting here with Finn so many times it was strange to think it was really happening. 'Unfortunately, the only singing in the show is weird and Shakespearean and I don't get to join in.'

'There's singing?'

'Yes, but don't get your hopes up, it's going to be awful. I'd bring ear muffs if I were you.' Finn laughed a low, throaty laugh and Sarah enjoyed the sound as it reverberated through her chest. 'Have you decided what to eat?'

'I think so.'

'Me too.'

They fell into easy conversation as they waited for the waiter to come and take their order. Sarah was in no hurry for that to happen, she was enjoying herself so much. Though a little nervous too, Finn was incredibly witty and clever, but not pompous or full of himself. He didn't think he was better than anyone else, not like some of the guys she'd met. His anecdotes about colleagues and patients made her giggle and, feeling at ease, she remembered the list of questions she'd imagined asking him in her fantasies. When the conversation lulled after the waiter had been over, she used one. 'So what made you go into medicine?'

'Ah.' He shifted in his chair. 'I hate answering that question, it always makes me sound like a massively pretentious snob.'

Sarah laughed. She couldn't imagine him ever sounding like that. 'I promise I won't judge.'

'Well, at the risk of sounding like a saint, I really wanted to help people, so being a doctor was the obvious choice. And being a GP I get to do different things every day. What about you?'

'Oh, I always wanted to be a doctor's receptionist and be shouted at by angry patients. It's my way of helping people too.' Thankfully Finn saw that she was joking and laughed.

'I thought you were going to say that.'

After a sip of wine she continued. 'I put a lot of my career aspirations on hold when Mum was sick. She died when I was 24 and I kind of fell into the job at the surgery after that.'

'What would you have done?' asked Finn. 'If things had been different?'

Sarah shrugged. 'I don't know really. I loved English and did an English degree at uni. Teaching maybe?'

The truth was that Sarah had taken her mum's death and her dad's betrayal so hard she'd locked herself away from the world, losing touch with most of her friends. It wasn't until a couple of years later, when Mayor Cunningham had been in the surgery one day saying that the position of secretary had come up on the theatre board that she'd started gingerly dipping her toe back into the pool of life and stepping outside the little safe world she'd created for herself. She'd been lucky to meet Lottie and the Greenley Players but, she thought regretfully, she'd wasted so much time. Looking up to see Finn and thinking of the amazing date they were having brought a beaming smile to her face and the tingle back to her skin. 'I'm just happy to have a job that I enjoy, good friends and a life full of fun things.'

'Like the am dram?'

Sarah nodded just as Finn's phone began to ring. He quickly pulled it from his pocket, blushing and apologising. The ringing stopped as he swiped the screen, clearly refusing the call. 'I'm so sorry, Sarah.' Sarah though, had caught sight of the screen. It was a pretty woman calling. She didn't know where the photo had been taken but the woman was pouting a little and Sarah had the vague feeling she'd seen her before in the surgery. Worry squirmed in her tummy. *Damn Vince*, she thought. If he hadn't betrayed her she wouldn't be so suspicious now. But Finn wasn't Vince, she reminded herself. 'I'm so sorry about that. It was my sister. I'll call her later.' Relief shot through her, relaxing every muscle in her body. His sister. Phew. She must have been mistaken about seeing her before.

Just then the waiter brought their food. Sarah's Pollo Milanese looked amazing and Finn's Fruitti di Mare was the biggest portion of food she'd ever seen, the bowl overflowing with succulent delights. 'I hope you're hungry,' she said, gesturing at his food with her fork.

'You might have to help me finish this.' His eyes sparkled in the candlelight. 'Either that or I'll have to hide some in your handbag.'

'There is no way you're putting prawns in my handbag,' Sarah laughed. 'Besides, have you seen this chicken breast? I've no idea where they get their chickens from but this one was a beast. Honestly. It's about the size of my head.' Finn laughed at her joke and Sarah relaxed even more. She'd never felt this comfortable on a first date before.

After a round of 'oohs' and 'mmm's' as they tasted their food, nodding at each other in approval, Sarah was able to find out all the things she had ever wanted to know about Dr Finn MacDonald. He came from a small family – just him, his mum and dad, and one younger sister. They still lived in Norfolk in the little town he'd grown up in, and he went to see them regularly. He thought moving to Greenley was the best thing he'd ever done and would be quite happy to stay there for the rest of his life. Another big thumbs up for Sarah. Greenley had a way of doing that to you. It sucked you in and crept into your soul, making itself a part of you until you couldn't bear to leave. In return, Sarah told him all about her, glossing over some of the things she didn't want to talk about. But what meant the most was that he didn't ask about her dad. Not once. Sarah was incredibly grateful for that. He must have been curious about their run-in the other day and the story behind it, but he respected her privacy and didn't ask.

Pushing their plates away at the same time, Sarah sat back in her chair. 'That was absolutely delicious.'

'Mmm, mine too. And look, no prawns left to smuggle out.'

'Thank goodness.' Sarah smiled. 'I didn't fancy a handbag

smelling of shellfish. I mean, I love living by the sea but carrying bits of it around with me is a step too far.'

The waiter approached. 'Can I interest you in the dessert menu?' he asked, placing them on the table and picking up the plates.

Finn gave a mischievous grin. 'It would be rude not to even look.'

'Very true,' replied Sarah. They were so in sync. So together. Sarah just knew this was the start of something special. Her first-date nerves had all but disappeared and it felt so natural being with him. Everything had been perfect so far.

'I'll give you a minute to choose,' said the waiter before disappearing off.

'This all sounds amazing too,' Sarah said when he'd left.

'No contest for me,' said Finn. 'Tiramisu. If it's as good as the main, it'll be the most amazing tiramisu I've ever had.'

Sarah took a sip of her wine as she read the options trying to narrow it down. She knew Finn was watching her and the quivering began in her chest as intense as pins and needles. She enjoyed having his eyes on her, but it was making it hard to choose a pudding. Eventually she said, 'Cheesecake for me. Nothing else comes close.'

He nodded. 'Good choice.'

The desserts were as delicious as the mains and gone even quicker. When they were waiting for the bill, Sarah realised with a worrying pull that though there'd been definite banter and a few glances, he hadn't reached for her hand, or tried playing footsie under the table. There'd been no accidentally-on-purpose touches and like a heavy stone had been dropped on her head, she realised that as much as he had enjoyed the evening, Finn probably didn't fancy her. He must have asked her out to try and cheer her up after the drama with her dad. Inwardly, Sarah cringed. It was a pity date. Yuck. A scream of frustration was building inside and reluctantly she prepared herself for the,

'Thanks for a lovely evening,' but no offer to do it again, and the weird day at work on Monday that would inevitably follow.

The waiter delivered the bill and Finn insisted on paying at first.

'What year is this?' asked Sarah, teasingly. Anything she could do to lessen the strange atmosphere on Monday was worth it.

'Okay, okay,' he held his hands up in surrender. 'Half and half it is, but I do insist on walking you home.'

She shook her head. 'You don't have to do that. I live in the opposite direction to you.'

'Non-negotiable, I'm afraid. If you don't let me walk beside you, I'll just follow you like a weirdo and be really annoying, like this ...' He started softly saying her name over and over again like a child saying 'mummy' until they got the attention they want.

'Fine, okay,' Sarah replied, laughing, with no expectations of anything other than a cordial handshake at the front door. Disappointment pulled at her again. She really quite fancied the pants off of Finn and would very much like to kiss him. He had a nice mouth and she'd always imagined his kisses would be soft and gentle, and not like having a sink plunger attached to her face, which she had, unfortunately, experienced before. Sarah grabbed her jacket from the back of her chair and Finn held the door open as they left. He held his arm out and she hesitated before threading hers through, unsure if it was the type of gesture she'd hoped for or if he was just being gentlemanly.

'That was a lovely evening, wasn't it?' he asked, his voice softer, almost uncertain.

'Yes it was. You did well with your enormous portion.' *What?* She felt her face grow red in the dusky light. Oh my God, she'd just said Finn had an enormous portion and now she was having a hot flush. She kept her eyes on the road in front of her and didn't risk looking at him. She'd never been so embarrassed. And now there was that tingling in her chest again. She really had to get control of herself. Was it her imagination or had he just squeezed his arm in, pressing her hand closer to him? She'd hadn't been this confused since she accidentally missed her turning on the M20 and drove all the way into London, going the wrong way round a one-way system and ending with a stern telling-off from a policeman. 'It's not far,' she said, hoping to move the conversation swiftly on.

The sky had become a mix of dark silhouettes against a vibrant back drop. On the horizon, bright pinks and lilacs filled the sky peppered here and there with lazy, unmoving, grey clouds. A short while later, after talking about the players and her next set of rehearsals, they were at her front door. Sarah scrabbled in her bag for her keys and turned back once she found them. Finn was leaning against the doorframe, his head dipped slightly forwards causing his hair to fall into his face. He swept it back and straightened up. 'Well, thank you for a lovely evening.'

Here it was. The end of the date and just as she had expected. 'It was fun.' Sarah tried to keep her eyes from his, but she just had to look at them one last time before the night ended and all hope of doing this again was lost. Before she could look away, Finn tilted forwards and his hand reached up – her heartbeat tripled in pace, pounding against her ribcage and her breathing grew erratic. His fingertips went from just under her ear, which she hadn't known before was an erogenous zone but it seemed to be right now, to threading through her hair resting at the back of her neck. He was drawing her in for a kiss. The kiss she'd imagined a million times. Her entire body was sparking, every muscle flooded with longing as his lips met hers. It was the gentlest, sweetest kiss she had ever felt and now her body was on fire. She opened one eye slightly to see if he was enjoying it and was overjoyed to see his were still closed, wrapped up in the moment. Sarah reached her arms up and around his neck. When Finn pulled away her voice was trembling as she risked asking, 'Do you want to come in?'

In a throaty whisper he replied, 'Yes, please,' before kissing her again.

***

Lottie opened the door and as soon as Sarah saw her face she sang, 'I slept with Finn last night,' waving the carrier bags of food she'd brought with her in the air and doing a happy dance, all thoughts of Vince forgotten.

'You did not!' Lottie's eyes widened.

'I did. I did. I did, I did, I did.' Sarah was twisting around on the spot while Lottie laughed. She'd never been so happy. Even the situation with her dad couldn't dampen her mood.

'You'd better come in and tell me all about it then.'

Finn had stayed the night and it had been the best sex Sarah had ever had. He'd been gentle but passionate. Just being near him made her happy. He was everything she'd been looking and hoping for. This morning they'd lazed in bed, making love one more time before he made them a cup of tea and some toast. And then, near lunchtime, he left, but there was no sneaking out as if it was all a horrible mistake, silently scrabbling around for clothes then doing a runner. He'd kissed her gently before getting dressed and then again on the doorstep as he said goodbye. The look in his eye had made her want to pull him back into the house and start all over again but he had to go. For the rest of the day Sarah had danced in her house while she cleaned, keeping herself busy just waiting for the evening to come so she could tell Lottie.

Lottie took one of the carrier bags from Sarah and led the way to the kitchen. Lottie's house had a wonderful, messy lived-in feel. She'd always lived there with her nan until she'd passed away last year, and Sarah could see why Lottie would never want to live somewhere else. Pictures adorned the walls and it was a wonderful, cluttered, untidy home, not just a place to live. 'I thought you had rules about not doing anything on a first date?' Lottie asked.

'Yeah, but that was with strangers. I've known Finn for a year already. And believe me, I've waited for this moment for a *long* time.' Lottie unpacked the ready meal Sarah had brought and turned the oven on to heat up. Sarah found the bottle opener in its usual drawer and uncorked the bottle of white wine. No screw tops today. She was treating them to a decent bottle worthy of Gregory and Cecil – they had something to celebrate.

'So are you seeing him again?' asked Lottie, looking over her shoulder as she found the plates and cutlery, and stacked them on the side.

'We haven't arranged anything yet, but I'm sure we will. Oh God, it was amazing, Lottie. He's just the nicest person I've ever met. He's so funny and kind and caring and—'

'Okay, okay, calm down,' Lottie teased. Dreamily replaying the night's events in her mind, Sarah stared out of the window. When she realised Lottie had left her in the kitchen and made her way back to the living room, Sarah grabbed her glass and hurried after her.

'So,' said Lottie. 'Do we think your heart has officially mended?'

Sarah smiled and plonked down on the sofa. 'I think it has.'

'Good. About blimmin' time. Vince the Prick doesn't deserve any more of your time.'

'I know.' And talking about him, her heart hadn't even twinged once. 'How's Sid enjoying his teaching job?' she asked, moving the conversation along. Since he and Lottie had got together, he'd been taking his life much more seriously and had quit mooching to start teaching journalism at the local adult education centre on a Saturday afternoon. Since then he'd been feeling much more fulfilled, according to Lottie, and had begun talking about their future which, Sarah hoped, might feature a wedding one day and a pretty bridesmaid's dress for her.

'He absolutely loves it,' said Lottie. 'He's got such a zest for life again. I'm so proud of him.'

Sarah moved a record from the arm of the sofa and put her glass on the floor. There were boxes and boxes of old vinyl records everywhere, along with some other boxes stuffed with his beloved Lego models. 'He's brought a lot of his stuff over, hasn't he?'

'Hmm?' A faint pinkness was beginning to colour Lottie's cheeks. Sarah narrowed her eyes.

'What's going on?'

'Nothing.' This was exactly why Lottie wasn't an actor in the Greenley Players. She was terrible. Utterly, utterly terrible. Especially when it came to telling lies, which was essentially what acting was. As their chairman she was fantastic, but she couldn't act if her life depended on it.

'Is Sid moving in?' asked Sarah, unable to keep the surprise from her voice.

The splotchy pinkness spread down Lottie's neck. 'Maybe.'

'Eeeeeeeeeeek!' Sarah grabbed Lottie in a bear hug, filled with happiness for them both. It had taken them long enough to get together so it was wonderful they were now taking the next step. Sarah sat back and picked up her glass again, proposing a toast. After they'd clinked glasses, she said, 'So Sid's moving in here, is he? What about his flat?'

'He's going to sell it.'

'I'm so happy for you.'

'Thanks.' Lottie beamed a big cheesy grin. 'Have you seen the posters in the outside poster cases? They're finally up.'

'No, are they hideous?'

'No. Look. I've got spares here.' Lottie grabbed a brown cardboard poster tube and wriggled out a poster. She unrolled it and Sarah winced. As feared, her face was absolutely enormous.

'My face is huge. And I can see that spot I tried to cover with a mountain of concealer.'

Lottie studied the poster again. 'It looks fine.'

'It looks like a second head. We could draw a face on it and it could have a part in the play.'

'Rubbish.' Lottie tutted then giggled. 'I think it looks really good actually.' It didn't but Sarah was in too good a mood to worry. Nothing could be done about it now anyway. 'How did the coaching go with Nate Thursday night?'

'Urgh.' Sarah sucked in a deep breath then blew it out puffing out her cheeks. She'd been tempted to phone Lottie Thursday night and explain what had happened, but her brain had been all over the place and by the time she'd calmed down she was exhausted and wanted nothing more than to climb into bed. Plus it was one of those things you had to explain face to face. 'It was disastrous.' She paused. 'Well no, maybe not that bad, but not good either. It was sort of terrible, but—'

Lottie shook her head. 'That makes absolutely no sense at all.'

Sarah laughed and explained what had happened, including her revelation and Gregory and Cecil's ridiculous interruptions. Lottie's expression changed from one of surprise to concern and then eventually back to surprise when Sarah described the scene with Nate at the beach. 'God, it's like something from a movie,' she said at last.

'I know. Just without the moving soundtrack and flattering lighting.'

'So you and Nate Hardy of the lovely bum had a moment on Greenley beach.'

'I wouldn't say we had a moment,' Sarah replied. 'Besides, he must think I'm gross because at one point he accidentally touched my hand and couldn't get his away fast enough. It was like I had the plague or hepatitis or something.' Thinking about it, it had all been so intense at the time. If they had had a moment it wasn't a *moment* moment. It was more a mutual appreciation for how shit life could be rather than anything else. 'Anyway, I think it may have actually helped. Now I know why I didn't like Miranda, I can deal with it and start actually playing her. It is just a part after all. Urgh, that sounds super pompous and acty, doesn't it?'

'Are you going to carry on with the coaching?'

Sarah had thought about it a lot since that night, unsure if it would be too awkward to see Nate again. But she wanted to talk to him. Maybe help him with what he was going through, the way he'd inadvertently helped her. 'Yeah, I think so. I hope so. I've got a lot to learn from Nate and he's a good teacher. He certainly made me see my character differently. I just hope Gregory and Cecil can control themselves next time.'

'Hey,' said Lottie, suddenly perking up. 'Why don't you use Sid's flat? It's just round the corner from Gregory and Cecil's place, so Nate could get there without being seen. And you'd be alone.' She raised one eyebrow suggestively. 'He's just as handsome up close and personal, isn't he? I found it quite off-putting talking to him at the theatre. How does a person actually go around being that attractive every day? Do you think they know that when they're having a conversation people are just staring and thinking, "My gosh, you are completely gorgeous."'

'It's horribly unfair, isn't it? Why should one person get that much gorgeousness and the rest of us have to go around with big noses, or wonky eyes, or double chins.' She pulled her head back to give herself a double chin which made Lottie giggle.

'Do you think *he* thinks he's attractive?'

Sarah pondered. The man she'd met wasn't affected with any sort of over-confidence or vanity. In fact, he'd been incredibly normal. 'I don't think so. I get the feeling he's a bit ... I don't know ... shy, maybe?'

Lottie sipped her wine and shook her head. 'How can you be shy if you're an actor? Your job is to literally stand up in front of loads of people and show off.'

'I know but, one-on-one he's different. More vulnerable. I don't think this whole situation with that model and his wife is as simple as the papers make it out to be.'

'Have you seen the latest?' asked Lottie, handing over a folded tabloid newspaper. On the front cover was a picture of Hannah Salgado who was quite attractive in a trashy, fake tan and brown lip liner kind of way. She pouted at the camera, resting a hand on her flat, rock hard stomach.

Sarah felt her mouth fall open. 'She's pregnant?' She scanned the pages, speed reading. They were making him out to be a neglectful husband and total scumbag who'd been shagging around for years and Hannah was saying Nate had offered her money to stay quiet. The back of Sarah's neck prickled as she read on, and yet, she couldn't reconcile the events she was reading with the man she'd started getting to know. He'd said it was complicated and that he wasn't the man he was being painted as. Was that true?

'Did you get Gregory's cryptic text message?' Lottie asked, finding it on her phone.

Sarah nodded, reciting the message. 'More bad news coming for Nate, but all is not what it seems. He needs our support. Please keep everything quiet.' Knowing Gregory's dramatic tendencies, she hadn't really paid that much attention. Obviously she'd been intrigued to know what the bad news was, but she had been too full of endorphins from her night with Finn to think on it. 'Do you think he'll be going back to London now?' asked Sarah. She hadn't realised how much she was looking forward to seeing Nate again. Or at least looking forward to their coaching session, she corrected herself.

'I don't know,' answered Lottie. 'I guess we'll find out more tomorrow at rehearsals.'

Sarah stared out of the open sash window. Lottie's house sat on the brow of a hill and the views reached out over the whole of Greenley like a still life in which nothing moved. A moment caught in time. In the distance she saw the sea and the small fishing boats moored in the harbour. The heat was astonishing this summer. She'd never known anything like it. Her time with Nate felt like a strange alternate reality totally devoid from her normal life but still it had affected her deeply. She'd felt a connection with him she couldn't explain or even fully understand. There was a strange tugging in her chest but Sarah put it down to the heat. It wouldn't be long until Nate returned to London and it all ended. With a shake of the head she dismissed the thought that she might miss him. She didn't even know him.

Chapter 15

'Don't forget to sniff him,' said Sarah with a nudge as Nate arrived at rehearsals Sunday morning alongside Gregory and Cecil. Lottie winked and a cheeky smile played on her lips.

'Good morning, everyone,' said Gregory, waving. Nate followed along behind, his head slightly bowed as if he was trying to make himself smaller, and his hands shoved deep into his jeans pockets. He was wearing a prosthetic nose Gregory had commandeered from the wardrobe department that looked more like a flesh-coloured sex toy purchased from a dubious online retailer. No wonder he was trying to make himself small. Once he was near the front he began peeling it off. The weather had cooled a touch lately and clouds were gathering in the sky threatening the first real rain of that summer. Sarah was wearing jeans and a vest top just in case the rain descended, and gave Nate a polite smile. She was feeling nervous but slightly less terrified about reciting her lines this time round. She had a long way to go yet but at least she was making progress. For the first time in ages they'd turned on all the theatre lights as the dense clouds darkened the sky outside.

Gregory, Nate, and Cecil formed a semi-circle, chatting to Conner, and Sarah watched from the corner of her eye as Lottie snuck up behind them. Swiftly, her head popped up behind Nate's shoulder, she sniffed, then ducked back down again out of sight. Nate spun around and Lottie, now bright pink, pretended to check a scratch in the floor before scrambling away without looking at him. Sarah turned and buried her head in her handbag she was giggling so much. Lottie then rounded to her side and in between bursts of laughter said, 'You're right, he smells lemony. I bet it's either a really expensive aftershave or lemon washing-up liquid.'

Sarah had to breathe deeply to gain control of herself, her whole body shaking with laughter. 'Why would he be wearing lemon washing-up liquid?'

'I don't know. Maybe he did the washing-up before they came out.'

'I can't believe you actually did that. That was the most sexually aggressive sniffing I've ever seen in my life. Your whole head shook.'

The colour was beginning to fade from Lottie's cheeks as she calmed down. 'Well, I wanted to get a good nose full, I might never get the chance again.'

'What are you two laughing about?' asked Sid, standing behind Lottie and resting his hands on her shoulders. She tipped her head back and he placed a gentle kiss on her forehead.

'Oh, nothing,' said Sarah, eyeing Lottie. It was their little secret. 'Can you believe it's only been two weeks since Nate arrived? It feels a lot longer.'

'I bet it does to him too,' Sid replied. Lottie took hold of his hands and intertwined her fingers with his.

'I don't know,' she said, still a little pink from laughing. 'I think he likes it here. Gregory said he seems very much at home.'

Before they could discuss it any further, Conner took to the stage. 'Okay, let's crack on then, we've got a lot to get through and we've only got a couple of weeks till showtime.' Inwardly, Sarah groaned, there were a lot of improvements to make in that time, but somehow she knew that if she continued coaching with Nate she'd make it. 'In a bit I'd like to work on the end of act one where Ferdinand and Miranda meet and get into act two but let's just quickly run through act one, scene one first. Scripts down though please. Joan, are you ready to prompt?'

No answer.

'Joan?' Conner asked a little louder, looking to where she was positioned on the side of the stage. When she didn't notice him, he resorted to shouting. 'Joan?' The old woman looked up, pushed her spectacles back up the bridge of her nose and waved her script in the air. Conner smiled but as he turned to Sarah he widened his eyes in a here-we-go-again way.

Mrs Andrews sauntered onto the stage in the strangest costume Sarah had ever seen. The Yoda kimono had gone and instead she'd decided to raid her wardrobe for every single scarf she owned and had somehow pinned them onto a white leotard, worn over black leggings. She was fanning herself with a tiny hand-held fan. Mouths fell open as everyone turned to look. She didn't look like a sprite or a spirit, she looked like there'd been an accident in a textile factory. After the initial shock had worn off, everyone went back to preparing for act one and Sarah gave Mrs Andrews the side eye.

'We really need to sort out a proper wardrobe person next year,' Lottie whispered.

'Definitely,' agreed Sarah as they walked onto the stage. 'And a new make-up person.' They were trying out hair and make-up styles ready for the full dress rehearsal. 'Betty's got the shakes so badly now she nearly had my eye out. I know she did it when your nan was in charge but she's a bit of a health hazard now. Look.' Sarah pointed to where Betty was waving an eye pencil perilously close to Kathryn's retina. Poor Kathryn had pinned herself so far back in the chair it was like a scene from a horror movie.

Lottie giggled. 'Poor old Betty.'

'Poor Kathryn, more like.'

Rehearsals began well with everyone remembering their lines, even Sarah. She was definitely feeling more at ease playing Miranda and was starting to move about the stage without thinking. It was all going very well. The scenery was helping her get into the role as well. Sean and Leonard, their two burly helpers were silently painting the rocks, and Sarah had to skip over one of their paint trays left in the middle of the stage. She gently nudged it to one side to get it out of the way and carried on with her lines. Sneaking a look, it seemed that Nate was enjoying the performance too; he was sitting in the front row next to Lottie who gave Sarah a big thumbs up.

Gregory began one of his longer speeches, moving around the stage like a real pro, showing everyone else how it should be done, but he was getting perilously close to the paint tray. Sarah tried to signal to him that it was there, but he just threw her a confused look and continued on with his speech. Then, taking a giant step back with his arms outstretched, his left foot went straight into the paint tray splattering his shiny white loafers and coating the bottom of his pale linen trousers. 'Oh, for crying out loud,' Gregory shouted then bent down and pulled up his trousers leg.

Debbie came out from backstage. 'Och, Gregory, you great plank. Why did you go and do that?'

'I didn't do it on purpose, Debbie, did I?'

Pushing her hands through her crazy red hair, unknowingly spreading a streak of magnolia through it, Debbie returned backstage, presumably to get more paint.

Sarah pressed her lips together to stifle the smile that was forcing its way out. Mrs Andrews wasn't even attempting to hide a mirthful laugh. 'Oh dear, you do seem to have put your foot in it, don't you?' Gregory flashed his eyes at her and took off his shoe, leaving it in the paint tray.

'Don't you have some builders to shout at, Mrs Andrews?' he fired back.

'No, it's a Sunday.'

'Oh, so even evil dictators give their staff one day off a week. How generous of you.' Mrs Andrews smiled gleefully while Gregory mustered his dignity, lifted his chin, and hobbled to the toilet to wash the paint off his trousers. He was followed swiftly by Cecil who picked up the shoe like Prince Charming holding the glass slipper and hurried off after him.

'Let's take a break, shall we?' said Conner, hiding behind his notes, clearly laughing too.

Sarah climbed down off the stage and sat in the front row with Lottie, Sid, and Nate. Lottie and Sid were deep in conversation and Nate leaned forwards, so he could turn and see her. 'You're doing really well today.' Sarah looked at him and the compliment warmed her from the inside, a large smile spreading over her face. 'Lottie was just saying we could use Sid's flat this week if you still wanted to meet? That way we shouldn't have so many interruptions.' Nate glanced down after saying it and it made him seem vulnerable and shy.

'I'd love to,' Sarah said. 'I've still got a lot to learn about performing Shakespeare.'

'There's not much to it once you understand his intentions.' The deepness of his voice was calming and powerful.

'I've been thinking about the questions you asked me the other day. I actually like Miranda a lot more now.'

'Good,' he replied with a grin. He peered around. 'This is quite a theatre you know, and a great bunch of people.'

'It is,' she agreed. 'I know I'm lucky to have my friends. Even Mrs Andrews isn't that bad once you get to know her.' They both peeked over to where she was waiting to come on, preening and puffing her hair. When she saw them staring, she stopped and gave Nate a sultry wave. Nate gave a polite smile in return and turned back. 'You look terrified,' Sarah giggled.

'I am. She looks like she'd eat me for breakfast.'

Sarah decided not to make a rather innuendo-laden joke, as

just the thought was making her blush. She dropped her eyes, remembering her and Lottie joking about seeing Nate's bum on TV. Trying to distract herself she said, 'Won't you be going back to London soon though?' His expression turned worried and seeing him upset made her feel distinctly uncomfortable. Unsure why, a part of her yearned to take his worries away. 'Sorry about the papers the other day. Are you okay?'

Nate nodded but it was unconvincing. 'I think so. I'm not really sure what's going to happen now. At first I was worried about my career.' Sarah raised her eyebrows as the words sounded callous. He must have noticed as he added, 'I know that sounds bad, but ... basically Emma already knew what had happened and our marriage has been over for a long time.' He pulled back a bit. 'I wish I could tell you everything, but I can't.' Hearing him say the words made it all so much more understandable. He seemed the loyal type. 'But now there's a child ...' A smile lifted the corners of his mouth, forming the deep lines in his cheeks. Then he shook his head. 'I love the idea of being a dad, but I don't know what's going to happen now.'

Seeing the way his face changed at the idea of a child, Sarah admired him for putting the baby first. 'I'm sure it'll be okay. Just give it time.' Without thinking she reached out and touched his arm. As she realised what she'd done she pulled her fingers away, but his eyes were locked on hers and something passed over his face. She wasn't sure if it was disgust, or surprise but she turned away quickly, embarrassed. Luckily, Sid and Lottie hadn't noticed.

Before long, Gregory was back, barefoot and with one damp rolled-up trouser leg, and rehearsals started again. Cecil placed the shoes on the floor along with their stuff. Sarah was able to take a break while they went through a scene she wasn't in but some of the new cast clearly hadn't been working that hard. One of the less experienced players shouted 'line' halfway through his bit to be met with stony silence. After a moment, he said, 'line' again.

More silence.

Everyone turned to where Joan was. The faint tapping of knitting needles carried on the air. 'Joan?' shouted Conner. 'Joan?' When no sound came back, he mounted the steps to the stage and made his way over to stage right. 'Joan, turn your hearing aid on,' yelled Conner. Sarah couldn't help but splutter and giggle.

'Oh, hello dear,' came a small, shaky voice.

'Toby needs his line, Joan.'

'Oh.' She was shouting back now, though she didn't realise it. 'Shouldn't he know it by now?'

'Yes, he should,' Conner replied. 'But still.' Sarah laughed and her hand shot to her mouth.

'Where was he, dear?'

'Don't worry, Joan. I've got it.' Conner came back onto the stage. 'It's "Set her two courses off to sea again. Lay her off."'

From the wings, Joan, in a surprisingly loud voice, repeated the same and Lottie and Sarah collapsed into giggles while Gregory muttered, 'Lord help us,' and the scene continued.

Mrs Andrews' portrayal of Ariel still involved a lot of wafting about the stage with an odd twirl thrown in here or there for good measure, but with the tinkling sound effects and soft lighting it seemed to work. Though they'd have to go back to the Yoda kaftan as she kept tripping over the scarves and nearly face-planted the floor. Soon it was Sarah's turn. In the scene where she met her love, Ferdinand, played by Cecil, all was going well until she had to say, '"I might call him A thing divine,' and an image of Nate popped into her brain. She quickly replaced it with an image of Finn. As she turned to Cecil, a sword that he was supposed to hold aloft hurtled through the air, out into the stalls, narrowly missing her nose and Nate's head. 'What the bloody hell, Cecil?' she shouted, her heart pounding. 'Watch what you're doing.'

'I'm okay,' came Nate's muffled response as he edged up from behind a seat, somehow smiling. Cecil charged to the edge of the stage.

'Oh, crikey O'Reilly, Nate, darling, I'm so sorry, it came loose in my hand.'

'You have to grip it tighter,' said Sarah, her heart falling back into her chest.

'Just imagine it's your wallet,' added Mrs Andrews and Cecil gave her an evil glare.

'I'm sorry, Nate,' he called out again. 'I was distracted by our lady of the scarves here, wafting towards me.' He turned back to Mrs Andrews. 'Though to be honest, you look more like a mad bag lady.'

'That's enough,' said Conner, walking into the middle of them all. 'Let's just start again, shall we?' Lottie took the sword and handed it back up to Cecil. Nate smiled at Sarah before sinking a little lower in his seat and Cecil began the scene again.

Conner seemed pleased. Everyone knew when to enter and exit the stage, but the musical segments were still tortuous, especially now someone had brought along a recorder they used to play at school. Used to, being the operative word. Lottie had suggested Sarah join in with the singing when she was off-stage as she was so good, which was a huge compliment, but added to the pressure a little because now she had a whole bunch of songs to learn on top of her lines.

Luke, playing Caliban, the beast-like witch's son, had decided against either Darth Vader asthma or the spit-spraying lisp and kept his speech normal but moved about the stage with a cat-like grace that suited the role much more. He really was very good.

Glad when rehearsals were finally over for the day, they all said their goodbyes. Before they left, Lottie said, 'Don't forget everyone, it's Sarah's birthday drinks Saturday the fourth.'

'We know, Lottie,' answered Mrs Andrews. 'You've told us about twenty million times.'

'She was never one to exaggerate,' Gregory whispered to Cecil.

'Yes, but,' continued Lottie, 'none of you have RSVP'd.'

'We didn't know we had to,' replied Debbie. 'Does it say it on the invitation?'

'No,' Lottie said. 'But you should do it anyway. It's polite. So, show of hands who's coming?' Everyone raised their hands except for a few of the newer players. Lottie fixed them with a stare. 'I expect you all to be there or be square. It's going to be heaps of fun.'

Sarah smiled at Lottie then left, glancing over her shoulder at Nate as she did so. He was watching her with a strange look on his face. A quiet ping from her pocket told her she had a text message. It was just a short one from Finn hoping rehearsals were going well. A warm glow grew inside her. She still couldn't believe how well things were going with Finn. It felt so natural being with him, like it was meant to be. As she pushed the revolving door and walked out into the sunlight, her eyes caught on something and she stumbled. Ben was standing there, leaning against the wall. He was wearing the same clothes again and they were grubby and dirty. He was squinting as the sun poked out from between the clouds and reflected on his glasses. She wondered where he was staying and what he was going to do for work now he was out of prison, but finding out would involve talking to him and she wasn't sure she wanted to do that. However, curiosity niggled at her brain.

'Sarah,' he said, walking forwards. She turned away from him and swung her bag onto her shoulder. 'Sarah, can we talk? Please?' She could smell his sweaty clothes before he approached and it turned her stomach. There were still a few bags of his clothes in the loft. There must be something there. She remembered angrily throwing his suits into a bag. It couldn't hurt to give them to him.

Another one of the players left and watched her as he went. Grey clouds gathered overhead and Sarah felt a few drops of rain on her shoulder. 'Where are you staying?' she asked, quickly finding her car keys.

'In Strawley, in a bedsit on Stockton Street.'

Strawley was the small city nearby where Conner went to university. It was fairly nice in places but nowhere near as nice as Greenley, and Stockton Street was in the scummiest part of town where all the drug addicts squatted. Sarah couldn't count the number of times Lottie and Sid had told her about things they'd heard of going on there– burglaries, drugs busts, overdoses – and how glad they were they didn't have to cover it for the newspaper. Sarah suppressed a shudder and a sadness rose up at the thought her dad had ended up there. For him to be so close and yet so far away from her was more than upsetting. 'You'd better come with me and have a shower. I think I've got some of your clothes in the loft.'

The smile that spread across Ben's face almost broke her heart and Sarah led the way to her car, him following along behind. The journey to her house was agony. She wound the window down to get some air in, the smell of stale sweat was so over-powering. Ben tried to make conversation but though this was a big step for Sarah, she still couldn't bring herself to give more than one-word answers, unsure of her emotions. Finally she pulled into her drive and opened the front door to let them in.

'I don't know what's in the attic, it could be jumpers for all I know, but you can't stay in those clothes for another day.' Ben looked down at his trousers and ran his hands down the front of his T-shirt. 'And you need a shower.'

'I know. I smell like a tramp's armpit.' This moment of humour was so like her old dad, Sarah spun to look at him in case they'd been transported back seven years. Her heart ached to see him standing there with a self-conscious smile on his face, and she turned her back, finding it hard to be reminded of the man he'd been.

'The bathroom's up on the right. Leave your clothes outside and I'll get them washed and dried. There's a bathrobe in the airing cupboard in the spare bedroom.' She hoped one of the bags contained spare pants. Unlike Gregory and Cecil, she didn't keep a supply just in case.

After half an hour Sarah had brought down three bin bags of stuff from the loft. One was of photos and things of her dad's, a golfing trophy and bits and pieces from his childhood. Thankfully one was a bag of clothes, including a couple of decent, if somewhat dated, suits. It surprised Sarah that she'd had the foresight to keep them. Had it been a glimmer of forgiveness among the rage and grief she'd felt at the time?

There were a couple of pairs of trousers and a few shirts, plus some underwear. It all smelled a little musty but would freshen up on the washing line when it stopped raining. Sarah left some things outside the bathroom and when Ben came down he appeared so much more like the dad she remembered. He was clean and smart in a fresh pair of trousers and a clean short sleeved shirt. They were a little big where he'd lost some weight and his hair was scruffy and a lot greyer. In the doorway, Ben fidgeted nervously adjusting his glasses.

The light rain was growing heavier and tapping gently at the windows. Without speaking, Sarah went to the kitchen and made them both a cup of tea. Ben followed and his frail 'thank you,' as he took a seat at the breakfast bar hurt her ears. The idea that he'd been punished enough rang around her head and Sarah watched her tea swirl in the cup. Her emotions swung so violently from anger to forgiveness that it was hard to get enough distance to think clearly. Lottie's advice kept popping into her thoughts but the flame of anger still smouldered inside her whenever she thought of his affair.

'What are your plans?' she asked eventually to break the uncomfortable silence.

'I want to get a job – any job, I don't care what. Then I can save up and get a decent place.' She nodded. It sounded simple enough but it wouldn't be with his criminal record. At least he was planning on getting his life back together. 'I went to your

169

mother's grave the other day, well, her plaque at the crematorium.' Her ribs constricted, squeezing her lungs. 'I told her I was sorry. I hoped you and I could try and start again.' Unable to speak, Sarah studied the flower pattern on her mug, tapping her fingers on the sides to focus her mind on something else. She couldn't talk about this now.

'What number Stockton Road are you staying at?'

'Forty-three.'

'Okay.' She thought of the spare room upstairs sitting empty. Her conscience told her she should offer it to him but as horrible as it was, it was too soon. Her dad was a stranger to her. It was only her memories that bonded them together and they were proving unreliable at best. Maybe one day she would offer but she wasn't ready yet.

'Thank you for the tea,' her dad said again.

A wave of sorrow so strong it nearly knocked her over crashed into her barriers. Without thinking Sarah said, 'I have to go out again soon.' It wasn't true but she didn't know how much longer she could sit here in this awkward bubble where everything around them had stopped. Despair emanated from her father and it pained her that she was partly responsible. Guilt flared again. Hadn't she made him suffer enough already? Wasn't he already struggling without a place to live, with the regret he felt over the family he'd lost? Because he did regret it, she was sure of that. She just couldn't figure out how to move on. If only she hadn't built her defences so high.

Her dad quickly finished his tea and Sarah stood up from her stool at the kitchen counter. 'Don't worry, I'll see myself out.'

He walked away and closed the door behind him as Sarah buried her head in her hands. What the hell had just happened? Had they taken a step forwards or back? Was she happy or sad? She knew where he lived now and still had the scrap of paper with his mobile number on. Acting on instinct, she took her phone out of her bag and texted him, letting him know her number in case he ever needed it. The tightness in her chest eased slightly, her conscience telling her she'd done the right thing. When he texted back saying he loved her and calling her sugarplum again she couldn't help the tears that stung her eyes and nose, eventually escaping down her face and into her cold cup of tea.

Chapter 16

It was hard for Nate to believe that he had been here two and a half weeks and the press still hadn't found him. It was Thursday evening and from the window of Sid's flat, he could see down to the beach. The sun was setting slowly, a giant ball of orange in a deep blue sky and magpies gathered in the trees up and down the street. He counted them. 'One for sorrow, two for joy, three for a girl, four for a boy …' Did that mean he'd be having a boy? He didn't mind if it was a girl or a boy.

That morning, Gregory had purchased some of the papers and Nate had taken a sneaky look. He wasn't looking good at the moment but Robin assured him it would pass. Emma, on the other hand, was quite happy to agree with the papers' verdict when she spoke to him on the phone but was thankfully shunning any attempt at a public comment, probably too worried the press might ferret out her own affairs.

For a moment, Nate thought about how settling in a flat like this, somewhere like Greenley, wouldn't be that bad after all. He'd love for his child to grow up somewhere like this. The place was full of wide-open spaces, green trees and blossoming flowers. The sound of the sea had filled his ears as he'd walked over. The perfect place for Sunday walks, skipping stones over the waves and good, clean air. Perfect and quiet. As the flat was just around the corner from Gregory and Cecil's he'd only had to keep the hood up on a sweat top Gregory had brought him. No weird disguises today. Though the bright pink hoodie wasn't exactly inconspicuous.

Sid's flat was in a large Victorian townhouse that had been converted into flats. He had the top-floor flat and the period features were all still there. A large tiled Victorian fireplace dominated the room in which Nate stood, and the high ceiling was decorated with plaster cornicing. It had a real homely feel and though he'd have loved to see the other rooms, Nate refused to pry, especially as they'd been so generous in letting him use the flat for his meeting with Sarah. He was even more surprised when they had happily handed over the keys for him to let himself in and out. The few short moments of freedom he'd experienced on the walk over had been blissful. If he was able to stroll around freely, he could certainly see himself settling here.

Through the window, Nate could see Sarah getting out of a car down the street, her glossy brown hair swishing around her face as she bounced along. She carried herself with an ease and grace Nate found attractive, and from above he could see her eyes darting to and fro as she watched the world go by. Her mouth naturally turned up in a small smile and Nate imagined running his thumb gently over her lips before moving in for a kiss, his breath lingering with hers. He'd met a lot of beautiful women in his time. Had even kissed some of them for TV, but none had this effect on him. When Sarah turned into the building and made her way up to the flat Nate discarded the image and ignored the fluttering in his chest. Flattening his hair he readied himself to say hello. Nerves churned in his stomach even though nothing was happening between them. There'd been an attraction on his part, but she didn't seem to reciprocate, and he couldn't act on it, even he wanted to. His life was complicated enough.

On hearing a gentle knock at the door, he went to answer.

173

Sarah stood there, shyly clutching her book and the script. 'Hi.'

'Hi. Come in.' Nate stood aside and she walked through into the living room. He caught the scent of her gentle perfume. 'How have you been? Have you seen your dad?'

Sarah sat down on the sofa, almost huddled over, and he worried he'd made some terrible mistake in asking. Her face was gloomy as she answered. 'I saw him the other day. He's trying to get a job. He wants to stay in the area and thinks we should try and rebuild our relationship.' Having studied voice work, the slight lift at the end of the sentence told him that perhaps she was growing more used to the idea of her dad being around.

'How do you feel about that?' Nate believed she should try and work it out with her dad, but it wasn't for him to say so. He didn't know everything about the situation, and he couldn't trust his own judgement, having made enough of a mess of his own life. When Sarah's eyes caught his, the sincerity in them tugged at his heart and he wanted to take her hand and comfort her.

'I'm not sure. I just don't know what would be best. Anyway, what are we working on today?'

Taking the hint that the subject was closed, Nate said, 'Well, I was going to ask you if there were any particular scenes you wanted to go through. The last rehearsal was so much better.' Gentle lines formed on her forehead as she flicked through the script. She looked cute. Nate scolded himself. He was in no position to find anyone attractive; his life was too much of a soap opera.

'What about act three? I've got such a lot to say I'm having troubling remembering it all.'

'Okay.'

Sarah offered him her copy of *The Tempest* while she read from the typed-up script. They began by talking through the scene and what Miranda's motivations were. Nate was surprised that Sarah was so astute, and her confidence seemed to have grown since their first, short coaching session a week ago. Just as they were beginning to go through the lines, his phone rang. With a sinking feeling he saw that it was Hannah and stared at his phone to make sure it wasn't lying to him. Robin had told him not to speak to her, but what if something had happened to the baby? To his child. She might need his help, or have something important to say.

'Everything all right?' asked Sarah.

Nate looked again at his phone, then back to Sarah who watched him quizzically. 'I'm sorry, I need to take this.' He moved out into the hall, swiping to accept the call as he went. 'Hello?'

'Hi, Nate, it's Hannah Salgado.' She sounded so supremely confident it reminded him of Emma and not the woman he'd met that night who'd been shy and overawed with the big city she found herself in. She was a better actor than he was, he thought sardonically. But she was still the mother of his child and he would do everything he could to make things work and give his baby a stable home.

'Is everything okay?' Nate tried to keep his tone even. 'Is the baby all right?'

'What? Oh, yes. Yes, everything's fine. But that's what I was calling about.' She paused and when he didn't enquire, she continued. 'Nate, I think we need to meet face to face, don't you? We need to decide what we're going to do. Don't *you* think so? We need to talk about how we're going to make this work.'

He nodded to himself. 'Yes. I think you're right. We do need to talk, there's a lot to sort out.'

'You're not in London at the moment, are you? You've done well to avoid the papers, they've been all over me.' She gave a false, hollow laugh and Nate resisted the urge to point out it was she who'd gone to the papers in the first place. As if pre-empting him she said, 'Look, I'm sorry for what I did, okay. I think it must have been the pregnancy hormones driving me crazy.'

'When did you find out you were pregnant?' he asked, ensuring his tone was even. He didn't want this to escalate into a row, but

175

with Robin's words ringing in his ears, a sliver of suspicion hit him.

'About a week ago. But your body starts changing straight away, doesn't it?' He supposed that was true, but it meant she'd gone to the papers pretty much immediately. 'So where are you? I could come down and we could talk there, away from everything.' Nate cocked his head. Though he wanted to speak to her, he couldn't give away his location. Not just for himself, but for Gregory and Cecil, Sarah, Lottie, and Sid. In fact, all of the Greenley Players who'd done everything they could to keep his presence there a secret. It had been a big ask from him, a stranger, and no one had let him down yet. They'd shown such loyalty it was truly heart-warming. 'Nate?' she asked again. 'I really think I should come to you so we can talk.'

'Listen, Hannah, I agree we need to talk and I'll be back soon. I'll ring you when I am, okay?'

There was a loaded pause as she considered his response. 'Come on, Nate. There's a lot to sort out for this child. Our child. Do you really want me to wait?' There was something mildly threatening in the way she'd said that, but he wasn't going to let down the friends he'd made here. 'I'm sorry, Hannah. I'll call you as soon as I'm back. I'm sure it won't be long.'

With a heavy sigh she said, 'Fine,' and hung up.

When he returned to the living room his legs were shaking and he flopped onto the sofa next to Sarah.

'Are you okay?' she asked, genuinely concerned.

'That was Hannah.'

'Oh.' Sarah dropped her eyes to her script and he felt a sharp pang of regret that she probably now thought he was everything the papers were making him out to be.

'She wanted to talk about the child.'

Sarah quickly shook her head and kept her gorgeous almond shaped eyes away from his. 'It's fine, Nate, you don't have to tell me anything. It's none of my business.'

It wasn't, but why did he want it to be? Why did the thought of her thinking so badly of him affect him so much? He'd be gone soon and then he'd never see her again so really, he shouldn't care what she or anyone else in Greenley thought, but he did. So much so it hurt. Thinking that if she knew the whole truth, maybe she wouldn't judge him so harshly, he said, 'Listen, I know it all looks really bad, but it's not what it seems. Like I said before, it's complicated.'

'I know, you said your marriage was already over.'

After a moment he said, 'Yes, it was, it had been for ages, but I did still cheat on my wife, and I know there's no excuse. We've only been together for show.' At this Sarah looked up. 'We fell out of love a long time ago. Emma had an affair – a few of them actually – and so we just agreed to stay married until the time was right to announce an amicable separation and divorce.' She looked confused and it was like a hot knife in his heart. 'I thought I was okay with the situation, throwing myself into work … I didn't realise how lonely I was. How broken until … Then, when I met Hannah I was stupid. She flattered me and I shouldn't have fallen for it, but I was drunk and …' He pressed his hands together in his lap until his fingertips where white. 'I was an idiot.' He was stuttering his words, sounding pathetic and Nate hated himself for it. 'I know I shouldn't have done it and my punishment is it's ruined my career and now she's saying she's pregnant, I don't know what to do.'

Sarah's mouth fell slightly open and Nate realised that rather than tell her everything in a grown-up manner he'd blurted it all out like a child having a tantrum. She must think him the lowest of the low. 'I made a stupid mistake, but now there's a child, I have to do something to fix this. If I'm going to be a father, I want my baby to be loved and to have a stable home, no matter what the circumstances.'

A quietness fell on the room. 'I think that's very …' Sarah paused and Nate held his breath wondering what she was going to say. 'Good. It's very decent … of you.' He didn't know why her words meant so much to him, but they did. 'Does it mean you're heading back to London then?' Sarah's voice was small and she kept her eyes away.

'Soon, I guess. I'm going to call Robin tonight.'

'What did you mean it's ruined your career? I thought you were just waiting for things to die down. Don't they say there's no such thing as bad publicity?'

'It depends on the publicity.' Nate cocked his head, now resigned to his fate. 'The work's drying up. All the roles I was asked to audition for are being withdrawn. They don't want someone with a bad reputation ruining their productions, especially for wholesome good guy parts. And I'm not Brad Pitt. I'm not a big enough name to just shake it off. Everyone thinks I'm a horrible cheat.'

'I don't.' By the time she'd said those words, she was already studying her script and the apples of her cheeks had turned pink. Nate wanted to reach out and take her hand but stopped himself. She glanced up and suddenly he was moving towards her, yearning for a kiss. She didn't pull away and he could feel the sweetness of her nervous, unsteady breath. His heart raced as he inched forwards. His fingertips brushed her hand. His eyes focused on her soft pink lips but before he could do anything she pulled back and cleared her throat. Tucking her hair behind her ear she said, 'Well, I hope you'll stay for my birthday drinks next Saturday. Lottie was secretly hoping you'd come.' Nate moved back and allowed himself to smile but his body was almost trembling. He hadn't felt such a longing for someone, or such a deep connection in an incredibly long time.

'How can I say no then?' he joked, running a hand through his hair, hoping she hadn't noticed the tremor in his fingers.

'Shall we get on?' Sarah asked, picking up her script, her voice overly bright and cheerful. 'I've got a lot to learn before you go.'

Sarah's head had been spinning all day since the nearly-kiss with Nate the night before and a horrible conflict was raging in her heart. She so desperately wanted to be happy with Finn after how she had longed for him, but this ... thing ... with Nate was confusing and exasperating. It didn't feel real, sitting somewhere between a dream and a strange alternate reality. It would never amount to anything, it couldn't, but still, in that moment last night she'd longed for Nate when she should have been longing for Finn, and that brought with it a whole tide of guilt. Even though it had only been a week since her first date with Finn, a date that had been absolutely perfect in every way. As far as she was concerned, they were at the start of something special. Something she'd wanted for such a long time. She wasn't about to ruin it now by not giving it her all. She had to forget about Nate and focus on reality. Up until the nearly-kiss everything had been going so well. She and Finn had agreed to be professional at work but despite their best efforts, there'd been several loaded glances across the crowded surgery waiting room and a few hot and steamy kisses whenever his consulting room was empty. He hadn't out-and-out flirted in front of patients but that just added to the excitement of these early days. He'd texted or phoned some evenings too and they'd chatted easily about the day's events. Sarah was beginning to feel that she knew him inside and out already.

Tonight, she and Finn were meeting again for what she knew would be another amazing date. House of Chocolat came into view, situated at the bottom of the old High Street, the tables full in the warm evening sunlight. Sarah struggled in her heels over the cobble stones and as she came closer, she spotted Finn already chatting to a tall, lithe, glamorous woman. The woman had thrown her head back and was laughing at something he'd said. The back of Sarah's neck tingled and she pushed down her suspiciousness, a horrible trait left over from her romance with Vince. Finn was just chatty, that was all. It was what she loved about him. He'd suggested this place for their second date because they often had jazz and poetry open mic nights. It was unusual, and Sarah felt it showed just how serious he was about their relationship, not doing run-of-the-mill dates. Thankfully, tonight was jazz. Sarah wasn't that keen on hearing badly rhyming limericks or serious existential poetry that she quite simply didn't understand and found horribly pretentious. But a bit of jazz she could definitely get into.

As she pushed the glass door and walked through, Finn turned. The gorgeous woman stepped back onto the small stage and Finn left her, flashing Sarah a dazzling smile. 'Hey,' she said, brightening at seeing his handsome face again, all thoughts of Nate banished as nothing more than make-believe. Bringing her attention to here and now with Finn, he gave a gentle kiss on the cheek and his skin was smooth and soft, sending a chill down her spine.

'Hi. You look gorgeous.'

'Thanks.' She'd made as much of an effort as she could today in an attempt to stop her brain thinking about the nearness of Nate's lips and the fact that he'd even wanted to kiss her in the first place. She'd worn her favourite super tight skinny jeans, red heels, and a plain black vest. A swipe of daring red lipstick and a fluff of her hair and she was all set. Glad that Finn approved, she surreptitiously admired his toned, athletic frame in a plain T-shirt and jeans. Behind them the small band were setting up. The gorgeous woman must be the singer. She had the most beautifully styled afro, cheek bones like Beyoncé and was testing the microphone. From the sound of her voice, Sarah knew it was going to be a good show. 'This was such a good idea. I've never been to one of their jazz nights before.'

Finn smiled. 'I'm glad you think so. It's not to everyone's taste, but I thought it might be fun.'

'It's fab. Plus there are absolutely no good films out at the moment.'

'That's true.' He pushed his long hair back and signalled a waitress. It was an amazing café that specialised in anything chocolate during the day, but at night the place transformed into a cocktail bar. Sarah ordered an espresso martini. She hadn't slept at all last night, re-living the moment Nate had looked at her, his eyes searching her face before settling on her mouth. It had taken everything she had not to tilt her head just a little so their lips met. This morning, absolutely knackered, she'd used an insane amount of concealer doing her make-up. She'd added a top-up for this evening. An espresso martini would wake her up and make sure she could give Finn her full attention. A twinge of guilt pulsed through her but she pushed it away. Nothing had happened. She'd made sure of that. She just had to forget about it. After ordering a French 75, Finn said, 'I heard you practising your lines in the surgery this afternoon.'

'Oh no! Did you? I didn't think anyone could hear me in the stationery cupboard.'

'I was making a round of tea and when you weren't at your desk I went to see if I could find you. I was tempted to jump in there with you but ...' Sarah felt her cheeks burn. 'Anyway, as you were mid-flow I decided not to bother you. You sounded very good.'

'I'm getting there.' Counting pencils for the week's stationery audit seemed as good a time as any to practise.

'I have no idea how you remember it all.'

'You just keep saying it over and over again and eventually it sticks.'

Finn gave a mischievous grin. 'That reminds me of a mnemonic we used to use for remembering the carpel bones. Some lovers try positions that they can't handle. Scaphoid, lunate, triquetral, pisiform, trapezium, trapezoid, capitate, hamate.'

Their drinks were delivered and Sarah took a sip. Christ, it nearly took her head off. She'd be awake for days if she had any more of those. 'Well remembered,' she said with a smile, starting to feel a bit zippy already.

'Not really. I don't think they'd let me practise medicine if I couldn't remember those.'

Everything began to quiet as the gorgeous singer introduced herself and her band. The music started and her warm, seductive voice echoed around the café as she sang some classic jazz songs. Sarah particularly liked her rendition of 'Summertime', where the slow, sultry tones were perfect for a warm summer night. The singer, Sarah was sure, cast a few glances in Finn's direction, eyeing him from under her long eyelashes, but later, when Finn reached out and covered her hand, she knew he hadn't even noticed. She enjoyed the comforting weight of it and knew there was nowhere else she'd rather be. The next time she saw Nate at rehearsals, if she ever did, she'd just have to ignore him.

* * *

It had been a long and tedious week in which all Nate could do was replay his and Sarah's moment over and over again, watch daytime TV, or raid Gregory and Cecil's library. Now it was mid Thursday morning and a dull funk had gathered in his mind. He supposed it was boredom and watching his career slowly slide down the toilet from the sidelines, unable to do anything to stop it, but a niggling feeling told him it had something to do with Sarah, with Greenley, and with the thought of saying good bye to it all. He wasn't quite ready to leave this life just yet. As much as he wanted to get back to London there was something special about Greenley-On-Sea, even if he had only seen a small amount of it. Nate knew that in another life he could have been happy here forever and he envied the Greenley Players for everything they had in this sweet little town. The rehearsals on Sunday and last night had gone well for the players, but he and Sarah had pretended nothing had happened between them. Being surrounded by people made it easier, but he'd really wanted to take her to one side and apologise. However much he'd wanted it, he shouldn't have let his feelings run away from him. Look at what had happened the last time he'd done that. No, he had to keep control of his emotions from now on. For his sake, and Sarah's.

The weather had grown incredibly warm again as another heat wave hit the UK. Being trapped inside in the stifling heat and rising temperatures was making Nate irritable. He paced the garden wanting to see the sea again and breathe the fresh air. Seeing Robin's name flash on his phone, he faked cheer as he answered.

'So, great news, Nate, things have really quietened down on the media front. I reckon you can come back to London whenever you like. Obviously they haven't found anything more about Emma. We'll have a bit of PR work to do to stage manage this whole thing. If Emma's determined to bring the divorce forwards you can go down the whole "conscious un-coupling" route – a few morning TV appearances, social media stuff, that sort of thing but it won't take long to get things moving again.'

'That's great,' he replied. As an actor he should have been able to hide his real emotions but he was weirdly disappointed as something inside urged him to stay. Then he remembered that it was Sarah's birthday celebrations at the weekend. If the papers had lost interest, he could actually attend without worrying about being snapped and even if someone did, he'd be gone the next day, so no one would bother Gregory and Cecil. 'I'll come back on Sunday, okay. There's something I want to do first.'

'Fair enough. It'll be good to have you back. Come in on Monday and we'll talk more about this baby and how we're going to handle it.'

'Okay. See you then.' The callousness of Robin's words made his stomach turn over. He was talking about the baby like it wasn't a life, just a problem to be solved. Like it wasn't *his* child. No matter what else had happened, the thought of being a parent still made Nate smile. He'd make it work and be the best dad he could be. His thoughts flew to Sarah and what she had said about her father. He would never let his child down like that and he wished he could reach in and take away her pain.

With his departure imminent, Nate decided to cook a meal for Gregory and Cecil to say thank you for their generosity. They normally got back from the bookshop at about half past five, so that gave him more than enough time to raid the cupboards and find something to cook. He wasn't seeing Sarah tonight as she had something else on. He didn't know what, he just hoped it wasn't with another man, then felt stupid for thinking it. Ignoring the heaviness in his heart at the prospect of never seeing her again, Nate made his way into the kitchen. Somehow she'd got under his skin. Blaming the strange bubble his life had become wrapped in, cutting him off from the outside world, he hoped when things went back to normal he'd forget about Sarah. But he wasn't quite sure that was going to happen.

Chapter 17

'Happy birthday to my bestest best friend, and singer extraordinaire Sarah!' announced Lottie, raising a glass of prosecco in the air. Lottie was already three sheets to the wind and followed with another announcement declaring that chip-shop chips with loads of salt and vinegar were the only chips worth paying for, and that restaurants could keep their pathetic thin cut French fries. Sid laughed, shushing her gently and helping her back into her seat after she nearly missed it. Sarah smiled self-consciously and raised her glass too. Last year she'd celebrated her birthday with a family-size bar of chocolate and a bottle of prosecco all to herself, alone in her house. The Greenley Players had only just formed and hadn't really bonded yet, plus with more disasters than successes, and a few tensions, she still felt lonely and not quite part of the group. This year couldn't be more different and she was ecstatically happy to be surrounded by friends. She hadn't invited Finn. It felt too early in their relationship for that and as the players had been through so much together, she wasn't ready to introduce anyone else into that world. Gregory had said Nate was coming and bubbles fizzed in her tummy that she tried to disregard as a side-effect of the prosecco.

The Greenley Players had taken over a corner of The Lazy Tankard, their favourite pub, the one they all went to whenever they got the chance. It wasn't the nicest pub in Greenley but it was the cheapest and the most old-fashioned. It didn't have airconditioning, and though all the doors and windows were open, hardly any breeze blew. The carpet had a dark-red swirly pattern and each table had a pile of beer mats. The walls were adorned with dried hops and old-fashioned metal signs. There was no chance of ordering a cocktail from the landlord, he'd simply look at you like you'd just spoken in Klingon and pour a pint. He'd only just started getting prosecco in after Lottie, with the aid of Gregory and Cecil, had nagged him continuously for the last six months.

Sarah lifted her glass to her lips and took a refreshing sip. Apart from one drizzly day last week the weather had grown hotter and hotter, reaching temperatures that amazed everyone. So much so, that the first ten minutes of rehearsals had been spent declaring how no one could believe how hot it was. Nate had come too dressed in his pink hoodie, and Sarah had done her best to never be alone with him, pretending nothing had happened. Ironically, it had been some of the best acting of her life.

All the Greenley Players were there this evening except for Gregory and Cecil who were yet to arrive. Mrs Andrews was doing what she normally did when they came here and was looking around with disdain as if drinking something from a place like this might give her cholera. Debbie was showing Sean and Leonard, the two stagehands, how to manipulate an imaginary paint brush, and Conner was head down, texting on his phone.

'Happy birthday,' shouted Cecil as he and Gregory approached through the usual Saturday night throng. 'Sorry we're late, darling.' He planted a kiss on Sarah's cheek, as did Gregory. 'Mr Bennett brought a mouse in, so we had to save it.'

'*I* had to save it,' said Nate, teasingly, following behind. 'These two spent most of the time standing on chairs, waving tea towels at me.'

Sarah's breath caught in her throat. He was still here. Her heart suddenly puffed up filling her chest and she took a breath. She was ridiculously happy to see him. Happier than she should be, but she put it down to surprise and pulled her eyes away. He was looking even more handsome tonight. Not especially different, but the tension had eased from his face and the crow's feet around his eyes were from smiling rather than worry. The deep lines that formed either side of his mouth were due to laughing. It was strange how in these few short weeks he had settled into the life of the players and become part of the group, and the time they spent together always passed so quickly.

'Happy birthday,' Nate said, and leaned forwards to give her a kiss on the cheek. The feel of his lips on her skin stiffened every muscle in her body, even down to the soles of her feet. He moved away and began telling them about the mouse incident leaving Sarah stuck to the spot. A moment later, gathering herself, she retook her seat.

As he finished regaling them with a full re-enactment, Cecil said, 'Right, that's enough, you. I'll get the drinks in, Nate, you sit down.' He squeezed in between Lottie and Sarah and her leg pressed against his in the small space. It sent a tingle up her thigh and she suddenly felt very self-conscious but there was nowhere to move to, everyone was so tightly packed in.

'How was your thing Thursday night?' Nate asked, bending closer so he could be heard above the noise. Unable to risk seeing him again, Sarah had called off the coaching session and arranged a third amazing date with Finn. But afterwards the same battle had waged, her mind comparing Finn to Nate, and self-loathing soaked her again. Here she was feeling exactly the same way about Nate as she did Finn, and she hated herself for it. She knew it was just a silly fan-girl crush, nothing more. It wasn't often you got to meet your favourite TV hunk, and it had gone to her head, that was all. Her relationship with Finn was wonderful and blossoming, not to mention real, this thing with Nate was just make-believe but the situation still made her feel rotten. 'It was fine,' she replied at last.

Nate scratched his cheek. 'I'm, umm, heading back to London tomorrow.' Sarah looked up, searching his eyes, trying to see how felt about it. 'Robin, my agent, said it's all clear to come home. The press seem to have lost interest. Well, as much as they're ever going to.'

'Right.' Sarah dipped her eyes and did her best to focus on the bubbles popping in her drink rather than think about what Nate had just said. A tug inside told her she wasn't ready to part with him yet. She'd only just begun to get to know him – the real him – under all the mess that had brought him down here in the first place. As much as she hated to admit it, she'd liked what she found.

'I've really enjoyed being here. And working with you,' Nate added after a slight pause.

'Yes, me too. I hope things work out for you.' Nate's eyes didn't leave hers, and there it was again, that fluttering in her heart and a deep yearning in her soul.

Cecil delivered a round of drinks. 'And one for the birthday girl,' he said handing it over. Sarah took it and thanked him. An easy conversation started into which they all fell. Nate was laughing and joking with everyone as they finally had the opportunity to quiz him about all the places he'd been and the people he'd worked with, but he was careful to ask questions about everyone he was talking to so the conversation wasn't just about him. It was endearing and sweet.

'What was it like,' asked Debbie, 'when you had to do that scene where you jumped off that balcony window? I heard you did your own stunts. Is that true?'

Once your ear had got used to Debbie's Scottish accent her voice carried a wonderful, musical lilt. 'Ah, I didn't actually do that one,' said Nate, looking uncomfortable. 'They asked me to, and I was all set up to do it, but the first time I looked down at how high the drop was, my legs went a bit wobbly and I chickened out.' Everyone laughed and Nate turned to Conner. 'I heard you were interested in directing as a career, Conner?'

Poor Conner coloured up under his long black fringe and wiggled his lip bar with his hand. 'Yeah, I was thinking about it.'

'I thought I could speak to some contacts of mine, see if they have any internships coming up. If you wanted, that is?'

Conner's eyes widened in surprise and a broad grin spread across his pale face. 'That would be amazing, yeah – great. Thanks.'

'No worries.' Nate pulled out his phone. 'Can you give me your email and I'll let you know how I get on.'

'Sure. Yeah.' Conner fumbled in his lap, his excited fingers missing the phone.

Sarah made her way over to Lottie who was laughing with Sid. 'Hey, you,' Sarah said, sitting on a low stool in front of her. 'Are you okay? You look a bit squiffy.'

'I am,' she giggled. 'I'm completely squiffy. Sid took me out for lunch earlier and we got a bit carried away. Did I tell you he's moving in?'

'Yes, you did,' said Sarah, smiling.

'I love Sid,' Lottie declared with a very serious expression.

'I know, sweetie. He's one in a million.'

'He's my one in a million.' Lottie pressed her hand to her heart almost spilling her drink in the process.

Sarah giggled. 'Shall I get you a glass of water?' She was met with a scowl at such a preposterous idea.

'It's your birthday. We can't drink water on your birthday. Nate will buy me a drink, won't you, Nate?' They both turned to see Nate watching them, a playful gleam in his eye and a smile pulling at his lips.

He nodded. 'I will. But only after you've had that glass of water from Sarah.'

'Shpoil-shport,' Lottie said and Sarah squeezed her shoulder before heading off to the bar to try and save Lottie from the worst hangover in history.

Just then the DJ for the night arrived, and a big flashing sign that said 'Karaoke' was switched on above the makeshift dance area. 'Oh, yay!' said Gregory, clapping his hands – he'd clearly had too many gins. 'It's karaoke time!'

Sarah returned with a pint of water for Lottie, and Gregory grabbed her arm, making her slosh it over her fingers.

'No, no,' said, Sarah, knowing full well everyone would want her to get up and sing first, which was sweet of them, but she really wasn't in the mood to have everyone – not to mention Nate Hardy – staring at her. The awful stage fright she always felt was beginning to mount.

'I insist,' Gregory replied, taking her wrist as soon as she'd put the water down and yanking her towards the DJ. 'DJ, the book, if you please?' He gave a slight bow. As the DJ was quite used to Gregory after he'd consumed a couple more than he should have, he simply grinned and handed it over.

'Karaoke! Karaoke!' chanted the group. Poor Nate looked terrified. This would be an experience for him, Sarah mused. Debbie McCray belting out Bonnie Tyler was a sight to behold.

'As long as you don't expect me to sing,' he added. 'I've got a voice like an out-of-tune fog horn.'

'Och, come on, Sarah,' said Debbie. 'You have to start us off. It's tradition.' It wasn't tradition. It wasn't tradition at all. That was an out-and-out lie. They just didn't want to be the first ones to sing. It was her own fault though. She'd been drunk and volunteered herself that one time, and now she was in for it. With Gregory offering suggestions as to what she should sing, it was clear she wasn't going to get out of it, so she chose a classic ABBA song and filled in the little slip. The DJ nodded approval as she handed it over, having heard her sing a couple of times before, and gave her the microphone.

Sarah always found it easier to stare at the TV screen showing the lyrics, even though she already knew them, rather than looking around at the people watching her. As the music started she swayed from side to side and was soon singing along. It was a surprise anyone could hear her from the shouting and whooping coming from the Greenley Players, but having them there made her smile, and before long she was actually enjoying herself. She finished to loud cheers before a very drunk Sid took to the stage singing 'I'm Too Sexy' in full comedic fashion, marching up and down the pub, and trying to pole dance with an oak beam. Thankfully he stopped short of taking his shirt off. Sarah and Nate watched on from their squeezed-in position in the corner, with him whistling and cheering along. When he leaned in and said, 'You really have an amazing voice,' his lips almost brushed her ear, sending a shiver down her spine.

'Thanks,' she replied, taking a nervous sip of her drink. 'I only got the courage to start singing in front of people last year, thanks to the players.'

'They're a really nice bunch.'

'They are.'

'They remind me of the am dram group I started with,' he replied, looking around with a fond expression.

'Really? I didn't know you'd been in a group.'

'I loved it. They were absolutely brilliant. Some were better actors than others, but we always had loads of fun and I learned so much.' A loud whoop caught their attention as Gregory and Cecil got up to sing the big end song from *Dirty Dancing*. 'Your friends are crazy by the way.'

Sarah nodded in resignation. 'They really are, but I love them anyway. Especially Gregory and Cecil. They're the heart of the group.'

'I can see.'

'And Lottie, of course. We wouldn't be here if it wasn't for her.'

No one else stepped up for karaoke and people headed back

to their seats. As the crowd broke apart Sarah saw Ben standing at the bar, looking nervously over. Pinned by panic, her stomach dropped and she sat still for a moment, unsure whether to approach him or wait for him to come over to her. Ben gave a tentative smile but stayed where he was. Strawley was twenty minutes away by car, longer on the bus; why was he here? It couldn't be a coincidence.

'That's your dad, isn't it?' Nate asked gently.

'Yes, it is.' Her mouth had gone dry and she felt her throat sticking together.

'Do you want me to ask him to leave?' Sarah glanced at him, unsure how she felt about the suggestion. It was a kind gesture and she appreciated his concern, but seeing her dad's face she felt she needed to speak to him herself.

After a large gulp of prosecco, Sarah went over. 'Dad? What are you doing here?' He was wearing the clothes she had laundered the other day rather than some of the other stuff she'd found in the loft. Perhaps he found it comforting to be in those clothes, and he couldn't really wear a suit to the pub. Keeping his eyes averted under his twisted frames, he scratched the back of his head.

'It's your birthday. I wanted to see you. I got you a card. Happy birthday, sugarplum.' He handed over a plain white envelope. 'I popped round earlier but you weren't in.' Surprisingly, she'd spent so many birthdays on her own it hadn't occurred to her that her dad might want to see her.

'Dad.' That was at least twice now she'd called him dad and it hadn't hurt, but he was pushing things between them, trying too hard and making it all move too fast. She could feel herself pulling back and rebuilding her defences. They were going up brick by brick, any holes made from their previous encounters being patched over and strengthened.

'I thought maybe we could have a drink together. I've been doing some window washing with a friend and I've got some money. Not much, but it's a start. And I've found a decent house-share to move to as well.' The lost puppy look in his eyes pierced but she just wasn't ready to sit down in a public place with him and have a heart-to-heart. Suddenly Ben's eyes dropped to his pint as someone Sarah didn't know approached.

'Ben? Ben Powell? I haven't seen you in years, mate. How've you been?' The guy was tall and dressed casually in jeans and a bright white shirt. 'It's Dennis, I used to live down the street from you and your Mrs.' He held out his hand for Ben to shake and he reluctantly took it.

'Nice to see you again,' Ben replied.

'I was sorry to see your old lady go. Tragic.' Sarah's eyes shot to her dad's face. His eyes had dipped in shame, but the idiot man kept talking. 'I heard you was working away just before she went. That's tough. Can I buy you a drink?'

'Umm, no, thank you. I'm good.' Ben showed his still half-full glass. 'I'm just having a drink with my daughter. Do you remember Sarah?'

'Yeah course.' He turned to Sarah and gave her a smile that made her skin crawl. 'I heard you singing earlier. Lovely. Lovely.'

'Thanks,' she replied curtly, wishing he'd leave.

'So are you re-married now or something?' he said to Ben.

'No. No I'm not.' The idea of it turned Sarah's stomach and surprisingly, Ben's bright blue eyes had hardened on Dennis.

'What you up to then? You still an accountant?' Dennis swigged his pint with his mouth wide open and Sarah could see the fillings in his top teeth. He eyed Ben's worn clothes.

'I'm umm ...' Ben faltered and Sarah wondered what he'd say. Would he admit he was reduced to window washing with a friend? Like a shaft of light piercing the darkness of her feelings Sarah felt her dad's shame and wanted to stand up for him.

Under Dennis' smug gaze, Sarah heard herself say, 'Dad's still working away at the moment, aren't you, Dad?'

'Umm ... yeah.'

'Oh, great,' Dennis replied and Sarah swore the dirty old perv brushed her back on purpose. She had to give Ben credit for what he was doing now. He hadn't been out long, he'd never work as an accountant again, but he was still trying to earn money. Before Dennis could ask anything else, Sarah said, 'Shall we sit down, Dad?' It was going to be hard for her dad to get his life back on track, especially with people he used to know asking what he was up to and judging him.

They found a table in the corner, Gregory and Mrs Andrews craning their necks as they went by. When they were alone, Sarah, still holding her card, said, 'Dad, you can't keep just turning up like this.'

'But you're my daughter. I just want to see you.'

'How did you know where I'd be anyway?'

He faltered and pushed his glasses up the bridge of his nose. 'Your bookmark was the invitation. When I knocked your copy of *The Tempest* over, I saw it. I hoped I'd get to see you this morning, but you weren't there.' She'd been at Finn's till the early afternoon.

Sarah felt a sudden surge of anger. He'd been snooping and it felt like a complete invasion of her privacy. 'I can't believe you'd go nosing around my stuff.'

Ben looked surprised. 'I wasn't nosing. I just saw it on the floor, that's all. Then when I popped round today and didn't see you, I thought—'

'You thought you could just come here and pull me away from my friends, from my party, to make things up to me?' Again a hot anger raged inside her. He couldn't just keep showing up in her life when he wanted to. After all she'd been through, she deserved for things to be on her terms and when she was ready. She'd been hurt so much he had to respect that, but clearly he was still only thinking of himself. 'There is no making things up to me, Dad. What's done is done, you can't undo it all and stop Mum from dying, or magic it so you didn't disappear and leave us to deal with everything on our own, or the—' She still couldn't bring herself to mention the affair to him as bile rose in her throat. She didn't want to hear his excuses or relive that pain. 'If you want to see me, call me and ask. Actually, don't bother calling me at all. If I want to see you, I'll call you.' She stood up, leaving the card on the table, and marched outside into the fresh air, letting the door bang behind her.

The sea air filled her lungs as she stomped down to the beach, hiding under the tall legs of the pier. The tide was out and Sarah backed onto the sea-worn pillar, gazing out over the calm water, the tide gently retreating leaving a wiggly line of froth on the pebbles. Behind her back, her hands traced the rough surface of barnacle shells. It was dark now and eerily quiet when the sound of shingle scrunched underfoot reached her. She turned to see Nate striding down the beach. A bright full moon lit his way. The breeze had picked up, gently lifting his hair, his brow furrowed in concern. He didn't approach straight away but once he had spied her, he paused at the water's edge, picked up a stone and skimmed it over the sea. It bounced a couple of times before plopping into the depths. Taking a few steps towards her, his deep voice echoed in the night as he asked, 'Are you okay?'

Sarah wanted to answer that she was fine, but it would have been a lie and she didn't want to lie to Nate. The rush of anger was fading, leaving guilt and regret in its wake. She'd pushed her dad away again. How much longer would he continue to make the effort if that was all he got in return? He shouldn't have just turned up, but what else could he do when she refused to let him break down her walls? If he hadn't bothered at all she'd have hated him even more. Realising she couldn't open her mouth without crying, she shook her head and sucked in a big breath. Suddenly Nate was at her side and turning her body to face him.

'It'll be okay,' he said gently. 'Just give it time. You said it to me and it's true. Just let things calm down.'

She lifted her head to see his angular features. He was studying her, memorising her face and she couldn't have felt more exposed if she'd been standing there naked. He gently brushed her chin, cupping it lightly in his fingertips and Sarah's heart beat with such a strange intensity she thought she might be dying. The moment didn't seem real and at his touch it was like a part of her soul melted onto his skin. He tilted her head up, his lips found hers and she kissed him back.

A tremor that began in her lips crept through every nerve ending in her body, lifting her arms so they were around his neck. Her hand was in his hair and her soul was illuminated like a bright shining star. A flash of light drew their attention and they looked up to see someone running away. It was probably just a teenager being stupid, but the moment was over and they separated. Where her hand rested gently on his chest she could feel the quick beat of his heart.

'Sorry,' Nate mumbled. 'I shouldn't have done that. I'm sorry.' Sarah wanted to say it was fine. More than fine. It had been the most amazing kiss she'd ever had, something more than just physical, but remembering Finn, shame-faced she cast her eyes down. Not only that, Nate was married. Even if that marriage was a sham, she should have left well alone.

Sarah's voice quivered as she pushed the words out, her heart hurting that she already regretted it. 'We'd better get back to the party.'

Nate's eyes were imploring and the way his heart had beat beneath her hand told her he felt something too. Sarah turned away and led the way back up the beach, walking quickly back to the party while Nate followed behind. Neither of them spoke. Though neither she nor Finn had officially called the other girl-friend or boyfriend, this wasn't school. You didn't send a note with a tick box. You had to wait for things to develop on their own and they were developing. But she'd just cheated on him. And now she was risking everything, making a mess of her life.

Gregory and Cecil were outside the pub waiting for them when they returned, sly smiles on their faces. But when Sarah glanced over her shoulder, she saw that Nate hadn't followed her back inside. He faintly asked Gregory and Cecil for the keys and strode away, back to their cottage. And with his return to London, out of her life forever.

Chapter 18

The next morning Sarah brought supplies for Sid and Lottie to the regular Sunday morning rehearsal. Only this was special, the first dress rehearsal. Dress rehearsals normally filled her with excitement but today she felt drained and grey. She had a feeling there would be a few sore heads after last night's fun. Her own was absolutely fine. Seeing her dad, then the kiss with Nate, had ensured it. Shortly after Nate left, she made her own apologies, claiming a migraine, and headed home. Lottie, she was sure, wouldn't have noticed, she was too busy singing 'Dancing Queen' at a volume that could be heard several towns away. The entire pub could have upped and left and she wouldn't have noticed, she was enjoying herself so much.

All Sarah needed this morning was coffee. She'd been awake until the small hours when the sun began to rise and the birds started their short, tentative chirps, thinking about Nate. He was heading back to London today and she'd never see him again. Occasionally her mind had strayed to her dad and she'd pick up her phone, thinking of texting him. But what could she say? Coming up blank she hid it under her pillow, rolled over and tried once more to sleep. Among all of this, Finn's sweet, kind face filled her with a disgrace that pounded her head and battered her heart.

She'd fallen asleep as the sun began to stream through the window, waking with just enough time to dress and gather supplies for the players. The only good thing with falling asleep when she did was that she could put off speaking to Finn for a little bit longer. It was cowardly, but until she'd figured out what to say, she just wanted to hide. Deep down she knew what she had to do but was reluctant to admit it. Not until she had Lottie's second opinion.

On the drive in this morning, the glorious sunshine and light breeze refreshed her skin, blowing the fog from her mind, but her eyes continued to burn with a hot grittiness. Using the spare set of theatre keys, she unlocked the revolving doors and went inside, turning on the lights as she went. A few minutes later, Lottie and Sid arrived looking the worst she had ever seen them. Lottie's voice had gone completely and from the way she was screwing up her face, daylight was proving painful. Sid's voice was barely audible, just a strained gravelly whisper punctuated by his occasional squeaks. Sarah put on her best smile and teasingly asked, 'Bit hungover, are we?'

'I don't think I've ever felt so rough,' replied Sid. Lottie nodded her agreement then immediately regretted it as her hand flew to her head.

Sarah laughed. 'Then you'd better drink this and take these.' She showed them the coffees and chocolate chip muffins she had brought, then pulled three bottles of water and some painkillers from her bag. Sid and Lottie grunted their thanks.

As the other players arrived including a rather subdued Debbie, a green-looking Conner and a strangely okay Mrs Andrews, the theatre came to life. Every time the door squeaked Sarah's head would lift involuntarily as she checked to see if it was Nate, or at the very least, Gregory and Cecil with news of him.

'How is Mrs Andrews okay?' asked Sid, taking a huge bite of his muffin. 'Even those hips were loosening up towards the end, and she actually smiled once or twice. She must have been off her face.' Mrs Andrews was shouting now into her phone, chastising someone, her face perfectly made up, without a hint of a dark circle in sight.

'I think she has a picture in an attic somewhere, like Dorian Gray,' said Sarah. Lottie managed a pathetic smile and Sarah gave her a cuddle, pushing down her disappointment that she wouldn't be able to speak to her about Finn. She needed her best friend's advice but right now all Lottie seemed capable of was vowing to never drink again. 'If I were you, I'd find a quiet corner and try and have a nap.' Lottie nodded and, hugging her coffee, shuffled off to find a quiet spot.

Before she'd made it very far down the aisle, Sean and Leonard came onto the stage and began hammering some bits of scenery into place. Lottie covered her ears and made a dash for the furthest, darkest corner while Debbie tried to stop them. 'Och, for the love of all things holy, will you please stop that. There must be something else you can be doing today?'

Smiling, Sarah turned to them. 'Guys, could you do some painting rather than the hammering? And how are you two not hungover as well? I saw you doing tequila slammers and Jaeger bombs with a bunch of 20-year-olds. Naughty boys.'

They gave wolfish grins. 'Always drink a pint of water before you go out and one before you go to bed,' said Sean.

'And have a big pasta dinner,' added Leonard before they disappeared into the wings, taking their hammers and nails with them.

The revolving door spun again and Gregory and Cecil came in, virtually running down to Sarah. They were waving something in the air and their eyes were wide with what Sarah could only describe as panic. 'Sarah, darling, have you seen?' shouted Gregory.

'You must have seen,' Cecil said, wiggling his hips like a speed walker. 'She must have seen, Gregory. How could she not have seen?'

'Because she doesn't read the papers, remember? And look at her, cool as a cucumber, she can't possibly have seen.'

Unable to get a word in, Sarah folded her arms over her chest, just as they reached the bottom of the aisle. 'What on earth are you two going on about?'

Cecil gasped and grabbed Gregory's arm. 'She hasn't seen. Gregory, she hasn't seen.'

'I know, dear.' He turned to Sarah. 'Sarah, darling, come here.' Gregory led them to one of the front-row seats and settled down to regain his breath. Sarah did as she was told and the rest of the players gathered too for good measure. It had been his phone he was waving in the air and Gregory showed them the front page of one of the tabloids. Sarah's heart somersaulted before shooting up into her throat and then settling at the bottom of her stomach. A large headline read, 'Lothario Nate Hardy at it again with mystery brunette', and underneath was a grainy picture of her and Nate kissing under the pier.

'Oh no.' Sarah pressed her hands against her forehead. The flash must have been someone snapping a picture of them and whoever had done it hadn't wasted any time selling it on. 'Oh, God. Does Nate know?' Gregory gave a slow shake of the head.

'I don't think so. He left early this morning. We saw him off from the station at half past seven. We only saw this after. I didn't have the heart to ring him yet.'

'Oh fuck.' Dropping her head into her hands she muttered, 'Oh, fuck,' again.

'You've already said that,' said Sid, helpfully. Sarah gave him a sharp stare. Lottie, who had come back when Gregory and Cecil arrived, slowly read the headline, her brain clearly trudging through the words. Then she turned to Sarah and squeaked.

'You kissed Nate Hardy last night?'

A rush of heat filled Sarah's cheeks running up from her neck as the players stared at her, some amused, some impressed, and Mrs Andrews scowling like it should have been her. Which was preposterous because she was evil. 'Only once,' Sarah clarified. 'And it was over very quickly.' But boy, what a kiss it had been.

201

Just the thought of it sent a bolt of lightning through her body, making her head spin, and there again was that strange sensation that her reaction hadn't been purely physical but something deeper. As her eyes settled on Gregory's phone, the screen black now, her reflection stared back at her. What was going to happen now? And what about Finn?

'You kissed Nate Hardy last night?' repeated Kathryn, jiggling on the spot. She'd missed the party as her teenage daughter had a stomach bug.

Gregory sighed dramatically. 'This might just be the end of his career, at the very least for the next few years.'

'Really?' asked Sid, surprised. 'Loads of celebs do this sort of thing though.'

'Yes, but it's his reputation isn't it? No one's going to want to watch a love rat playing a hero. And it doesn't matter how good he is, people don't watch things with actors they don't like. And the papers are saying he cheated on his wife with this model, then skulked off to another mistress during the media frenzy. They'll eat him alive when they find him.'

'What can we do?' asked Sarah.

'Nothing, my love.' Gregory placed a hand gently on her shoulder. 'It's unfortunate, but he's just going to have to ride it out and try to rebuild his career afterwards.'

'And his life,' added Cecil.

'But that's so unfair. Okay so he made a mistake with the model but—'

'He cheated on his wife, Sarah,' said Sid, gently.

'But …' Sarah fell silent. She couldn't break Nate's confidence, but she didn't want everyone to think he was such a shit. He was a good man. 'Like he said, it's complicated.'

After a pause Gregory said, 'Ah, I see you know the truth too.' Sarah nodded.

'What truth?' asked Sid. Cecil, Gregory, and Sarah all looked at each other. 'Oh, come on, you can't keep us out. Haven't we kept his being here a secret like you asked? None of us gave him away, surely you can trust us with whatever this secret is.' Again, all three stared at the others before Sarah spoke.

'His marriage was already over way before he slept with that model. He said it had been for months and months. She even cheated on him first.'

'Och, I've heard men say that before,' answered Debbie, folding her arms over her chest.

'You?' asked Mrs Andrews, attempting to frown.

'Aye. I've had my fair share of romance afore.' The idea of mad Debbie having any sort of love life was both intriguing and frightening but Sarah decided not to press for details.

'Honestly, Debbie,' Sarah said.

'It is true,' said Cecil. Debbie harrumphed.

'He said they were planning on announcing their divorce, they were just waiting a few more weeks.'

'And the model?' asked Sid.

'He was lonely,' Sarah replied, her heart hurting thinking of how low Nate must have felt then, how alone, and she yearned to take away his pain. She'd spent a long time feeling the same way too. Feeling lonely because her mum was gone and her dad had left them, alone because she'd closed herself off from the world, then alone when she'd fallen so hard for Vince only to have her heart crushed.

Gregory also came to Nate's defence. 'He was desperately lonely from what we could see. And he wasn't lying to us.'

'No way,' added Cecil. 'We can tell.'

'Poor Nate,' croaked Lottie. 'And poor you,' she added, reaching out for Sarah's hand. 'I really liked him.'

'Me too,' added Conner, speaking for the first time.

'Me too,' Sarah replied, realising just how much. It wasn't just some crush, it felt even stronger and more powerful than her feelings for Finn, who she still had to talk to. She owed him an explanation. All this time she'd told herself her feelings for Nate were heightened by the soap-opera-style events surrounding them both, but they weren't. Now Nate wasn't here, she wanted him to be. She missed him already. Missed talking to him, missed hearing his voice. The thought that he'd be hurting alone in London hurt her too. There must be something she could do to help him.

In the silence the Greenley Players watched on. Debbie still looked harsh and disapproving, Conner, sad. An idea occurred to Sarah and she turned to Lottie and Sid. 'You're journalists, what if I go to the papers and say it was all my fault?'

Lottie seemed confused so Sarah explained. 'What if I act like I'm some crazy fan-girl and say I kissed him and he didn't kiss me back?'

'They'd leap on the story,' said Sid.

'But the picture?' Lottie replied, her voice quiet and strained. She cleared her throat but it made little difference.

'It's as grainy as my sister's custard,' interrupted Cecil.

Sarah smiled. 'Not a saying I've heard before but okay. Cecil's still right and that's the point. It's really grainy, you can only just tell it's me.'

'That's because Nate has his tongue down your throat,' teased Sid and Lottie batted him with her script.

'I'm not named in the article either, so they still don't know who it is – it would be a scoop.'

'It could work,' said Gregory, nodding. 'He'd still have to deal with the fall-out, but in a way, it might actually help him.'

'How?' asked Conner who had been lurking at the back and was even paler than usual with his hangover.

'It'll show people that he's still got a fan base, that he's still desirable in the eyes of the public. That people still want to meet him and snog him and see him naked on TV. That sort of thing.'

'I think you got a bit carried away there, didn't you?' said Sid, and Gregory nodded, pretending to fan himself. Then Sid turned to Sarah. 'If you do this, we can help find some contacts.'

'Cecil and I will help you practise,' added Gregory. 'Mrs Andrews can advise on the crazy-person aspect, can't you, darling?'

Mrs Andrews narrowed her eyes and smiled. 'Of course. I've learned so much from you over the years, Gregory.'

Overwhelmed by all the support she was getting, Sarah grinned at them. For once something felt right. 'But what about the play? This is supposed to be our first dress rehearsal.'

'I'm sure we can miss one rehearsal,' said Conner, giving a single nod.

'Are you doing it then?' asked Lottie, and without hesitation Sarah stood up.

'Yes. Definitely, yes.'

* * *

Walking back into his house after four weeks away was one of the strangest feelings Nate had ever experienced. It didn't feel like home anymore and the eerie silence he was met with made the large mews house feel empty, just like his heart. A bunch of reporters were waiting outside as his taxi pulled up but with only one small bag to deal with, he was able to get in and unlock the door without too much trouble.

As he went through to the kitchen, he noticed for the first time how bereft of colour his home was. There were period features, but all the furnishings were grey, modern and very, very expensive. The kitchen had every possible convenience and swanky gadgets, but nothing made it feel comfortable. He missed the homely feel of Gregory and Cecil's cottage, the smell of the sea and the bright, vivacious colours of their small chaotic court-yard garden. Perhaps when he and Emma sold the house he would find somewhere in Greenley. Somewhere he could disappear to when he wasn't filming. In his head he saw Sarah's smile. If he moved there with his child, it would be hard seeing her then leaving all the time. He was missing her already, but he dropped his bag and forced himself to think of something else. No, Greenley was out of the question. The doorbell sounded and after a quick look through the spy hole he was relieved to see it was Robin.

Opening the door but hiding behind it so the reporters couldn't snap him, he let Robin squeeze in through the gap. Nate had forgotten just how rotund he was and almost trapped his belly in the door. Robin, dressed in pale beige trousers and a huge voluminous shirt that made him look even shorter and rounder, pulled Nate in for a hug. 'Come here, mate. Christ, you are one lucky sod.'

'Me? What do you mean?' he asked as Robin released him. The last he'd seen the papers had gone up a gear in their loathing and were pulling out their thesaurus' to find new names to call him.

'I don't know how you managed it. You should have just told me she was a nut and I could have issued a statement.'

Ignoring the empty feeling in his heart, Nate said, 'Robin, what the fuck are you talking about?'

'The fan-girl.' Nate shrugged. 'The crazy lady who kissed you on the beach.'

'Sarah?'

'Sarah? Don't tell me you actually talked to her?' What the hell was he talking about? Sarah wasn't crazy. He'd met deranged fans before, ones who tried to lick his face or pinch his bum, but she wasn't one of them. Seeing his nonplussed reaction, Robin took out his phone, tapped and swiped at the screen for a moment before showing it to him. 'Look. I assumed you already knew about this.'

Nate took it and read a newspaper article. He had no idea that the silly photo someone took of him last night had hit the papers but somehow it had. Sarah had got in touch with the tabloids and was acting like some loopy, psycho fan claiming to have attacked him on the beach. She was saying she'd kissed him, rather than the other way around. From the demented way Sarah had repeated herself over and over again in the article, she was acting like an absolute loon. A swirl of emotions swept around his brain in mounting confusion. Why? Why would she do that for him? He already knew that she was a lovely person but why make herself look like that just for *him*? Could it possibly be she had feelings for him too? Deeper feelings than he'd ever thought possible. No, it couldn't. She was just starting to see someone. Gregory and Cecil had mentioned it in passing. She'd pulled back from his kiss the first time and the second was just a mistake. Her hasty retreat had told him so, and the way she'd marched off without looking back. But Nate couldn't think about the kiss or the way it had rocked his body and soul, sending his heart pounding against his ribcage with a deep heavy yearning.

'You've certainly got a way with the ladies,' Robin said, then laughed to himself. 'Anyway, this crazy lady might just have saved your bacon.'

Nate handed back the phone. 'What do you mean?'

'I can't tell you the amount of phone calls I've had this morning asking where you are, when you'll be working again, what you've got lined up – people are going mad for you again. And in a good way this time. I'm being sent a million and one scripts for you to read and consider, but we can go through all that later.' Robin's phone rang again and he answered straight away. 'What? Really?' Robin moved up and down the hallway. 'Are you joking? Danny, mate, I owe you big time.' He hung up, a huge grin on his face and let out a deep laugh. 'It is your lucky day, fella.'

'What now?' Nate rubbed his forehead, pinching his temples. He had no idea what was happening. Robin's small eyes behind large glasses pinned on Nate.

'*Hot News* are breaking the story that Hannah Salgado is not, in fact, pregnant.'

Nate stared at him, unable to speak, and his tongue fell to the bottom of his mouth as a mixture of relief and disappointment flooded his system. Relief at the thought that he hadn't created a child with someone he didn't respect. If he was going to be a father with anyone, he'd want it to be Sarah. Wait, what? He shook his head, unsure where that thought had come from. Then disappointment struck because he'd come to like the idea of being a father, of the idea of tiny hands holding his own. 'How do they know?' he asked at last.

'Her assistant's gone on the record and exposed her as making it all up. Hannah won't be able to deny it either. She'll probably come up with some excuse that she just thought she was and it was a genuine mistake, but no one's going to buy it, and in terms of public support, you'll be the one everyone sides with.' Robin's balding head was becoming shiny from the excitement and his top lip had beaded with sweat. He took his handkerchief out and wiped. 'Right, you call Emma and let her know what's going on, try and get her to come back, it'll look better. And I'll get on with sorting out some of these job offers.' Robin marched through to the kitchen and Nate heard him fill the kettle and switch it on.

Turning on the spot, Nate ran both hands through his hair and rested them on the back of his head, linking his fingers. He felt muzzy and lightheaded. In the last five minutes everything in his life had turned around. The life he thought was crumbling around him was suddenly patched back up. He knew he should be smiling. He knew he should be happy. But his face didn't want to move and his soul felt leaden. The simple fact was when he took a step back and examined his life, there was a Sarah-sized hole and he had no idea how to fill it.

Half an hour later they were on their second cup of coffee and had moved to the living room. 'So what do you think?' asked Robin.

Nate threw the script down onto the sofa and checked the clock again. It had moved on by just under two minutes since the last time he'd looked. Nate wondered how Sarah was feeling now and banished the thought away. Stretching his arms above his head he moved his neck from side to side. The air-con was up high, and large floor-to-ceiling windows overlooked a mani-cured-to-within-an-inch-of-its-life back garden, bereft of life or character.

Robin threw his hands in frustration. 'Don't any of these appeal? They're all great opportunities.' Robin's phone hadn't stopped ringing or pinging with email notifications and Nate was inundated with offers both here and across the pond. Hannah would disappear back into obscurity, and Emma had said she was staying with her mum. Divorce would follow and for once, life was settling a little. All he had to do was decide which jobs he was genuinely interested in, but for some reason he felt empty and bored.

Nate was glad to be back in London among the hustle and bustle of the city but every sound rang hollow and ironically, coming back to the large, empty house felt claustrophobic. As he sat there with Robin the walls closed in on him and he found himself wishing for pebble beaches and the sea.

'Come on, Nate. There must be something here you fancy doing. Look.' He tossed a script over and it landed in Nate's lap. 'This one's produced by Jeffrey Rolo. You've always wanted to do one of his films and he's emailed to say it's back on the table.' Nate sighed. 'Or this one. It'd be great to get you back into costume dramas.'

Thinking of costumes, he wondered what the Greenley Players were wearing for *The Tempest*. He hadn't had a chance to see them all, only Mrs Andrews' crazy creations. Gregory had been doing such a good job as Prospero, Nate wished he'd talked to him more and learned more about him and his time on the stage. And Cecil too was so kind and caring. He missed sitting in their garden, a glass of crisp white wine in his hand, listening to bird-song and chatting about this and that. 'What was Gregory like back in the day?' asked Nate to Robin's surprise. His eyebrows were lifted high in his crinkled forehead.

'He was great. Did you like him?'

'Yeah. He's a nice bloke. Cecil too.'

Robin let the papers in his hands tip towards his belly. 'Gregory was a very good actor. If he'd have really put the effort in, he'd have made it big.'

'What happened?' Nate straightened a little.

'He wasn't cut-throat enough, really. And he was also too busy enjoying himself.' Nate smiled. Now that, he could believe.

Actually, Nate missed all the Greenley Players, now he thought about it, and the town, and especially Mr Bennett. He wanted to go back and see all the parts of Greenley he'd missed. Take walks along the pier breathing the salty air, listening to the sea. A picture of him strolling hand-in-hand with Sarah formed in his mind. She wouldn't stop popping up. Her laugh echoed in his brain even though she was miles away, a siren's call to make him charge back to Greenley.

'Nate? Nate?' How long had Robin been calling his name? 'Nate, wake up, fella. Come on, get your head in the game. You're not the only one they're looking at. Not anymore. I really don't think you can pass up this one.' Robin threw another script at him that landed on the floor. 'This could be the new *James Bond*. And the money's good too. In fact, the money's great.'

Nate looked down and tried to muster some sort of enthusiasm. 'It's in America.'

'So?' Robin shrugged. 'There's nothing to keep you here is there? It's too good an opportunity to miss. You turn this down now and you may never get the chance again. This is a real once-in-a-lifetime type thing.'

Picking up the script he glanced at it again. It was true there was nothing to keep him here anymore and a complete change of location might be just what he needed. A chance to move on. To forget all about the last month and everything that had happened. A niggling at the back of his mind told him something

210

wasn't right, but he put it down to nerves. It felt like a lifetime since he'd acted. He'd spent so long sitting around thinking, he'd forgotten to actually get on with life. Time to start making decisions again. And a fresh start in the US was about as fresh as it got. If Sarah was seeing someone else, as Gregory and Cecil had said, there really was nothing for him to stay for. 'Okay then,' he said to Robin. 'You'll make the call tomorrow?'

Robin smiled and clapped his hands together. 'Get packing tonight and I'll tell them you're flying out immediately.'

* * *

Sarah parked just down the road from Finn's house and took a moment to collect herself. As he hadn't called, she presumed he hadn't seen the news but then he probably didn't read the celeb pages. Still, it had given her time to figure out what she needed to do and what she was going to say. It was just after lunch now, but the morning had been manic with activity. Everyone had been spurred into action finding telephone numbers and contacts, and calling like crazy trying to sell the story. Sarah had been interviewed over the phone by a few papers with Gregory by her side, coaching. She'd nearly lost her temper a couple of times as he'd been writing down things she should say, or making crazy person gestures, telling her she needed to sound more bonkers. It had been hectic and had left her with a pounding headache and a tightness at the base of her skull. It was too hot to be getting worked up like this. Even her ear was sweaty where the phone had been pressed against it for such a long time. When it was all over, everyone had disappeared to the pub, the all-important dress rehearsal abandoned, but Sarah had something more important to do and she was not looking forward to it.

Finn's house was on a row of Victorian villas with bright white walls and beautiful architecture. As she neared, she took a deep breath before climbing the stairs to the front door. Using the large lion-shaped knocker, she banged it down. Guilt thudded through her and squeezed her throat. It was all such a mess. She liked Finn a lot, but she'd liked Nate too – though 'like' didn't seem a strong enough word to describe it.

This morning Sarah had decided she had to call it quits with Finn. She clearly wasn't ready for their relationship. Finn had been all she'd wanted for the past year, but Nate had gone and messed everything up and she wouldn't lead Finn on. He deserved so much more, so much better than her. And even though Nate had gone back to London and out of her life altogether, she couldn't be with Finn while her heart longed for someone else.

When Finn opened the door, his strawberry blond hair was slightly messy where he hadn't combed it and he still seemed half asleep. He was wearing joggers and a T-shirt that looked like it had been slept in. He was clearly having a lazy Sunday. 'Oh, Sarah. Hi.'

'Hi,' Sarah said tentatively, still unsure what else she was going to say, or how she was going say it. 'Can I come in?'

He hesitated, casting a glance over his shoulder. 'Umm, sorry but now's not really a good time.'

That was odd. He didn't seem that pleased to see her and something about him was different. His normally easy, relaxed manner had gone and there was a tightness to his features and voice. Had he already read the papers but not called? God, she hated herself right now. 'Please? It's really important.'

With another swift glance over his shoulder, in a weirdly loud voice he said, 'Okay. But it'll have to be quick, I'm afraid.' They went through to the living room and Sarah gingerly lowered herself onto the sofa. A noise from upstairs caught her attention but before she could mention it Finn said, 'So, what's up?'

Sarah's stomach erupted into a fizzing mess. This was it. She wondered if Vince had ever felt this guilty and he'd gone full-on bedroom gymnastics level of cheating. She doubted it. 'Umm, I really need to talk you about something.' Sarah took a deep breath for courage then outlined everything that had happened, beginning with Nate appearing at rehearsals, finishing with the kiss last night. The words tumbled out at lightning speed. When she finished, unable to meet his eye she looked away. At first Finn didn't speak and Sarah cast her eyes around to avoid looking at him. The plain cream walls of the living room were bare apart from a large art print above the period fireplace and some photos in an alcove. The painting was of a lake, the waters calm and still. The exact opposite of how she felt right now. Her fingers were clenched so tightly they were about to cramp up, but then her eyes settled on the floor at the corner of the sofa.

Two wine glasses, stained at the bottom with red wine, stood next to an empty bottle. One of the glasses was rimmed with lipstick. A perfect imprint in red. There was another noise from upstairs and Sarah looked up at Finn her stomach knotting tighter. A redness was coming into his cheeks. *Not again*, she thought. *Please not again.* 'Who's upstairs?' she asked quickly. He'd never mentioned having a cleaner.

'Listen, Sarah, I said it wasn't a good time.'

Her eyebrows knitted together. 'After everything I've just told you, that's all you have to say?' He should be livid, hurt, or at the very least mildly disappointed. He shrugged and raked a hand through his hair.

'What do you want me to say? You're a grown woman who can do what she likes. It's not like we were an item or anything?'

'Wh-what?' Sarah felt a burn in the back of her throat. Weren't they? Hadn't they been? She'd stupidly assumed they were since that first night they'd spent together. That it was the start of something. He held up his hands in surrender.

'Look, Sarah, I'm sorry but I didn't know we'd gone exclusive. And to be honest that's not what I'm looking for right now.'

'But—' The room spun and all Sarah could think was that she needed to get out. How had she been such an idiot?

'Come on, don't overreact.' He was giving her that carefree

smile. 'You kissed someone else and I'm telling you it's fine. You should be pleased.' How had she got him so wrong? She'd completely misread him. Anger suddenly burst through her as she thought of all the time she'd spent feeling guilty and beating herself up for being a bad person. All for this jackass. Helplessly looking around Sarah spied a photo of him and his sister – she couldn't be anyone else, they were almost identical, both with curly strawberry blond hair and brown eyes. They could have been twins. Which meant the pouty woman who'd phoned during their dinner date, the woman he'd claimed was his sister, wasn't.

Suddenly, Sarah questioned why now? Finn had only become more interested in her since her dad's arrival. Had he sensed an opportunity as she was at such a low ebb? Or perhaps he simply had an opening in his busy schedule. Whatever it was, the thought made her sick to her stomach. She'd spent so long crushing on Finn she'd failed to see what he was really like, and whether he admitted it or not, he let her believe they were headed somewhere when they weren't. And if this was what he was like at home, what on earth had he got up to at the conference? The pouty woman who wasn't his sister was probably some woman he'd met there and duped too.

Sarah stood up. 'You're an absolute shit, Finn MacDonald. You might play the good guy but it's just an act. How many women have you got on the go, hey? How many irons in the fire apart from me?'

'Sarah, come on.' He stood too, cocking his head. Footsteps descended the stairs, and in the doorway appeared the gorgeous singer from the café. The one who'd been giving him the eye that night. She'd clearly got dressed hastily, wearing the same clothes as she had the night before. They were wrinkled, thrown off, Sarah presumed, in a moment of passion. Her hair was messy and the remnants of make-up around her eyes made her look seductive rather than like the tired panda Sarah always did.

Lifting her chin, Sarah picked up her bag and walked to the

door. Finn followed, ushering the other woman into the living room and closing the door behind him so he could speak to Sarah in private. 'Listen, Sarah, it doesn't have to be like this.'

'Oh, I think it does.'

'Why?' He leaned against the wall, relaxed and confident like he'd done nothing wrong. Sarah wanted to punch him in the balls. 'I like you, you like me. We could still have some fun.'

Sarah turned back and gave Finn her best smile, all the anger bubbling up to fill her with confidence. 'Finn MacDonald, I'd rather eat my own eyelids than go out with you.'

'Well, it's your loss.'

Had he really just said that? Pausing first for dramatic effect, she replied, 'It's not, Finn. It's really, really not.'

And with that she stormed out, slamming the door behind her. Only once she was in her car did she allow tears to form in her eyes, willing them back with all the strength she had left. He didn't deserve her tears. If anyone did, it was Nate Hardy whose heart had been broken and had now left her life forever. As her feelings for Nate threatened to overwhelm her, she threw the car into gear and sped off home, wondering how she'd let her life become such a catastrophic mess. She could only imagine what Lottie was going to say when she told her.

Chapter 19

Mandy was in first on Monday morning and Sarah gave a half-hearted wave through the glass of the surgery's automatic doors before unlocking them and heading inside. Not only was today the first night they'd be unleashing *The Tempest* on Greenley, but it was also the first time she'd be seeing Finn since their, for want of a better word, break-up. She had the worst stage fright anyway, beginning as soon as she woke up, building during the day and now there was all this on top. Nausea rose in her stomach. Yesterday afternoon she'd gone home and let herself have a good cry. She'd cried at her own stupidity, cried that she was pushing her dad further and further away by not allowing herself to forgive him, cried that a part of her was missing Nate, cried that she'd been so completely blind to the real Finn. And now, all this anxiety was affecting her appetite. This morning she hadn't been able to eat anything, worried about how embarrassing it was going to be to see him in the office.

The surgery was already getting stuffy and Sarah fiddled with the air-con controls. She was feeling sick enough without that adding to it. If she had to sit in hot air all day she really would throw up. Then knowing her luck, the rumour mill would start that Nate had got her pregnant.

From the way Mandy was jostling in her seat it was clear she wanted to ask her about what had happened. The cold fingers of embarrassment inched up Sarah's spine. Her loony plan to contact the papers had seemed such a good idea at the time but she hadn't thought about the consequences afterwards. The mortifying shame as she walked down the street and people stared. The questions she'd have to endure from friends and patients alike. On the plus side, if some of the patients thought she was a bit mental they might not shout at her so much. Gregory was doing a good job as a stand-in agent, stopping the press from visiting by pretending she'd left town. If only she actually could. Sarah hung her cardigan over the back of her chair, placed her handbag on the floor then took a seat next to Mandy. For about three seconds Mandy was able to keep the smile from her lips before she spun around and exploded with glee. 'Oh. My. God. You kissed Nate Hardy? I thought you and Finn were … you know. Was it good?'

Unsure if Finn had arrived yet, Sarah looked around quickly. 'I did kiss Nate Hardy, but it was only once and I was a bit drunk.' She hadn't been, but it was what she'd told the papers. That, and that she was a deranged lunatic stalker with a life-size cut-out she dressed in different outfits and talked to at night.

'And have you really been obsessed with him for the last five years?'

'No.' She sighed. 'It's complicated.' Everything was complicated. Her relationship with her dad, her relationship with Nate. 'Complicated' didn't even begin to cover her life right now. 'Messy and a complete disaster' were better descriptions. Her friends would be better off retiring to a safe distance or keeping away entirely.

'And what about Finn?' asked Mandy, leaning in.

Sarah had wondered how she was going to deal with this question. Mandy had a lot of great qualities, but Sarah knew she couldn't trust her to keep quiet. Patient confidentiality was one thing, but when it came to her friends, Mandy had a fierce loyalty and wouldn't be afraid to let Finn know what she thought of him. Sarah had decided discretion was the way forward. Working with him was going to be hard enough without Mandy making it harder. 'We've decided we want different things so we're calling it quits.'

'Oh right.' She looked surprised, but Sarah didn't explain any further.

'Look, I don't mean to be rude, Mandy, but can we not talk about this right now, please? I'm not feeling great at the moment.'

Mandy nodded and switched on her computer. 'All right, chuck. But at some point you have to tell me everything.'

'I will. I promise. What's this anyway?' Sarah tapped the cool box she'd discovered hidden under their desk.

'I've had this great idea,' Mandy replied, popping the lid. There was no food inside, just lots and lots of the cool packs you'd find in the freezer. She picked one out and wrapped it in a tea towel that had been resting on the arm of her chair and handed it to Sarah.

'What am I supposed to do with this?'

Mandy smiled and stood up. She'd been sitting on one! 'It keeps me lovely and cool.'

'I bet it does,' Sarah replied with a giggle. She was tempted to try it but decided to rest it on her lap instead. 'Genius,' she said to Mandy's gratified smile.

Finn arrived shortly afterwards, and the day began as it always had, like nothing had happened between them. He cheerfully waved and his normal, 'Morning ladies,' and cheeky smile made Sarah grip her pencil in anger. Then he disappeared into his office, only emerging to call his first patient. All the flirtatious banter of the last month was gone and as much as Sarah hated him now, the place felt empty without it.

For Sarah, the morning was more like an endurance trial and it was clear from the whispered chatter and sly glances that came her way that everyone knew what she'd done. The patients who hadn't read the papers were told all about it by those who had. Some even made snide comments, sometimes to her face, sometimes behind their hands, but Sarah did her best to ignore them.

Mid-morning, when it was Sarah's turn to make a round of tea, she hesitated by Finn's door. If she left him out everyone would know that something was up and she didn't want to seem spiteful. Hesitantly, she knocked.

'Come in.' His voice was bright and cheery. 'Oh, Sarah. Hi. How's your morning going?'

Instead of saying it was agony and she'd quite happily hole-punch him and some of their patients to death, she kept her voice casual. 'I wondered if you wanted tea?'

'Oh. Yes, please.'

'Okay.' She grabbed his cup and walked back to the door.

'Sarah, wait.' The pleading tone caught her off guard. 'Can you wait for a minute please?' A week ago, being in the same room as him would have resulted in kisses and … she blushed as her imagination re-lived some of those moments. Or perhaps she was getting a bit pre-menopausal, now might be a good time to discuss some HRT. 'Listen, I'm truly sorry we seem to have crossed wires—'

'Crossed wires? What are you talking about?' It wasn't crossed bloody wires. 'Crossed wires my behind!' she said a little more loudly than intended. She could feel herself getting cross. He was doing that face doctors pulled when they were being sympathetic but didn't actually give a flying fuck. 'You led me on, Finn. And you know you did. You let me think we were having a monogamous relationship that had a future when in fact you were shagging around behind my back—'

'Sarah, I really don't think I did.' He ran a hand through his hair. It seemed to be his signature move. 'But if you think I did, I'm sorry.'

'Sorry doesn't quite cut it.' She spun on her heel.

'This really doesn't have to be the end, Sarah. We could carry on having a good time. You had fun with me, didn't you?'

Fun. Fun! Fun was all it had been, she thought with a pang of sadness. Resisting the urge to throw his empty tea cup at him, she carried on towards the door. 'Next time I want your type of fun, Finn, I'll ask Sid to tell me about his ingrown toenail.'

By lunchtime, after more snide comments from patients, Sarah was ready to leave her desk and get some fresh air. 'Do you mind if I have lunch outside, Mandy? If I don't, I might end up murdering someone.'

'No, you go ahead, honey. You've had a hell of a morning. Tomorrow will be better though, once they've got it out of their systems. Besides, it could be worse.'

'Oh yeah? How's that?'

'You could have Mr Grainger's rash or Mrs Bolton's … you know …' Mandy grimaced and pointed at her crotch. Sarah didn't know and didn't want to either, but she giggled and gave Mandy's shoulder a squeeze as she went past, thankful for her support.

Out in the refreshing air, Sarah walked across the road to the seafront. She took a deep full breath, filling her lungs with the salty tang from the sea, and sat on one of the benches looking out at the harbour as the sun beat down on her face. Small fishing boats bobbed about on the high tide and she read their names, just as she had a hundred times before. With no appetite Sarah took her packed lunch from her bag and rested it on her lap. Unwrapping her sandwiches, she felt the bench shift with the weight of someone sitting down beside her. It was Ben. 'Dad? What are you doing here?'

'I saw the headlines,' he said gravely.

'Oh.' She took a bite of her ham sandwich, but it tasted dry and stale in her mouth. When she swallowed, it stuck in her throat and she had to force it down.

'I thought I'd better come and see you,' Ben began. 'Maybe give you some advice.'

'Excuse me?' Sarah spun to look at him and her stomach churned with rage. She could understand him coming to see if she was all right or to offer some support, but advice? He really was in no position to offer her guidance considering he'd turned his life into such a shit-show. Just because he'd been allowed out of prison and they'd had a cup of tea together, didn't mean he could act like a parent. It was too late for that, or too soon, depending on how you looked at it. Ben mumbled at first, but as he spoke his features took on that stern father expression he used to have when telling her off as a child. 'Look, I know you might not want to hear this, but it's my duty as your father to tell you—'

'Your duty to tell me what?' Sarah pinned him with angry eyes and had to force the tension from her mouth.

Ben lifted his chin. 'That you shouldn't have done it. You shouldn't have made yourself look an idiot just for some man.'

'Umm ... what now? Sarah's brain overloaded with anger, short-circuiting, and it took a second to catch up with Ben's lecture. 'An idiot? An idiot? How bloody dare you.' She stood up so quickly the lid to her lunch box flew off and onto the grass. *It wasn't just for some man*, she wanted to shout. *It was for lo*— She stopped herself from thinking it just in time. She wasn't getting caught up in a make-believe romance again. 'It was to help a friend. To help someone get their life back together.'

'But that wasn't you,' Ben said a little more gently. 'I know you.'

'No, you don't. You have no idea who I am or what I'm like now. You have no idea about me or my life, or anything at all.'

'Please, Sarah ...' He stayed sitting, his hands gently clasped in his lap, but Sarah wasn't having any of it.

'No. I won't have you coming here and telling me how to live my life. You haven't been here for the past six years, have you?'

Ben looked up at her and his bright blue eyes were dulled with sadness. 'Sarah, I'm your dad.'

'No, you're not. You gave up that right when you not only got yourself sent to prison but you cheated on Mum with that woman from work.' The look in his eyes was one of pure shock. Shock that she knew, no doubt. It was the first time she'd said it out loud to him, but unexpectedly, the world hadn't ended. Indeed, among the anger there was a tiny sense of release.

An old couple ambled by arminarm, chatting about the weather. Sarah smiled as they bid her good morning. 'Morning,' she replied, with fake cheer. But once they'd passed, Sarah stood in silence until they were completely out of earshot. Greenley was a wonderful, friendly place, but it really needed to work on its timing. When Sarah turned back around, Ben was standing up and he was angry. His face was tight and it was an expression she'd never seen before.

'You think I had an affair? With Mrs Arnold? She looks like a garden gnome! How could you ever believe something like that, Sarah? I'd never, ever cheat on your mother.' He'd slipped back into speaking like her mum was still alive and Sarah wondered if, after all these years, he'd finished grieving. 'So that's what all this is about? You think I had an affair with another woman?'

Sarah's stomach had vaulted and crumpled in on itself. 'There were rumours,' she said quietly, keeping her eyes down.

'And you believed them? How could you believe something like that of me?' He studied her face.

'Didn't you?' Oh God, had she been wrong? She'd been so sure. But there was such sincerity in his expression. Terror shot through her.

His quiet calm voice exploded with anger. 'No, Sarah, I didn't. I would never betray your mother like that. I was stupid, yes, taking money that wasn't mine, but I loved your mother through and through. She was the only woman in the world for me. Maybe if you'd let me actually speak to you, read my letters or written to me we could have sorted this out years ago. All I get from you is hate and anger.' Sarah flushed and couldn't look at him, feeling

222

ashamed. 'Sometimes, Sarah, you have to admit when you're wrong and move on. I'm trying, maybe you should too.' He started to walk away and Sarah felt trapped. She had been wrong. So, so wrong, pushing him away for something he hadn't even done. She'd based so much of her anger on something that wasn't true. Just like Finn. How was she getting it all so wrong? He paused and said 'Goodbye, Sarah,' then walked away from her. His final words were said with such a cold finality Sarah knew she'd pushed him too far.

Watching his retreating back, she flopped down on the bench, the strength in her legs gone, gripping the edge tightly in her fingertips. She'd been so inflexible, so indignant in her emotions and just as with Finn, she'd been blinkered. Tears fell this time, but not hot, angry tears, the ones that fell now were full of sorrow and regret because seeing Ben walk away she realised that among the chaos she was sure of at least one thing: if her dad hadn't had an affair she could bring herself to forgive him everything else. She wanted her dad in her life and had only herself to blame if this time he didn't come back.

Chapter 20

That evening, Greenley Theatre was alive with the buzz of opening night. It was glorious and warm outside which made it hot and stuffy inside, and from the wings Sarah could see through a tiny gap in the curtain all the people gathering in their seats, chatting and smiling and fanning themselves with the programmes. Backstage, Gregory rested on a chair with an ice pack on the back of his neck, his thick, brightly coloured robe was so warm. Cecil hovered over him cooing and fussing, they were still so in love after all these years together, and it made Sarah smile. Her heart still yearned for a love like that and it was Nate she pictured herself with.

Behind the curtain, last-minute preparations were underway. Costumes were checked, twisted and tucked, and all mobile phones had been switched off and locked away in the basement. For the actors, nerves were swallowed down as the players either quietly went through their lines or paced around, trying to control the buzzing energy that made their legs shake until they finally walked on stage and the exhilaration of performing took over. Everyone had got used to Sarah's stage fright by now and they'd designated a sick bucket, that Sid had kindly labelled. Conner kept glancing over to see if she was okay, which strangely, she was. Butterflies were fighting in her stomach, but she didn't feel the overwhelming fear and queasiness that usually absorbed her at this time. It was either down to Nate's guidance or the fact that her dad wasn't the bad guy she thought he was, she wasn't sure which. Her hankering for Nate hadn't changed and the thought of him caused her bruised heart to ache and disturbed her sleep, no matter how hard she tried to forget him.

Fiddling with the back of Sarah's simple linen smock, Lottie said, 'Have you got some shorts to wear with this, or really, really, big pants, otherwise people aren't going to see your talent, they're going to see your chu—'

'All right, thank you. I get the idea.' Sarah pulled it down and made a mental note to keep her legs crossed.

Letting go of the bottom of the dress, Lottie asked tentatively, 'Are you okay about Finn the absolute shitbag? I'd still like to rip his testicles off and stuff them in his ears.'

Sarah slumped back against the main piece of scenery on the stage, then straightened as it gave a wobble.

'Hey,' said Debbie, poking her head out from under the sparse tree in the centre. 'No leaning against the scenery, you wee dollop! You'll send the whole lot over.'

'Sorry, Debbie,' Sarah and Lottie said together before edging a little further away. 'I'm fine,' she began again. 'No, I'm not. The thing is, I know it could never have worked with Nate. He's an actor on TV and I'm a nobody, but … it just felt like there was something kind of special there. Oh, I don't know. Maybe I imagined it all. And as far as Finn goes, I just need to forget about him, or staple his nuts to his desk.' Sarah went back to fussing with her costume.

'Come on, let's get started and show this town how fab you are.' Lottie held out the sick bucket. 'Are you sure you're all right? You seem very calm tonight.'

'I am, actually,' Sarah replied. 'I'm kind of looking forward to it.' Lottie looked worried. 'I'm honestly fine. I think with everything being so mad and shitty these last two days, a few first night nerves are paling into insignificance.'

'Even if half the town still thinks you're crazy?'

Sarah smirked. 'At least if they think I'm crazy they'll be too scared to boo.'

'That's true,' Lottie giggled. 'Well, five minutes to go.'

Sarah nodded and passed those who were on first as they took their places on the stage, giving cheeky last-second grins and nervously wiggling eyebrows. Sarah wished them good luck and a minute later the curtain parted, the opening lines were said, and the play was underway. Everyone calmed down as the moment had actually come. It was like waiting for a job interview; you spent all day tying yourself up in knots but as soon as it started you felt calm. The only real concern was whether the new sound equipment would work, which it did, very loudly, deafening those who were directly in front of the speakers. The crew turned it down straight away so the sounds of the raging tempest gave a sense of atmosphere rather than bursting an eardrum. Sneaking a peep, ready to come on, Sarah could see two of the actors were so busy pretending to fall to and fro, showing how the boat was crashing about, that they fell into each other with a clunk of heads loud enough to be heard backstage. Luckily, the audience thought it was planned. As they came off stage Gregory handed over the ice pack which the two sore heads shared between them.

Gregory and Sarah's acting was pretty marvellous, even if she said so herself. She was able to play Miranda with true heartfelt emotion. But her mind kept finding its way back to Nate. However much she pretended otherwise, whatever they'd had had been special and had forged a deep bond between them she couldn't easily forget.

Mrs Andrews soon joined them on stage back in her Yoda outfit, the scarves abandoned, and in all her make-up, with her crazy costume and random swirling movements she made a pretty decent Ariel, though listening to her sing was painful and distressing. And the weird combination of maraca, triangle, and recorder played with far too much enthusiasm was an odd, slightly unpleasant mix. Sarah just hoped the audience thought it was part of their interpretation. Even better, Cecil managed to keep hold of his sword and not lob it out, decapitating members of the audience.

Before long it was time for the intermission and in the stuffy heat of the evening the players flocked to the bottles of water Conner and Lottie had ready to hand out. A loud chatter erupted from the other side of the curtain and the players congratulated themselves on how well things were going so far. Last year's Shakespeare hadn't gone nearly this well. In fact, it had been a disaster and one none of them wanted to repeat. After fifteen minutes it was time to get back on stage. The second half went well apart from a mistimed forward roll from Luke that almost sent him off the edge of the stage, and a strange adlibbed whoop from Mrs Andrews when Gregory set her character free.

The standing ovation at the end was more than they could ever have hoped for. Standing shoulder to shoulder with her friends, Sarah took a bow and silently thanked Nate. Her performance wouldn't have been as good without him. Wherever he was, though her heart ached, she wished him luck. She wondered what it would be like to have her dad there in the audience and if he'd be proud of her. Would she ever get the chance to find out?

A silence fell on the theatre as the audience left and the players, now changed into their normal clothes, came out to chat. 'All of you were absolutely brilliant,' Gregory said as the others came out and dropped into the seats that only a few hours earlier had been full of people waiting with anticipation. The players were relaxed and not a little relieved. 'Conner, you've done an amazing job.'

'Thanks, Gregory. Do you think Nate would have been impressed?' he asked, looking at Lottie.

'Yes, I think he would,' she replied, smiling but with a sideways glance at Sarah.

'Gregory, darling,' said Cecil. 'You were simply marvellous.'

'You really were,' Lottie added.

'Oh, thank you so much,' he replied, wiping away a few beads of sweat that remained. 'And you, Sarah, my sweet, were just fabulous! One of the best Mirandas I've ever seen I'd say.'

'Yes,' added Mrs Andrews. 'You were very good, Sarah. I was worried you'd be absolutely frightful after some of those rehearsals, but you really pulled it out of the bag.' Sarah suppressed a smile. Mrs Andrews' backhanded compliments were legendary.

Debbie clapped her hands together. 'All of you were absolutely grand.'

'Well, the scenery made it, dear,' said Gregory.

Kathryn came up grinning. 'Guys, I am absolutely buzzing! My first performance! Did you see my kids waving at me? Proud as punch they were. And I only slipped up on that one line.'

'You were great,' said Lottie, giving her shoulder a squeeze.

A loud pop made them jump and Sarah turned to see Gregory opening a bottle of champagne, beside him, Cecil held plastic glasses ready to be filled. 'Come on,' Cecil said. 'Let's have a celebratory drink.'

Sarah took one and sipped, but as everyone rejoiced and the sound of laughing and chatter grew louder, her heart grew empty. Everyone was gone: Nate, her dad. Finn was no great loss but it didn't stop the empty hole left in her life. Only a couple of days ago it had seemed that everything was coming together but now it had all crashed down. Smiling and backing away slowly, she slipped outside into the fresh air.

In the cool dusky evening, as the lights from the harbour twinkled in the night, a shiver shot down her spine. A second later, Lottie came through the revolving door. 'What is it, honey?'

'Oh, I just wanted a bit of fresh air,' Sarah replied gazing up at the stars. The sky was clear and she could see all the constellations her dad had taught her. 'I just didn't quite feel like celebrating.'

'You were fantastic tonight,' Lottie replied, and Sarah gave a small smile.

'Thanks.'

Lottie nudged towards her. 'Want to talk about it?'

'No, you should be celebrating. Don't worry about me.'

'No way. Come on, talk to me.'

Sarah sighed a deep heavy sigh. 'It's just that everything feels so empty.'

'Because of Finn?'

'No, not because of him. As stupid as it sounds, I feel like I'm over him already. He wasn't what I thought he was, but I refuse to waste any more time feeling guilty or blaming myself.'

'Because of your dad, then?'

'Partly.' She sighed again. 'Have I blown it, do you think? Should I call him and apologise?'

'I don't know. Maybe give him some time to calm down? You said he was really angry.' Sarah nodded.

'It's mostly because of Nate,' Sarah finally admitted. Lottie paused then took Sarah's arm and led her across the road to the promenade. They found a bench opposite the beach and sat down together. The streetlights cast shadows over the town and the echo of a slow-moving tide murmured in the dark. 'What are you going to do?'

Sarah thought for a moment, wondering if things could ever have worked out between them. Her head said no but from the pain in her chest she'd have to wait a little longer for her feelings to fade. Right now, it didn't feel like they ever would. They'd connected on such a deep level, and it felt like a piece of her was missing, lost out there in the world, never to come back. Turning to Lottie, the only person she could be truly honest with, Sarah said, 'I think I've fallen in love with him.' Lottie's eyes widened. 'I thought it was just a crush at first, a silly dream. Nothing was

229

real, was it? It was all so odd him being down here. But the more I got to know him, the more I felt … something. And it was so strong and powerful that it felt like it couldn't be real. But he's gone now.' She gave a sarcastic laugh. 'I'll never see him again.'

Lottie took her hand and squeezed it. 'Does he know how you feel?'

Sarah shook her head. 'I don't think so.'

'But the kiss? He must know from that. He might even be feeling the same.' Lottie's eyes were pleading on Sarah's behalf and Sarah so wanted her to be right, but she wasn't.

'It was just a silly moment, Lottie. I was upset, he was stressed … it just … happened.' She sighed. 'Things like this don't happen to people like us.' Thinking of her whirlwind romance with Vince she added, 'And if they do, they don't end well. Besides, we're just normal and he's—'

'What? Not normal? Like an alien?'

Sarah cocked her head at Lottie's silly joke. She was turning into Sid. 'You know what I mean. He's an actor.'

'So? He's still a person with thoughts and feelings. He still puts his trousers on one leg at a time, as my nan would have said. Which is another way of saying he still poos, brushes his teeth—'

'I get the idea.'

Lottie gripped her hand. 'He's just a man, Sarah. Like any other bloke in town.'

She returned the smile but just couldn't bring herself to feel it. 'It could never work, Lottie, even if he did feel the same way.'

'Why not?'

'Because he'd be away all the time acting with gorgeous leggy actresses.' She threw her hands in frustration. Why was Lottie encouraging her? 'And let's face it, he's completely out of my league.'

'Oh, don't talk nonsense.' Lottie scowled. 'How do you think people survive when their other half's in the army or something? People's husbands and wives work away all the time and they manage perfectly well.'

'Why are we even talking about this? It's not even a possibility. He's gone.'

'Why isn't it? Stop being so negative, Sarah. Anything is possible. This *could* be a possibility if you told him how you feel.'

'Don't be silly, Lottie. Now who looks like the crazy one? What would be the point in telling him? He's not going to stop being an actor. And if he doesn't feel the same way I've made a fool of myself.'

'You've done that already.' Lottie nudged her with her shoulder.

'Fair point, but—'

'But nothing! A very wise man once said to me to be brave. Maybe you need to do the same thing.'

Sarah smiled. 'And who was that?'

'Gregory.'

'Gregory? Are you kidding? Three months ago, he told me to go blonde and we all know how that turned out.' She'd had orange hair for three days and had to wear a hat to hide it.

'Okay, so maybe he isn't that great on hair. But he does know about love. Just look at him and Cecil. No one could be happier than those two.'

'Except for you and Sid.'

Lottie gave a silly, soppy grin. 'See, he was right about us. Maybe you should take his advice and be brave. Like I did.' Lottie got up and went back inside leaving Sarah alone.

Could she do it? Could she call Nate and let him know just how deeply she felt for him? More to the point, *should* she do it? She'd continued pushing her dad away and regretted that deeply. Would she regret it if she didn't at least try? What did she have to lose, anyway? The town, the whole country, thought she was a bit of a lunatic, her heart was already in tatters, she didn't have much left to worry about. A tiny flicker of courage was sparking into life. If he didn't feel the same, she'd never see him again. Embarrassed or not he'd never be there to remind her. She pulled her phone from her pocket and stared at the screen. But just as the flicker grew stronger, it dimmed. The thought that he'd be out there feeling sorry for her for getting it all so wrong was too much to bear.

No. She'd sworn off whirlwind romances after Vince had broken her heart, and had she still not learned her lesson after the debacle with Finn? There was no getting away from the fact she was a failure at relationships, reading all the signals wrong, not picking up on the things in front of her face. Nope. She was pleased Lottie had been brave and things had worked out for her and Sid, but they'd known each other for forever. She wasn't going to rush into any hasty decisions, no matter what. Not this time. Placing her phone back in her pocket she told her heart to stop trying to rule her head. It never ended well when she let it. She took a deep breath in through her nose, squeezed her eyes shut, and let it slowly out. Then, alone, she sat there on the bench amid the night's deathly silence.

Chapter 21

Nate stood in his bedroom in nothing but his boxers, and even though it was hot his skin had erupted in goosebumps. The Greenley Players' opening night would be over now and he wondered how they'd all got on.

A fractured beam of light slid through a gap in the curtain illuminating the room just a little. However much he tried, his thoughts roamed back to Sarah and all that she'd done for him. She must have found something in him she liked, why else would she have done what she did? Not only kissed him but saved him. He'd asked himself this question over and over again. Was it too much to hope she had feelings for him? Could she be falling in love with *him*? His confidence had been so battered by self-loathing and damaged by guilt that he felt he had nothing to offer her. Emma had fallen out of love with him, and Hannah had used him. He'd grown so used to feeling that he had nothing worthwhile to offer anyone. Or did he? Could he? And *love*? Could it be love? The word swam around his head. A glimmer of hope brought a smile to Nate's face because he loved Sarah, he realised now. He'd loved her even before he'd left Greenley. What a complete idiot he'd been. It would have been so easy to say the words while he was in Greenley – open his mouth and let them tumble out. For fuck's sake, he'd said them enough times on set to women he really didn't love, so why hadn't he when he'd actually meant it? Was it because it was *true* love? A love he felt so deeply he was scared it would all end the same way as he and Emma had, with them barely tolerating each other. Was it because he didn't want to drag Sarah into the mess that was his life? Whatever it was he didn't know but he hated himself for his spinelessness and for letting his first real chance at happiness fall from his grasp.

Nate grasped the curtains and opened them fully to look out of the window at the dark garden below. Realising the full extent of his feelings, he didn't know whether to laugh or cry, and his face veered between one emotion and the other. He'd been falling in love with Sarah from the first moment he saw her on the beach. There was just something about her that his soul was drawn to. Two spirits that only by joining together would finally make each of them whole. They'd connected in a way he never had with anyone before. He couldn't deny it any longer, his feelings for Sarah were more than he'd allowed himself to realise. She'd haunted his thoughts like a ghost, ever present and unforgettable. Imagining a life lived with Sarah at his side he was sure they were meant to be. He'd been so stupid to swear off love. It wasn't that love couldn't exist for him, he'd just needed to find the right woman.

Robin's voice burst into his head shouting, 'What about America?' He'd be there for months. Maybe longer. And it was a once-in-a-lifetime opportunity that could sky-rocket his career to a new level. The career he'd worked so hard to build, had nearly lost and only just recovered. Thanks to Sarah, a voice murmured. Nate scratched the back of his head, lifting his eyes to the ceiling and hoping for an answer. When none came he slumped down on the edge of the bed. Why did his life have to be so bloody complicated? The thought of him and Sarah together filled his heart with a love so intense he couldn't believe it was real. Surely love was the only thing that mattered. Real, true love didn't come along very often. Of all the opportunities he'd had in his life this was the one he couldn't miss.

Sod it all. Sod America. Nate raised his eyes again and laughed to himself as a weight lifted from his mind. He had to tell her how he felt. Even if Sarah was seeing someone else and rejected him, at least he would have tried. But if she said yes, well … he'd do whatever it took. He'd move to Greenley and become an acting teacher, a dustman – anything, anything at all to be with Sarah. Nate took his phone from the bedside cabinet to call Sarah, but paused. This wasn't something he could say over the phone. He wanted to tell her face to face. To look into her eyes and see her smile. And afterwards, he'd cup her face and kiss her, feeling her soft smooth skin again.

But he couldn't leave now. Too many whiskies meant he couldn't drive and the trains wouldn't get there till the early hours. He couldn't rock up in the middle of the night at Sarah's, it would ruin the moment, and he didn't actually know where she lived. And he'd inconvenienced Gregory and Cecil enough. Plus he owed it to Robin, after everything he'd done, to speak to him face to face and explain. Robin and Anna had been married for forty years, he'd understand. Tomorrow morning he'd put everything on hold and head down to Greenley.

The night was long and restless, bereft of sleep. Nate tossed and turned in bed, the sheets wrapping around his legs so he had to fight to get out. He climbed out of bed just as dawn broke and a pale lemon sky lit the world. Once dressed, Nate drew back the curtains. It was too early to call Robin, barely five o'clock in fact, so Nate headed to the kitchen for a coffee. He should have felt tired and cranky but a strange elation had taken over his body, like a kid on Christmas morning. Too excited to remain in the house he went for a run to burn off some energy. At nine, Nate couldn't hold back any longer and called.

Unfortunately, Robin didn't understand as well as Nate had

hoped he would and went absolutely mental, insisting on coming round there straight away to talk some sense into him. Nate knew it didn't make sense as far as his career was concerned. It didn't make sense at all. But it was the right decision for his heart and soul. Nothing had ever felt so right to him before.

Half an hour later, the doorbell rang and through the spy hole Nate saw Robin's frowning face. As he opened the door, Robin, with unusual stealth, flew in, waving his arms around as he spoke. 'What the bloody hell do you think you're doing? Have you gone absolutely fucking mental?' Nate had expected a level of shock and surprise, but was taken aback by just how furious Robin was. 'After everything I've done for you, clearing up the mess you got yourself into, you're going to turn down the best opportunity of your life for some bit of stuff you've known for a month?'

Having grown used to Robin's flashes of bad temper over the years Nate knew he'd calm down after he'd said, or rather shouted, all the things he'd thought of on the way over. Remaining calm, Nate replied, 'I'm not turning it down, Robin, I just want to have a couple more days to sort something out.'

'What? What do you need to sort out? What the fuck could be so important? She'll still be here when you get back.' Sweat dropped from his forehead as he spun around to face Nate. It was warm today but this early in the morning it wasn't so warm Robin should be that red, hot and sweaty.

'Robin, calm down. Just chill out for a second, okay? Like I said on the phone, I need to head down to Greenley to speak to Sarah and tell her—' Robin scoffed. 'Robin, just calm down. I think you're over-reacting a bit.'

'Over-reacting? Over-fucking-reacting? You want me to ask some of the US's top producers to postpone a meeting so you can nip down to Greenley-On-Sea and chat up a girl?'

Nate frowned but not at Robin's words, though his flippancy was beginning to grate. His eyes were wide and white, and sweat gathered in the deep wrinkles of his forehead. 'Robin, are you okay? I think you should sit down, I'll get you a glass of water.'

'I don't need to sit down. I need you tell me why the hell you're doing this?' Robin rammed his hand into his pocket trying to find a handkerchief. Nate led the way into the kitchen. He was getting that glass of water whether Robin wanted it or not.

'Here, drink this first.' Nate handed Robin the glass of water and he begrudgingly took it, drinking half in one go. He was still very red and a little unsteady on his feet, swaying as he tipped his head back to drink. Finally he sat down. 'Listen, Robin, you know how grateful I am for everything you've done but I'm only asking for a couple of days. I need to find Sarah. And I need to tell her that I love her.'

Robin gazed up but didn't speak. Then, unexpectedly, an amused squeak escaped from his mouth before a full-on belly laugh came out. It faded as his face grew stern and angry once more. 'You're putting your entire career on hold – a career that has only just crawled out of the toilet – for some silly tart from Greenley-On-Fucking-Sea?'

Okay, that was a step too far. 'Robin, hang on. I know you might be a bit … disappointed that I'm not doing this after I've been to America, but you have to understand that this is spec—'

'I don't have to understand anything. After everything I've done for you, you're not throwing it away now. Do you realise how lucky you are?'

'Yes I do!' Nate shouted. 'Just not in the way you think. I know I'm lucky that things are picking up again work-wise, but I'm even luckier because I think I might have found someone special. Someone who loves me – the real me. Surely, after all your years with Anna you can understand that? I don't see why we can't just say I've sprained an ankle or something.' His tone was imploring, but Robin's face remained fierce.

'Because then you'd be the next box office action hero with weak ankles! The flights are booked, the time and date's been set for the meeting. They've even asked me what sort of cookies you like!'

'I'm sorry Robin, but my mind's made up. This has to come first.'

Robin's shoulders stiffened. 'If you go, I can't guarantee that I'll be your agent when you get back.'

'What? Seriously?' A heaviness fell on Nate's chest. How could Robin force him to make such a choice.

Robin didn't answer, just nodded. Exasperated, and feeling like he'd been blindsided, Nate couldn't think what to say. Robin's breathing had calmed and his face was slowly returning to a normal colour, but his mouth was set in a grim line and the skin around his eyes was pinched. For a millisecond Nate questioned himself, but all it did was reinforce that he was making the right decision.

'I'm sorry, Robin, but I have to do this first.'

Robin stood up, sending his chair flying backwards. Without speaking he went to the hall and slammed the front door shut behind him. Nate bent and picked up the chair then flopped down on one of the stools himself and pushed the heel of his hand into his forehead. A sharp pain stabbed just above his right eye and a stress headache pounded his skull. So that was it. He'd made his choice. And yet, though he was sad it had to end this way, he was still sure he was doing the right thing.

Once he'd calmed and his legs had stopped shaking Nate went to pack. This time he could pack properly. Gregory and Cecil had let him use the washing machine, but living in the same three pairs of jeans, pants and T-shirts had involved a lot of laundry. Almost an hour and a half later he was just grabbing the things he needed from the bathroom when the doorbell rang. Nate hoped it was Robin. Maybe now he'd had a chance to take his blood pressure tablets and chill out he'd see it wasn't really that big a deal, and if the Americans weren't happy with a few days' delay then so be it.

Stepping off the final stair he went to the spy hole and looked through. Pulling back in confusion, he unlatched the door. 'Anna, is everything all right? Is Robin okay?'

The petite woman smiled and pushed a strand of silky-grey hair that had escaped from its bun out of her face. 'Robin's fine. I wanted to talk to you about him, actually.' Her voice had always reminded Nate of a yoga instructor, soft and gentle, and she emanated an endless patience and serenity. Nate closed the door behind her and gestured towards the kitchen.

'Would you like a coffee?'

'Yes, please. That'd be nice.' She was wearing jeans and a large, baggy striped shirt that could have been one of Robin's. It swamped her tiny frame, but she wore it well, making it look stylish, and her tiny feet were encased in flat ballet pumps.

Nate put the kettle on and found the cafetière, measuring in the ground coffee. The rich, deep smell filled the kitchen making him feel instantly calmer, as Anna hopped onto the stool with an easy, pleasant smile that Nate found slightly unnerving. He'd never seen her on her own. It was always with Robin at some event or other and occasionally at their house when he'd been over for dinner. Finding some milk and the sugar bowl, he put two mugs in front of them and sat opposite her at the island unit in the middle of the vast kitchen. Trying to keep his voice level he said, 'So what's up?'

'Robin told me what had happened between you.'

'Right.'

'Robin's a good agent, but he's a complete idiot sometimes.' Nate paused, pouring the hot water onto the coffee. Steam rose in the air between them but through it he could see Anna's gentle smile. 'I'm not sure we'd have ever got married if I hadn't asked him.'

'You asked him?' asked Nate in surprise. He pushed the plunger on the coffee and poured some into Anna's cup, then his own. 'Robin's always had it the other way round. A romantic dinner for two—'

'Which I booked.'

'A ring you'd hinted at?'

'Which I bought.' She added a splash of milk and a sugar cube as the gentle smile became a wide grin and a distant look glazed her eye. But then she looked at Nate and the mist cleared. 'You have to understand, Robin's brain can only focus on one thing at a time, either work or play. Not both. But he cares about you, Nate. He cares very deeply.'

Nate felt a heat rise up from his chest. 'Then why did he threaten to quit working with me?'

'Because he's a stubborn old fool who needs to take his blood pressure tablets and calm down a bit.' At this Nate smiled. 'After he left you, he really was feeling quite unwell so he came home.' She must have seen the concern on Nate's face as she waved her hand dismissively. 'Don't worry, he's okay. I called our doctor and he's going for a check-up tomorrow. He'll get a telling-off for drinking too much and not losing any weight yet, but he's fine.' Her features tightened a little and Nate could see she'd been worried, more worried than her voice implied. 'But the reason I'm here is to say that Robin won't be dropping you.' Nate stared wide-eyed and she reached out gently resting her small hand on his larger one. 'I want you to go to Greenley and see this lady of yours, see how it works out. Robin will call the States and let them know there's been an unexpected delay. We can say I'm ill, I don't mind.'

Coffee almost spilled from his cup where he was tipping it in surprise. 'Anna …' He shook his head, speechless.

'When Robin's calmed down he'll realise that there's more to life. His doctor will remind him of that tomorrow too. Sometimes he just gets so caught up with work he forgets it's not the most important thing in the world. Love is. And if you think you've found someone special, just like I did with Robin, then you have to do everything you can to make it happen.'

'Anna, I don't know what to say.' Nate's throat tightened and he pushed down the lump of emotion. 'You know how much I

240

respect Robin. He's been like a second father to me for a long time.'

Her kindly smile was as warm as an embrace. 'I know. And he'll remember that too. Go to Greenley. Be happy.' She finished her coffee and stood to leave, carefully tucking in her chair. Nate did the same and as he accompanied her to the door, he couldn't help but hug her.

'Thank you.'

Once she'd gone, a grin tugged at his face and Nate ran upstairs to finish packing. Checking his watch he saw that it was almost lunchtime. How could it be lunchtime already? Only two minutes ago it had been barely dawn. Time to get down to Greenley.

Should he take flowers? he wondered. No, that would be cheesy and they'd probably wilt on the train. Tomorrow he and Sarah could go to the florist and he'd buy her some flowers. The biggest bunch imaginable. He smiled at the thought as he closed the front door behind him and made his way to the tube station.

A few people took surreptitious snaps of him on the tube, but he pretended not to notice. It didn't matter anyway, his heart and his mind were so full of thoughts of Sarah, of what he'd say to her, of how he'd hold her and kiss her the way they'd kissed on the beach that night, that nothing could bother him. Racing up the escalator steps he hurried through St Pancras to the ticket booth. How could there be a queue at this time of day? Impatiently he tapped his foot, slowly edging forwards until he'd bought his ticket. Then he sped past the cafés and bars and through the barriers just as the train pulled away.

Inwardly cursing and embarrassed under the watchful eye of the staff, he made his way to a bench and checked the departures board. Half an hour till the next train. Half an hour of hell. Giving himself a mental shake, he determined to not be so dramatic. It was only half an hour then he'd be on his way to Greenley. Just the thought of going back to that wonderful little place calmed him down. He looked forward to seeing Gregory and Cecil again. He hoped to see Sarah before tonight's performance started but now he'd be cutting it fine. It was just gone three-thirty so it would be around five by the time he got the next train there.

Finally the train arrived. It was busy but by walking to the furthest carriage he was able to grab a table. After stowing his bag and collapsing back into his chair he realised he was thirsty. The day had been so fraught he hadn't thought to eat or drink much and his appetite had been swallowed by adrenaline. The train rattled down the tracks for almost half an hour when a text message appeared on his phone. It was Robin with two small words that meant the absolute world. 'Good luck.' A smile spread across Nate's face and he relaxed, closing his eyes and savouring the moment of relief. A few seconds later another text popped up from Robin.

Emma's lost the presenting job. Some wife contacted Daddy accusing Emma of sleeping with her husband. Emma's in the dog house and been told to stay out of the limelight! Karma.

Maybe the wife had followed Hannah's example, maybe Marcus had something to do with it. He could guess whose wife it was. Those odd emails and questions from Marcus suddenly made sense. Marcus could never stand an injustice. All the time Nate had thought it was just a bad attempt to make him feel better. Now he smiled at the thought of his friend's loyalty. With Gregory and Cecil, and the Greenley Players, perhaps he wasn't as alone as he'd thought. The unhappy ex would get paid off, of course, but if Emma had lost the job then rumours couldn't be far behind. It goes to show that what goes around comes around. Nate went back to enjoying the journey, watching fields and grazing animals shoot by.

Then the worst happened. Halfway through the journey, the train stopped and a signal failure had him stuck in the middle of nowhere for almost an hour. He thought about getting out at the next station and taking a cab the rest of the way, but he really had no idea which would be quicker and the small village they'd stopped at didn't seem to be busy enough to have a taxi rank outside it. All he could do was sit and wait.

When the train finally pulled into Greenley at six o'clock, Nate ran from the platform, out of the station and grabbed a taxi. 'Greenley theatre, please.' This time he was able to see the streets of Greenley in the evening sunshine. Watching the strange mix of modern and period houses, tree-lined streets, and beautiful seafront, he relaxed his shoulders. The sun was dipping behind the pier and a golden glow spread out into the surrounding cloud backlighting them, casting shadows on the water. The tide was high, gently soaking the bottom deck of the pier and all the fishermen had made their way to the top. The taxi stopped outside the majestic theatre and Nate handed over a ten-pound note, wishing the driver a good evening.

For a moment, he paused outside the beautiful Victorian building. The poster cases had been filled with large posters of the players dressed in costume. Sarah's pretty face stared out at him, as did Gregory, and he smiled. Nate felt like he'd come home. It was almost six-thirty. The theatre doors weren't open to the public yet and Nate began to panic. He hadn't thought much beyond getting here or what he'd say in the pivotal moment he saw her again. He didn't want Sarah to see him now for only half an hour, and for them then to have to part while she went on stage. No, call it melodramatic, but when he saw Sarah he wanted them to have time to talk and just be together. He still had to find somewhere to stay tonight, so picking up his bag he strolled along the seafront taking big deep breaths, stopping at the bed and breakfast he'd spied on the taxi ride over. Once he'd settled in he'd come back for the performance.

Later that evening, showered and shaved, when Nate entered the theatre, it was to be met by someone he didn't recognise selling tickets. He bought one and a programme before finding a seat at the back. It was soon filling up and with only a few minutes to go there weren't many seats left. The atmosphere was buzzing with anticipation and he slunk down in the chair not wanting to be noticed by anyone, least of all Sarah. Spying her name printed on the programme, he ran a finger over the type, picturing her smiling face. A sudden rush of emotion filled him, longing to hold her and admit the truth of his feelings. Finally, the curtains parted and the crash of thunder and lightning rang around the theatre as the play began.

* * *

Sarah waited in the wings for her scene to begin. Next to her, Gregory whispered to Mrs Andrews with excited anticipation but she couldn't feel it. It was the final night of *The Tempest* and Sarah found it odd that they put in all that work for just two performances. It seemed that just as they got it right it was over and on to the next play. Usually, she'd find the prospect of the next show exciting, but there wasn't room in her heart or her head for anything else right now. It was roasting hot again tonight and that made everything feel even more horrible. Fanning herself with the programme, she wondered again where her dad was, and the weight of her regrets nearly stole the air from her lungs. She so desperately wanted to call but what could she say except 'sorry', and that little word didn't seem anywhere big enough.

Just then she felt Gregory's elbow in her ribs and turned to see him pointing to the very back of the stage where Lottie stood. Ben was at her side, smiling. Sarah's heart almost exploded with joy. She shivered despite the stuffy heat. Edging back from the wings she went to her dad and following her instincts, wrapped him in a hug.

'Dad, I'm sorry. I'm so, so, sorry.'

'Shhh, sugarplum. Shh.' He stroked her hair and she raised her head just enough to see his face, tears stinging her eyes.

'I'm so sorry for everything. I've been such a horrible daughter.'

'No, you haven't.' He stood back and pushed his glasses up his nose. 'You're just stubborn, like your mum was.

'What are you doing here?'

Her father had caught the sun where he'd been working outside and the eyes that had seemed dull with sadness were bright and clear.' You didn't think I'd miss your final performance, did you? I tried to come last night but I wasn't sure you'd want me there.'

'Oh, Dad, thank you.' She placed a kiss on his cheek. 'I'm sorry I said you're not my dad anymore. I was wrong. I was so angry I let it take over everything—'

'I'll always be your dad, sweetheart, whether you want me to be or not.' Sarah laughed with a heart full of relief that he hadn't let her push him away. 'I'm sorry I kept saying everything wrong.'

'You didn't, Dad. It was me—'

Ben shook his head. 'No, sometimes when I tried to talk to you it came out all backwards or I'd say the wrong thing. I just didn't want the whole town laughing at you, like they do me.' At this Sarah floundered. 'I haven't been able to be a father to you for a long time, and I know that was all my own fault. I regret my actions every single day and I'm paying the price now. But I won't let the rest of my life pass by without doing everything I can to make it up to you. Please, let me be there for you now.'

Sarah nodded and kissed his cheek again. 'Can I give you one tip though, Dad? If you do want to be there for me, it might be best not to turn up to my work and tell me I'm an idiot on my lunch break? I know this might shock you, but I do already know that.'

He smiled back. 'And can I give you a tip?' Sarah nodded. 'Let people in, Sarah. I want to help you. To love you. I'm sorry I said you made yourself look like an idiot, it was a bad choice of words, but you know what I meant. You made yourself look crazy. Why? The Sarah I know is smart, funny, clever – I couldn't be prouder of you.'

245

Emotionally exhausted, Sarah felt her shoulders flop. The walls she'd put up began to crumble, tumbling down brick by brick. She wasn't just ready to take one, small, tentative step forwards, she wanted to take a huge, giant leap. To make up the ground they'd lost because of her stubbornness and bad judgement. 'Can I tell you after the show? I'm due on stage in a minute.' He nodded, placed a kiss on her cheek and backed away but she pulled him into a close hug again. 'I've missed you, Dad,' she whispered.

'I've missed you too, sugarplum.' And just as he had when she was a child, he handed her his handkerchief for her to dab her eyes. Ben left to take his seat, guided by Debbie, and Sarah silently mouthed 'thank you' to Lottie before heading back towards the stage.

Waiting in the wings she looked out at the audience clothed in semi-darkness. There was no feeling of excitement for her tonight, no last-minute crippling nerves. She felt numb and there was nothing left in her used-up, empty heart to give. Making up with her dad had taken the last drops of her energy and Sarah shook her head and took a long, deep breath in. Every person in that audience had paid for a ticket and deserved a good performance, even if she was falling apart on the inside. She wasn't going to let the Greenley Players, her friends, down, or Nate who had done so much for her. Summoning up her courage she pulled her shoulders back ready to walk on stage. The audience were watching eagerly, ready for a good show. And she was damn well going to give them one. For her dad and for Nate Hardy. Wherever he was.

* * *

Nate sank down in his seat as Lottie and Ben took their seats in the front row. Did that mean Ben and Sarah had made up? He hoped so. The sound of the raging tempest rang out from the speakers and slowly, the curtains parted. The players on stage were some of the newer ones and there was a bit of over-acting with weird jerky movements and eyes that constantly searched the crowd for people they knew, like children in the school nativity play. But as their scene drew to a close Nate paused, sitting as still as possible so as not to miss a moment; Sarah and Gregory were on next. *Enter Prospero and Miranda*, he thought.

Sarah, with a confidence he knew she had but hadn't seen surface during rehearsals, marched onto the stage, staring out into the crowd. He ducked down not wanting her to spot him and as he did so, she ran back to Gregory. 'If by your art, my dearest father, you have put the wild waters in this roar, allay them.' She was good. More than good, she was almost the equal of Gregory. Nate's breath caught and he smiled. She moved about the stage with the graceful gestures of a ballerina. He worried now he'd made a mistake in coming down, she seemed so together, so happy, and he didn't want to ruin it. Even if she rejected him he had to try.

The normal friendly teasing between Gregory and Mrs Andrews played out beautifully. Nate wondered if Gregory was enjoying himself a little too much, particularly when he said, 'How now? Moody?' pausing dramatically and giving the moody part a bit too much emphasis. Nate was impressed by all the players' hard work. There was one mishap with a spotlight where the wrong part of the stage was lit, leaving Mrs Andrews in the dark, but she handled it well like it had been intentional all along. Even the singing wasn't that bad. He could hear Sarah's voice from the wings when she joined in and it was glorious.

During the intermission Nate relaxed back into his chair. They'd all been fantastic. He couldn't wait for the second half to begin.

'Excuse me, are you the guy from the telly?' asked the lady to his right.

'Yes, that's right.' He held out his hand. 'Nate Hardy, pleased to meet you.' The young woman blushed and shook his hand but no great fuss was made. No one really cared. Everyone was so eager for the second half to begin.

The second half began with a great monologue from Luke. He really was fantastic. He teased the audience, staying on the edge of the stage, reciting the monologue as if speaking directly to them. But the moment that stood out most for Nate was when Prospero destroyed his staff. The perfect rise and fall of Gregory's voice, the pauses that were pushed past the point of dramatic, verging on the uncomfortable, made the moment unforgettable. Conner had done an amazing job. The standing ovation at the end was well deserved, and though he wanted to stand tall, whoop and holla, he kept ducked down so Sarah didn't spot him, his own sense of the dramatic taking over.

When the curtains finally closed and the audience filed out, he had to decide what to do, his lack of planning showing again. Did he follow with everyone else and wait for Sarah outside or did he ask to stay there? He hadn't thought that far ahead. Knowing how long it could take to get changed after a performance, especially a final one, Nate decided to stay and speak to Sarah inside, whenever she emerged. He'd waited this long, an hour more wouldn't matter.

Lottie was at the door saying goodbye to everyone, Ben waiting at her side. As Nate made his way over, she saw him and frowned. 'What are *you* doing here?' Even though she was short, her narrowed eyes and sharp tone were quite intimidating and scary.

'I'm here to see Sarah.' He tried to smile, but Lottie wasn't impressed and her face grew tenser.

'Oh, are you now?' Nate nodded and looked at his shoes, feeling like he was being told off by the head teacher. She crossed her arms over her chest. 'Bit late, isn't it?'

'Is it?' he asked, searching her face for a clue, a gnarling feeling in his stomach.

'Well, no,' Lottie conceded. 'Maybe not. But it could have been, couldn't it? She made herself look like a loon for you, you know.'

Lottie had resorted to wagging her finger at him and the tone of her voice made him shrink back. For a friendly girl, he would bet she was quite formidable when she wanted to be, she certainly was being now. No wonder she'd got them registered as a charity, which wasn't an easy task. She could probably work for the United Nations if she wanted to. Lottie could scare anyone into doing anything. Ben watched on, a sympathetic look in his eye. She paused to say a cheery goodbye to the last person leaving and then turned back, scowling.

Nate scrunched his hair in his hand. 'I've come to tell Sarah I love her.'

'Oh, well … good.' Her eyes began to twinkle as she smiled.

'I know it took me a while. After everything that had happened, I just couldn't believe I'd be that lucky.'

Lottie smiled and pointed at the stage where Sarah had just come out from the wings. She hadn't spotted him yet and was chatting to a flushed-looking Gregory, and though she laughed, her eyes carried a sadness the polite smile couldn't hide. This was it. This was the moment he'd been waiting for. His chest had tightened around his lungs, stealing his breath, but he felt an inner calm. He skirted behind the last row of seats and paused at the top of the central aisle. Sarah's hair was still messy, as her character wore it, and it suited her. He watched her step down the stairs at the front of the stage and sling her bag onto her shoulder, distraction keeping her gaze from him. As Nate began to walk down the aisle, his legs wobbling beneath him with every step, she finally looked up, and her eyes widened as she came to a stop.

Nate kept going like a string was pulling him closer. Gregory and Cecil, he noticed, had stopped talking. Gregory was watching him with one hand over his mouth and the other holding an ice pack on the back of his neck. Cecil held his hands over his heart, his smile radiating happiness for them both. The rest of the players followed until the stage was full.

Now that Nate was opposite Sarah, with only a small space between them, he couldn't believe he hadn't admitted his feelings for her before. He'd been so stupid. And though he'd rehearsed the things he wanted to say time and time again throughout the night and on the train journey down here, he just couldn't find the words now they were face to face. He opened his mouth to say something – anything – when at that precise moment Gregory fainted.

* * *

The first Sarah knew of Gregory passing out was a giant clunk behind her and Cecil screaming like a girl. Before that, her mind had been frozen and all she could think was, *Nate's here. He's here. Standing in front of me.* A dozen questions ran through her mind. Why was he there? Had he simply come to thank her? She didn't know what to say, or what to do. She'd walked towards him without thinking or speaking. The look in his eyes was so intense, like he was looking right into her soul and it had pulled her close. She wanted to reach out and touch his face but her fingers stayed at her side. She wanted to lift her head and kiss him again but couldn't move. Deep creases formed either side of his mouth as he smiled at her.

Cecil's scream pierced her reverie and she spun to see Gregory in a heap on the ground. After a quick glance back at Nate to make sure she wasn't imagining him, she fled to Gregory. Nate followed and Lottie ran down the aisle as all the players gathered round with worried glances.

'Oh, my darling,' cried Cecil, holding Gregory's hand and patting it like they were in some 1950's movie. Gregory came too almost immediately and rolled onto his side, clutching the back of his head.

'Urgh, what happened?'

'You fainted, darling,' said Cecil, becoming a little tearful. 'You fainted, but you'll be all right.' Sarah rubbed his back to try and calm him down.

Gregory looked up, bleary eyed. 'Nate?' he said, in a croaky voice like he was doing some dramatic death scene. Sarah was sure he was putting it on while Cecil looked a bit miffed at not being spoken to first. 'Nate? You came back.'

'I did,' he said matter-of-factly.

Gregory gently touched the back of his head feeling the size of the lump. 'Ouch.'

'It's okay,' Sarah said. 'You'll be fine. I think you just got a bit overheated.' Sid's long arm reached over her shoulder and handed Gregory a bottle of water.

'Let me stand up,' said Gregory.

'No,' Cecil commanded. 'You stay where you are. You should be in the recovery position.'

'Honestly, darling, I'm absolutely fine. I don't feel dizzy or anything. It's just a bit sore.'

'No.'

'But I'm fine! At least let me sit up, I'm getting cramp in my shoulder.' Cecil conceded with a disapproving huff and helped Gregory to sitting.

'At least you didn't pass out during the performance,' Sarah offered to cheer him up. She glanced at Nate who was watching her every move. It was disconcerting, but making her go all tingly in a lot of different places. Why did Gregory have to faint now?

A few minutes later, after sipping some water and telling Cecil how many fingers he was holding up, Gregory was allowed to stand, and everyone turned their attention back to Nate.

'Did you see the show?' asked Conner. 'What did you think?'

'You came back just for us,' said Mrs Andrews, clapping her hands together. 'Oh, just wait till I tell my husband. He's an MP you know, perhaps he can put in a good word for you for the New Year's Honours List.' Gregory rolled his eyes, clearly feeling better.

'We didn't do too badly, did we?' asked Kathryn. Though it was more of a rhetorical question.

'Och, laddie,' said Debbie, and from the look on Nate's face he was still struggling with the accent. 'I knew you wouldn't miss our last show. How wonderful of ye to come all the way here just for us.'

Sarah watched, unsure what to say, while her stomach bubbled with nervous anticipation and her heart pounded in her chest. With Nate stood before her she recognised now that even if the circumstances were strange, intense and, she had to face it, crazy, the love she felt for him was real. Deep. A love unlike anything she'd felt before. Her feelings for Vince and Finn hadn't even come close to this. Her connection with Nate wasn't just in her heart, it was in her soul, in the very essence of who she was and who he was. It was everything and it was perfect. It was certainly worth the risk.

'It wasn't *just* for you,' Nate said, turning back to Sarah and her heart stopped beating. He gently took her hands in his. 'I'm so sorry I didn't tell you how much you mean to me before I left. I was stupid.'

'Nate I—'*Nate I what? Nate, I'd like you to do the laundry. Nate I'd like you to love me for forever.* She hadn't thought that sentence through. Her brain was a mess of crazy emotions. Could she actually say out loud what she'd been thinking? Because she didn't need a string of pointless dates to get to know him. She knew everything she needed to know already. She knew he had a strong moral core, even if he had made mistakes. She knew he was the one for her. 'Nate, I love you.'

A heavy, oppressive and disheartening silence began to form in the second before he answered. Her heart was beating so fast her lungs fluttered and her body trembled. Then a smile formed on his face and taking it as a good sign, she carried on. Her throat was terribly dry and she wondered how she'd ever get the words out, but after swallowing she said, 'I mean, I know we haven't known each other for that long, but I thought there was something between us – a connection. Something really special.'

'I'm in love with you too. I have been since the first time I saw you. But I didn't think I deserved someone like you – someone so kind and caring. And my life's been such a mess. It's still a mess ...' He laughed and rubbed the back of his head. 'It's crazy and up and down but I want to be with you, Sarah. If you'll let me. I really do love you.' There was a nervous quiver to his voice. 'Or I'll give it all up if you want me to – become a dustman, a taxi driver ...'

The players all said, 'Awww,' and Sarah stifled a giggle. 'I don't think you need to go that far, though I'm sure you'd make a very good dustman.' Lifting her head, Sarah kissed him as a chorus of cheers and hoorays surrounded them. Just as Sid was Lottie's one in a million, Nate was hers, and the intensity of his kiss only reassured her of that fact. She could feel the longing emanating from his heart.

'About bloody time,' muttered Cecil.

And when Sarah and Nate parted, she turned to Cecil and tutted. 'Everyone's a critic.'

Chapter 22

FOUR MONTHS LATER

Sarah supervised as Nate dragged a box up the stairs and into Sid's, now his, flat then headed straight back out for another. He was finally back from America and it had been a tough few months being apart, especially as their relationship was so new. But he'd flown back and forward as much as he could, and they'd spoken every day. They were steadily getting to know each other and the slow, easy pace suited Sarah. It was like their hearts were joined by a string and when they were together, they wrapped around each other, linking them together forever. When they were apart, the string simply stretched but remained unbreakable.

Emma and Nate had publicly announced their split, and after he'd moved out he'd decided to buy a place down in Greenley. With Sid having moved into Lottie's, his flat had gone on the market and when Sarah mentioned it to Nate in one late-night phone call, Nate had immediately made an offer to Sid. She hadn't realised how much he'd fallen in love with the town, or the flat after their single coaching session there. The sale had gone through nice and quickly and Nate was happy to be moving in just before Christmas. He wasn't due back in America for a month and even then, Sarah thought she might go with him this time for a little holiday.

'Shall I get the kettle on?' asked Lottie who was helping him move in too, along with Sid who'd been roped in for some heavy lifting.

'Ooh, yes please,' Sarah replied. 'I could murder a cuppa. It's freezing out there.' The December rain battered the window and the strong winds blew through the bare branches of the trees. She peered down at the removal van parked on the kerb and admired Nate's strong body as he took a box from the van.

Life in Greenley had settled down nicely since that wonderful night four months ago. The players were getting ready for the opening night of the panto in just over a week's time. And this time, Mrs Andrews had a starring role and not as the pantomime dame, or the wicked witch. Gregory was having a go at directing as Conner was off on an internship with a production company, arranged by Nate. Sid and Lottie were happier than ever, and wedding bells seemed a step closer. Lottie had even press-ganged Nate into becoming a patron of the theatre. Ben had a job as a delivery driver for the local supermarket and was absolutely loving it. He'd even moved into a small one bedroom flat in Greenley.

As far as Finn was concerned, he'd got his comeuppance when he'd double booked a lunch date and received a swift knee to the groin in the surgery waiting area. Sarah and Mandy had enjoyed the spectacle, especially his hobbling back to his consulting room wincing in pain.

A sudden gust of wind whistled around the building as she heard Sid and Nate climb the stairs and come in through the open door. They were becoming firm friends, which wasn't a surprise as everyone liked Sid, but it was still wonderful that Nate was settling in so well. 'How are you doing, boys?' Sarah asked, pulling one of the many boxes towards her to try and make room for the others.

'Fine,' Nate replied. 'You just stand there and supervise, don't worry, we'll do everything.' Sarah smiled at him.

'If you're nice to me I might let you have a biscuit when you're done.'

Sid rested his hands on his hips and shouted to Lottie in the kitchen. 'Any chance of tea for the workers?'

'Maybe when you're done,' Lottie called back. 'No skiving.'

With the divorce underway, Nate and Sarah had made their relationship public. Not that the papers had really cared that much. Sarah didn't go to flashy awards things with Nate, he always went on his own, and with nothing salacious going on the press couldn't be bothered to schlep all the way down to Greenley when there was much more interesting stuff happening in the city. As a result, they were left pretty much alone.

'That's the last big box,' said Sid, pointing at the box he'd placed on the floor.

'Yep,' Nate confirmed. 'Just a couple of suitcases now.'

Sid offered his hand to Nate. 'I hope you'll be really happy here, mate.' Nate smiled and shook it before pulling Sid in for a hug and a manly pat on the back.

'I'm sure I will be. This place is beautiful. I couldn't be happier.'

'Nor me,' Sarah added, going to Nate's side and sliding her arm around his waist. 'But you do realise you'll be involved in the panto next year if you're back in time.'

'No, no, no,' said Nate, shaking his head. 'No I won't. Being here is downtime for me.'

'Oh yes you will,' Sarah and Sid chorused. Nate rolled his eyes just as Lottie came in carrying four cups of tea.

'Didn't I tell you? You and Sid are the pantomime horse.' Nate and Sid looked at each other in shock.

'But, because we like you so much,' added Sarah, 'we'll let you decide who's the front and who's the back.'

They both gave a resigned shrug and with the clink of four mugs tapped together in cheers, they toasted the Greenley Players and the new year that was soon to be ahead of them. Sarah was absolutely sure it was going to be the best year of her life.

Acknowledgements

Wow! To be writing the acknowledgements for my second book is something I never, ever thought would happen to me. Thank you so much to everyone who decided to read *Summer Season on the Seafront*, I really hope you liked it!

This book wouldn't have been anywhere near as good if it wasn't for the amazing team at HQ Digital. You are all amazing but I'm incredibly grateful to my editor, Emily Kitchin (who is super lovely), for her brilliant insight, advice and guidance in making this story the best it could be. I'd also really like to take a minute to appreciate all the book bloggers out there who do so much to spread the word about books. You guys are utterly, utterly fabulous!

My family have been unwavering in their support and I owe them so much. Your love and encouragement mean the world to me, so thank you! But really my biggest thanks go to every single person who decided to spend some time with me and my characters. Being an author is all I ever wanted and it's only thanks to you that it's possible. I hope I haven't let you down!

Keep an eye out for Katie Ginger's next book,
Snowflakes at Mistletoe Cottage, coming in October 2019! …

Turn the page for and extract of *The Little Theatre on the Seafront* by Katie Ginger …

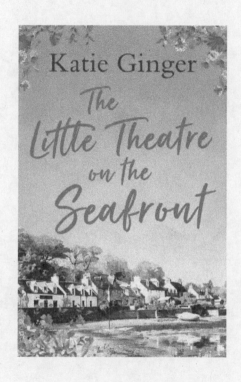

Prologue

To my dearest girl,

What a wonderful life we've had together, my darling Lottie. I'm so sorry that I'll miss so many things, such as seeing you get married and have children, but my time has come and I'm off to see your granddad. It's been a long time since we last saw each other so we should have a lot to talk about, which will be a pleasant change from our married life together.

With all this death business I've been thinking about you and what you'll do after I'm gone, and I've decided something – you need a shake up, my girl!

I love you, dear, but all you do is go to work, come home again, and that's it. You're thirty years old and you should be doing more with your life than spending your evenings with a little old lady like me.

If you remember, I have tried to get you enjoying life a bit more, but to no avail. Last year I set you up with that lovely handsome window cleaner, but you didn't bat an eyelid. In fact, I'm not entirely sure you even knew what was happening. And then there was that time at Christmas, when I tried to get you to go to your school reunion ... but you stubbornly refuse to enjoy anything that takes you out of yourself and out into the world. To be frank, dear, it's no way to live.

So, I've decided that a bit of emotional blackmail is in order. And as spending your evenings fussing over me won't be an option anymore, you're going to take over my place as chairman of Greenley Theatre and carry on my, dare I say it, good work, on the 'Save Greenley Theatre' campaign.

Think of it as one of those New Year, New You, type things! Good luck, my dear. I know you'll make me proud.

Lots of love,

Nan

P.S. I haven't actually arranged this with the committee yet so that will be your first job. Have fun!

Chapter 1

Lottie waited outside her house for Sid, her colleague and best friend, to pick her up. She checked her watch and rolled her eyes. He was late, as usual. In all the years she'd known him he'd never been able to get anywhere on time – even primary school. After five more minutes of shuffling to stay warm she saw his battered old car round the corner and hid the box behind her back.

'Here you go,' she said as she climbed in.

'You got me an Easter egg,' Sid replied, smiling. It was an *Incredible Hulk* one.

'I couldn't resist.'

'Me neither.' He handed over a large posh box.

Lottie giggled and had a quick look at the huge milk chocolate egg covered in a white chocolate drizzle. Her mouth began to water. 'You're the best.' Sid's grin grew wider. Lottie tucked the egg down by her feet while Sid tossed his onto the backseat where it was cushioned by a mound of rubbish and they headed to the first job of the day.

Lottie leaned forward and peeked at the picture on his top. 'Don't you think that T-shirt's a bit off for meeting an old lady?'

Sid pulled it to his nose and sniffed 'What's wrong with it?'

'I don't mean it's skanky. It's the picture.'

265

'What's wrong with the picture? Dragon Slaying Vampires are a great band.'

She raised her eyebrows. 'I'm not sure a half-naked woman with enormous breasticles, standing on top of a dragon's severed head in a giant pool of blood, is really appropriate for an octogenarian. Do you?'

'Oh,' said Sid. 'I suppose not.' He shrugged. 'I'll keep my jacket on.'

'Yeah, good luck with that.'

Sid was the reporter on the *Greenley Gazette* and Lottie was his photographer. Over the years they had covered every sort of local issue from the first day at school to hardcore crime and had learnt that old ladies over the age of seventy love to have the heating on. And it was already turning into a surprisingly sunny February day.

Lottie peered up at the clear blue sky and soft white clouds overhead. She loved living in Greenley-On-Sea, especially on days like this. The sun shone brightly, and the air was crisp and clean carrying a hint of salt from the sea. The streets were full of children on their way to school, laughing and giggling at what the day might hold in store.

'You were late again,' she said, teasingly.

Sid pointed to two takeaway cups in the cup holders. 'I stopped to get coffee.'

'Aww, thanks.' She sipped the skinny mocha savouring the tang of coffee and sweet hit of chocolate, then removed the lid to swipe up some of the whipped cream.

'I have no idea why you have it made with skimmed milk and then put cream on top.'

'Because,' said Lottie, popping the lid back on, 'I can convince my brain that whipped cream is mostly air and therefore has no calories and skinny milk is mostly water, so really, it's not that bad for me. In fact, on a day like this it's actually good for me. I'm hydrating.'

Sid's deep set hazel eyes under slightly too bushy eyebrows looked at her sceptically. She'd known him all her life and he knew her better than anyone else in the entire world, especially since Elsie, her nan, had passed away just after Christmas. She felt a familiar stab of grief tighten her throat but pushed it down. 'Do you want to have lunch at mine today?'

'Have you got any decent grub?'

'Sidney Evans, you only ever think about your stomach.' Lottie smiled and considered the sparse remains in the fridge. 'Beans on toast?'

'Yeah, alright.'

They were now in the posh part of town where old white Georgian houses with large sash windows lined the roads, but before long they would be out the other side back to the normal houses. 'So who's this old dear we're seeing this morning?'

He bobbed up and down in excitement. 'Mrs Harker and her opera-singing parrot.'

Lottie stared. 'Opera?'

'Yep.'

She blinked. 'Oh.'

'I know. I love my job,' Sid replied, beaming as if it was Christmas.

Sid parked the car in front of an ordinary mid-terrace house. A neat front garden with a small path led them to a plain white front door. Lottie climbed out first. 'I think I'll get a photo of Mrs Harker outside holding the parrot. It'll be a nice juxtaposition of the ordinary and the extraordinary.'

Sid tutted. 'You take this all far too seriously sometimes.'

They walked to the door and Sid gave a cheerful knock. A petite woman in her eighties wearing a floral dress and long beige cardigan opened the door. 'Good morning.'

'Good morning, Mrs Harker. I'm Sid Evans, from the *Greenley Gazette*, and this is my photographer, Lottie Webster.'

'Come in, won't you?' asked Mrs Harker, leading the way.

Lottie followed Sid into the porch and was immediately struck by the heat. It was like having a boiling hot flannel shoved on her face. She looked at Sid and grinned as a redness crept over his cheeks. It was going to be fun watching him cook, a little bit of payback for last week when they'd done the weekly shop together and he'd kept secretly adding things to other people's baskets. She'd giggled at the time but it was quite embarrassing when he got caught. Of course, he'd come clean and charmed his way out of it while Lottie hid at the end of the aisle, peering round from the pick 'n' mix.

As they entered the living room, Lottie slipped her coat from her shoulders and spotted a cage with a bright red parrot perched inside. The bird didn't move and for a moment, Lottie worried it was stuffed. It wouldn't be the first time they'd interviewed a crazy person.

'I understand,' said Sid, 'that you have a very unusual parrot, Mrs Harker?'

'Oh, yes, Mr Neville is very talented.'

'Mr Neville?' repeated Sid. Lottie recognised from the twitch in his cheek a grin was pulling at his mouth.

'Yes, Mr Neville's my parrot. He sings Tosca.'

Sid nodded. 'And can we see this talent in action?'

Lottie readied her camera as Mrs Harker approached the CD player and switched it on. The music started and Mr Neville, as if by magic, came to life. He opened his wings and rocked on his feet as he screeched in unison with the music. Lottie lifted her camera and took some shots. Calling it singing was going a bit far, but it was certainly entertaining. A moment later, Mrs Harker switched off the music and Sid conducted the interview.

'Well, thank you very much, Mrs Harker,' he said when he'd finished. 'That's quite a parrot you've got there.'

'He's great, isn't he?' she replied, opening his cage to take him out. 'Did you want to take your coat off, young man? You look a little bit hot.'

'No, thanks. I'm fine,' said Sid, wiping his top lip.

Lottie repressed a laugh.

'I was so sorry to hear about your grandmother passing, Miss Webster,' said Mrs Harker.

Lottie paused as a shiver ran down her spine. 'You knew my nan?'

'Yes, dear, I went to school with her and we played bingo together for years. She was a lovely woman.'

'Yes, she was.'

'It was wonderful what she was trying to do for the town, she was always working hard to make a difference. Such a shame she never quite got the theatre going again.'

Lottie opened her mouth, but nothing came out. Grabbing the bottle of water Sid offered, she took a big drink.

'Did Mrs Webster talk much about the theatre?' Sid asked. He must have seen her impression of a goldfish and stepped in.

'Oh yes, she had grand plans. Elsie was going to make it like it was when we were young. Get the community involved again. I think that was where she met your granddad, Miss Webster.'

Lottie's eyes darted to Mrs Harker's face. She had no idea that was why the theatre meant so much to her nan. From the depths of her mind she remembered Elsie telling her the story. How she spotted him from across the aisle and that was that. Love at first sight. Lottie had responded by saying how lovely and picking up her book, burying herself in another time, another place. She bit her lip feeling ashamed.

'All the bingo club were behind her, you know. Johnnie, the caller – the guy who calls out legs eleven and two fat ladies, and all that – he said that we could move back there when Elsie finished renovating it.'

Lottie tightened her grip on the water bottle and swallowed. She needed to get outside into the fresh air. 'I think, Mrs Harker, it would be a lovely idea to get a picture of you and Mr Neville in front of your house, if you don't mind?'

'Not at all, dear,' she replied, admiring Mr Neville and stroking his feathers. 'Are you sure you're alright? You look quite pale.'

'Yes, I'm fine, thank you.' Lottie's voice was high and squeaky. Her hand shook as she clicked the camera, but finally, after a few attempts, she had the shot.

Sid escorted Mrs Harker back to her door and said goodbye as Lottie climbed into the car and pulled another bottle of water from her camera bag. She watched Sid remove his jacket and move round to the driver's side to get in.

'Okay, you were right,' he said, wiping his forehead with the back of his hand. 'I was absolutely roasting in there. Why do old dears always have the heating on? I mean, I know it's still chilly, but come on.' He looked at Lottie, his furrowed brow accentuating his crooked nose. 'Are you alright?'

'I am now I'm out of there.'

'Was it the bit about your nan?'

Lottie stared at him in disbelief. 'Of course it was! I wasn't so impressed by an opera-singing parrot I nearly fainted.'

'Alright,' he said sarcastically. 'I was just checking.'

Lottie pushed a stray lock of hair behind her ear. If Sid wasn't so genuinely clueless when it came to women she would have been cross with him. 'Sorry. I know I'm being unbearable at the moment.'

His cheeky grin returned. 'That's okay.'

'It's just that, I knew the theatre meant a lot to Nan, but I …'

'What?' asked Sid, softly.

She shook her head, unable to steer her brain into forming a sentence. A familiar wave of grief and sadness washed over her, tinged with panic and fear at what she was being asked to do.

'Listen, Lots. I know you don't want to deal with your nan's letter but I think we have to. You can't keep ignoring it.'

Elsie's final gift to her hadn't been at all what Lottie had expected and she had no idea how to deal with it. 'There's nothing to talk about, Sid. I'm not doing it and that's final.'

'But, Lottie, your nan must have thought this was what you needed. You can't keep shoving your head in the sand and pretending it never happened.'

She crossed her arms over her chest. 'Yes, I can.'

'No, you can't.' Sid ran his hand through dark curls that maintained a stubborn unruliness no matter how short they were cut. If Sid was her type – which he wasn't – she might have thought him handsome in a geeky way. 'I'm not trying to annoy you.'

'I know you're not. You don't need to try.' She gave a weak smile.

Sid started the engine and began to drive off. 'But why leave you a letter? Why not just ask?'

Lottie shrugged. 'Nan knew full well that if she asked me face to face I'd tell her to bog off.'

'And stomp off out of the room,' he said teasingly.

She turned to him and widened her eyes in fake surprise. 'I don't do that.'

'Yes, you do.' He smiled. 'But it's fine, I don't mind. I just don't understand what you're afraid of.'

Lottie opened her Easter egg and broke off a piece of chocolate, waving it in the air as she spoke. 'Oh, I don't know, making a fool of myself in front of the entire town, letting Nan down, everyone laughing at me.'

'No one would laugh at you, Lottie.'

'Despite what Nan thinks—' Lottie felt her heart twinge, the words catching in her throat. 'What Nan thought, I quite like my life.'

Sid looked at her sceptically. 'You like being safe, Lottie, that's not the same thing.'

'But what if I take over the theatre and make things worse?'

'How can you?' Sid glanced at her quickly before turning his eyes back to the road. 'What could you possibly do to make it worse? Burn the place down? Blow it up? You're not planning on blowing it up, are you?'

271

Lottie scowled.

'Oh, I know,' he continued in a mocking tone. 'You're going to run National Front rallies, or host puppy kicking competitions?'

'No, but—'

'It's a small local theatre for a small quiet town. Not a top notch, swanky London showbiz place.'

Lottie cocked her head and broke off another piece of chocolate. 'But I don't know how to do this.' Her voice was rising and she pulled it back. It wasn't Sid's fault. 'I'm not a project manager, I have no idea how to be a chairman and do chairman-type things. And, I know absolutely nothing about theatres.'

'But you are ridiculously bossy.'

'No I'm not, I'm just … organised.'

Sid's face broke into a wide grin and he grabbed her hand, giving it a squeeze. 'You can do this, Lottie, I know you can. Just give it a chance.'

Lottie ate another piece of chocolate.

'The thing is, Lottie,' he continued, 'your nan was right. You do need to get out more. I mean, when was the last time you had a boyfriend?'

'When was the last time you had a girlfriend?' she countered.

'It was 2003, but this isn't about me.'

Lottie repressed a smile. 'You were twelve in 2003.'

'Yep, but I'm perfectly happy with my life; you're not and you haven't been for ages.'

Lottie folded her arms over her chest. It was true. She had been feeling restless for a long time now. But when her nan became ill, she'd retreated even further into her safe, quiet life. It wasn't that she didn't like people, she did. She'd just never quite got around to getting a social life, that was all. 'What's your point?'

'I think if you stopped looking at everything so negatively you'd see this could be good fun.' Sid was always trying to chivvy her up.

Lottie toyed with her camera, opening and closing the lens,

her mind racing. 'I've got to do this, haven't I?'

'We have,' said Sid, smiling at her. 'I'll be there for you.' He stopped at a junction. 'Shall we head to yours now? We can have lunch and start coming up with a plan to get you on the committee.'

Lottie checked her watch. 'It's only half eleven.'

'I know, but I'm starving. Please?' He stuck his lower lip out just as her stomach rumbled.

'Alright then. Just for you.'

Well, hello again! How are you guys doing? Still looking AMAZING, I see!

Thank you so much for reading *Summer Season on the Seafront*, my second book with HQ Digital! I hope you enjoyed your visit to Greenley-On-Sea. If you haven't read the first book, *The Little Theatre on the Seafront*, please think about it. If you did, I hope you enjoyed seeing everyone again.

Lovely reader, would you please consider spending a couple of minutes and leaving a review? They really help authors find new readers and mean the world to us. It would be amazing if you'd consider it. Thank you!

If you fancied having a chat about all things book related, or just seeing random posts about my dog and the weird things my kids do, then you can find me on my social media channels. My website's: www.keginger.com; or I'm on Facebook at: www.Facebook.com/KatieGAuthor. And I also prefer to put off housework by distracting myself with Twitter! I'm @KatieGAuthor if you fancy helping me ignore the hoover or the ever-growing mountain of washing.

HQ Digital are amazing and publish loads of awesome writers, so if you're eager to find your next read, please check them out! I guarantee you'll find something you like.

Until then, I'm going to leave you with a little bit of a tease about my next book! It's set at Christmas and will get you in the festive spirit in no time! So bring on the Christmas songs, find your terrible reindeer jumpers and get ready for some yuletide fun!

Thank you for reading!

Thank you so much for taking the time to read this book – we hope you enjoyed it! If you did, we'd be so appreciative if you left a review.

Here at HQ Digital we are dedicated to publishing fiction that will keep you turning the pages into the early hours. We publish a variety of genres, from heartwarming romance, to thrilling crime and sweeping historical fiction.

To find out more about our books, enter competitions and discover exclusive content, please join our community of readers by following us at:

🐦 @HQDigitalUK

f facebook.com/HQDigitalUK

Are you a budding writer? We're also looking for authors to join the HQ Digital family! Please submit your manuscript to:

HQDigital@harpercollins.co.uk.

Hope to hear from you soon!

DIGITAL H|Q

If you enjoyed *Summer Season on the Seafront*, then why not try another delightfully uplifting romance from HQ Digital?